Pug Ugly and Pretty Dead

Bill Coates

For Cindy, dear wife and best friend

Inspired by Primo, Pug No. 1
In the hearts of Bill and Mary McClellan
Of St. Louis

Also by Bill Coates

Needles Arizona

Rancho Javelina

People, Places and Dogs:
Columns from the Casa Grande Dispatch

Chapter One

1997

The ex-con and the pug dwelt in the land of the dispossessed. Most people called it the river bottom. Mesquite Suzy knew the way. She knew how to find Rhino Holloran. Ray Canin spotted her domicile, just off the shoulder. It was half-shaded by a half-dead mesquite tree. He slowed the car.

The photographer, Danny Stewart, leaned out the passenger window.

"Hey, that'd make good Page One color," Danny said. "Can't beat pink paisley on a blue bedspread for a front door. Or is that a table cloth? Maybe one shot with the old woman peering out, and another with her standing in front of her, uh, house."

"She's not that old," Canin said. "The social worker said she was in her late thirties."

Canin had called the Maricopa County Welfare Department, which had an outreach office for the homeless. He told the social worker he was looking for guy named Rhino and his pug. The social worker told him he meant Rhino Holloran, the ex-con. Canin replied, "That's the one." In turn, the social worker told Canin to keep an eye out for the bedspread hut of one Mesquite Suzy, as she was affectionately known by the welfare workers.

She could tell him how to find Rhino Holloran. Ray Canin was looking for Rhino Holloran because the city editor thought it would

1

be a good idea. Canin didn't.

"What'd that welfare worker say?" Danny replied. "She was a woman twice her age?"

Danny blew some air through his nose. It was how he laughed, often with a shake of his head.

Canin pulled up alongside the roadside hut, sheets and blankets tossed over a frame of plywood and cardboard. It was not quite eight-thirty, a.m. and – Canin guessed – not quite ninety-eight degrees. So it went for August in Phoenix, when coarse massive clouds built up in the afternoon and evening, bottling up a day's worth of solar radiation. Now, the clouds had lifted, letting in more sun. Piling heat on top of heat. It was like putting a sauna in a toaster oven.

"Yep, great color," Danny said.

Ray couldn't argue with that. Dirt-poor people were usually found in dirt-colored dwellings. But not Mesquite Suzy. Her patently humble home had all the colors of a rainbow – a faded rainbow at that. Blankets, towels and bed sheets were draped over cardboard boxes, weathered slabs of plywood and a few well-splintered two-by-fours. Standing on the edge of a cotton field, it looked as sturdy as a child's pillow-fort.

Perhaps fitting for a woman who, as Canin learned, was a little off her nut. Suzy's previous address was a psychiatric hospital. She spent a year or two there, until the money ran out. She drifted to Phoenix. She ended up standing in the middle of a downtown freeway, having declared herself the state tree. She had put down roots as a mesquite, and wasn't moving.

A state-appointed psychiatrist reported that Suzy was extremely delusional, noting that the state tree was actually a paloverde. On the other hand, her life really was a mess, so her behavior wasn't entirely unexpected. Loading her up with psychotropic drugs, the shrink sent her on her way. She ended up back on the street, fending for herself. It didn't get much better than that for the mentally ill in Arizona.

2

Her current residence sat about a hundred yards from the river bottom. Here, she kept her distance from the other unwashed masses. But more to the point for Canin, she knew her way around. She knew Rhino Holloran. She knew how to find him, so said the social worker, who didn't have time to show Canin around himself – due to budget cuts and all.

Danny squeezed out the car door, aimed his Nikon at the blanket hut and fired away.

Canin was looking for something solid to knock on, when Suzy pushed aside a quilted flap and stepped out. Canin caught a faint odor of incontinence. It smelled – unhealthy. He took a step backward. Mesquite Suzy, saying nothing, sat down in a weather-beaten rocker near the shoulder of the road, facing the river bottom but looking at nothing in particular.

She wore maroon Bermuda shorts and a sleeveless top. They seemed to match, unlike what usually passed as fashion for the homeless. Mesquite Suzy sat in full sunlight without squinting. She was used to the sun. Repeated, prolonged exposure to Arizona's Chamber of Commerce sunshine, in fact, had baked her into a human raisin. Danny was right, Mesquite Suzy was shriveled up beyond her years.

Other than that, she seemed as normal as suicide in Sweden.

Canin identified himself as a reporter for the *Scottsdale Monument* (Slogan above the flag: A *Monument* to the truth). He asked if she knew how to find Holloran. She replied she didn't give guided tours.

"But you look clean enough, so I'll tell you. Once you hit bottom, just turn left. You'll see something of a road. About a hundred yards up, that's where you'll find 'em. Big man, little dog. Right at the bottom," she said. She smiled slightly, perhaps knowingly. She had pretty good teeth for a woman with no fixed address.

So, Canin thought, Rhino Holloran was truly a bottom dweller, a river rat. It wasn't that hard, in the practical sense. The Salt River had

3

no water by the time it reached Phoenix. Maps labeled it a river, but it was really a bone-dry geologic scar separating north Phoenix from south.

The year-round flow had been channeled to farms, factories and homes. This wasn't an entirely new idea.

Some 1,500 years ago, the Hohokam people – long since gone – built an elaborate network of canals to deliver river water to their fields. They somehow managed to do it without massive federal reclamation projects. Those came later, about 1910. Big federal money built big federal dams and stopped up the water. A blue-green ribbon of life became a large, ugly ditch. The industrious Anglo settlers of Phoenix did their share to uglify what was left. They gouged out stone quarries, built garbage dumps and, later, the Ninety-First Avenue Sewage Treatment Plant.

Well, the sewage plant wasn't all that ugly, at least not evidently. Towering oleanders hid it from view. Like a mansion on the hill, it overlooked the stretch of bottom land that Rhino Holloran called home.

Settled into her rocker, Mesquite Suzy continued to point down the road, nodding slightly. She kept her arm suspended in the air, perhaps because Canin hadn't paid it sufficient attention. He shrugged and, turning his head, tracked the course suggested by the leathery limb, following Ninety-First Avenue as it dipped down into the stream bed. Crossing the Salt River here was only a problem during flooding, and that happened maybe once every ten years or so. Climbing up the far bank, the road entered the Gila River Indian Reservation, disappearing into a stand of trees.

Canin had a fleeting thought: He, too, would like to disappear behind the trees, out of sight of Clay Sommerfield, the managing editor who put him up to this story. A dog story. It seemed like punishment. Canin didn't particularly like dogs. He didn't like writing about dogs. And he didn't like the idea of doing a story in a place that

4

didn't have grass or air-conditioning.

He had gotten the assignment just yesterday, by way of an e-mail. As he scrolled down it, Canin cursed under his breath – comparing Sommerfield to the orifice responsible for waste management.

Sommerfield happened to be walking past, and heard the curse. Sommerfield did not reply under his breath. It wasn't his style. He shouted in soprano. He was about five-seven, 135 pounds, with his vocal cords taking up half his ballast.

"We're a local paper, Canin! It's a local angle! Ex-con and his dog gets Best Pug in Scottsdale dog show. Scottsdale! Ever heard of that? That's the city we cover. And everything it touches! And it touched a dog. Everybody loves dogs. And this story has pathos, lots of pathos. Ex-con finds meaning of life through his dog."

"Ex-con? I like ex-cons even less than I like dogs."

"Don't worry. From what I'm told, he's a gentle giant."

"What'd he do? What was his crime?"

"I don't know. Probably a drug charge."

"And what's pathos? Is that plural? One patho, two pathos?"

"Just find that bum and his dog, will you?"

"Ask somebody else. The other reporters love dogs. And they probably even know what pathos is."

"I like your style. It's your kind of story. And frankly, you haven't shown me much lately. I used to count on you for whimsical, funny stories – like the time you went skydiving with the mayor."

"He didn't have a dog with him."

"He broke his leg, and you turned it into a humor piece. I almost fell out of my chair laughing. And now what are you writing about? Girl Scouts fluffing pillows for hospice patients."

"It had pathos," Canin said.

Sommerfield unfolded a scrap of paper.

"You can start here, with this number. Call Brian Flattery."

"The city flak?"

5

Canin didn't look Sommerfield in the eye. If he didn't make eye contact, maybe the whole thing would go away. But Sommerfield kept talking.

"Flattery was there, at the dog show last week. He called me up and told me all about this pug being led around by this guy who looked like a cross between a pro wrestler and sasquatch."

"I thought they were same."

"Look, the ex-con and the pug won a ribbon. And Flattery said the guy lived somewhere in the river bottom and was named Rhino, because he had horns growing out of him."

"You're getting story ideas from a flak?" Canin asked.

"Flattery used to be in the business," Sommerfield said. "He used to be a reporter."

"Christ, I'm not sure I even know what a pug is."

"You would if you had covered the god damn dog show like I asked you. You flat out blew it off, claiming all those dogs would drive you into a fetal-prone panic! Fine. This is one dog. One fucking dog!"

"Why didn't you just send out a photographer, get some wild art. Who's on duty that Saturday … oh, right, Shine."

"George had a scheduling conflict," Sommerfield said.

"Yeah, he had a date with three beers. Besides, that was a good story about the hospice pillow fluffers. They were Brownie Scouts. And talk about a good photo. Did you see the smile on that dying woman's face when that little girl gently lifted her head to puff up her pillow?"

"Dying? She was already dead. We had to write a correction."

"Now, I remember."

"I want the pug story, with art, by tomorrow. Early p.m., as in two. We'll put it up on the Web."

Right, thought Canin. *Sommerfield didn't say the magic words:* "Or you're fired!" *But, even unspoken, they hung in the air.*

So here Canin stood, sopped in sweat on the edge of a dry river,

6

twenty-five miles from Scottsdale, half regretting he took the assignment, just to keep his job.

Mesquite Suzy lowered her arm, but continued peering on down the road. Canin thought he saw something behind the prune-dried face. But he couldn't tell if it was a question – or an answer. Without a word, she rose from her chair and went inside. Ray Canin and Danny Stewart got back in the car and headed on down the road, past the high oleanders and – half-hidden by them – high walls topped with rolls of razor wire. And behind the walls, the sewage treatment plant. This much Canin knew about it: The plant was fed by the city's main sewer line, a large collector that followed the Salt River downstream to Ninety-First Avenue. And here, the shit stopped, right at Mesquite Suzy's doorstep.

But there was an upside. The treated effluent went into the river bottom and created an oasis. Wild grasses grew alongside large, shaggy tamarisk and mesquite trees. In turn, the shade and privacy they provided attracted people like Rhino Holloran and other hardy settlers.

A whole village came into existence. With no zoning restrictions, people parked their broken-down campers and obsolete school buses and put up plywood shelters wherever they could find space.

Where Ninety-First Avenue hit its low point, Canin made a left. The tires rolled off the pavement, and the car headed upstream, lurching up a rise of fist-sized stones smoothed and polished by waters past.

Canin nursed his nearly paid-off eight-year-old Toyota in first gear, anticipating the sound of a rock penetrating a vital organ. He had just spent eight hundred on a new clutch. *Dear Jesus, no more repairs.* His knuckles went white on the steering wheel.

Too bad Danny's brand-new pickup wasn't ready yet. As for his old one, it just wouldn't start – after a quarter-million miles in the name of photojournalism. Canin, reluctantly, volunteered his Corolla.

7

It had front-wheel drive, so – with any luck – wouldn't get stuck. The cassette player still worked, though his selection of tapes wasn't what it used to be. Most of what he owned had – one by one – melted to the dashboard. And there they remained. Salvador Dali goes 3-D.

And, as the sun rose higher, the cassettes went soft again. Canin could feel his shirt – where it touched the seatback – drenched in sweat.

The ride didn't start out that way. He and Danny had been as cool as radishes in the crisper drawer, until they got halfway from the newspaper. That's when the air-conditioning broke down. The car became a rolling rotisserie, and Canin's glasses kept sliding down his nose on a sheet of sweat. Repeatedly, he pushed them back in place with a fingertip, up over a scar that looked like stitching on a baseball.

As the car pitched side to side, Canin glanced over at Danny, thinking he'd see a young combo Pima-Navajo too tall for a compact and clinging to the door handle like a bad subway ride.

Canin got the too-tall part right. But the ride didn't bother Danny Stewart. He grew up on the Salt River reservation east of Phoenix and Scottsdale. After college, though, he went north and became a prize-winning photographer for the Navajo Times. Crisscrossing the Navajo Rez, he had banged up his pickup on far rougher grades than this. To Danny Stewart, this was nothing.

Danny glanced out the window – the wind tussling his smooth, jet-black hair. He appeared to be scanning the terrain for possible shots. Then he rummaged through his camera bag, taking inventory on lenses or something. The heat didn't seem to bother Danny either. Maybe that just was part of being a photographer. Getting the picture trumped complaining about the conditions. Maybe it was just Danny. Perhaps some combination of the two.

Danny pulled out a stubby lens, held it up.

"Wide-angle lens, for wide-angled Anglos," he said.

Canin chuckled. Danny often joked about Anglos, if mildly so.

8

Canin guessed it was a humor borne of a lingering, trace resentment all Indians likely held toward whites – like background radiation left over from the Big Bang.

But Danny revered one white man. The guy who took the first picture. Some Frenchman named Niepce. To Danny, first was important. Neil Armstrong was first. Niepce was first. Indians were first. And, maybe, Danny figured this assignment was a first. A homeless man and his dog, on the river, without the water.

For Canin, the assignment was a test. Muddle through or get fired. Get fired and give his wife even more of a reason never to move back. She had filed for divorce. But it wasn't final, and there was always hope. Unless he got fired. He took a deep breath and realized – *here was his motivation.* He'd do the responsible thing, swallow his pride and keep his job. And maybe Renee would give him a second look and give up the orthodontist.

What did he ever do for her? Besides make her teeth look perfect – just like the rest of her. And take her to Europe three times.

For Renee, Canin thought. He'd do it for Renee.

So Canin pushed on. Soon, the stream bed leveled out, and the Toyota crawled past a broken-down school bus. Near the back, a pair of sunken eyes stared back at them through a window tinted in dirt. The man looked like someone good at playing a banjo.

The bus slid out of sight behind a stand of tall tamarisks and cottonwood trees. The rocky surface beneath the tires gave way to a fine, tightly packed silt. It made for a kind of road, kept clear by the local traffic. Grasses and weeds grew along the shoulders. The air in the river bottom was heavy, warm and wet, smelling of sewer gas and serving as a constant reminder that this was not the high-rent district.

Canin could now see a half-dozen settlements, homes, whatever you wanted to call them. Most clung to the slightly higher ground near the river bank. Some people built on grassy plateaus running through the middle of the river bottom, elevated just enough to keep the

9

tenants dry on the few occasions that a little rain prompted a little runoff. Of course, when the river flooded, as it sometimes did, no place down here was safe.

Nothing Canin saw fit the description of Rhino Holloran's domicile. Canin began to wonder if he had missed it. There was no sign of the plywood shack described by the social worker, or the rusting Ford falcon or some kind of a small squat dog, the show dog.

Something clicked. Canin turned to see Danny snapping a doughnut of a lens on one of the two camera bodies nestled in his lap.

"Now if we only find the person you're supposed to shoot," Canin added.

"Maybe we should ask that guy up there."

"Yeah."

The guy "up there" sat in a metal-frame folding chair in the shade of a mesquite tree. He was small, but his car was big – a late-50s Plymouth station wagon that weighed less than the space shuttle but had bigger fins. There was no shack of any kind about, suggesting the man slept in his car. Certainly, it was roomy enough. Canin stopped the Toyota and got out. So did Danny, all the while waving around a light meter to gauge exposure. Probably hard to figure, Canin thought. On one hand, it was getting overcast with mountains of fat, gray clouds. On the other hand, the sky was still so bright, he had to squint through his clear lenses.

If only Renee hadn't run his sunglasses through the garbage disposal.

The small man with the big car stood up. He looked to be eighty, but it was hard to tell. He was pale, short and wiry, and wore an army-green T-shirt stretched across a cantaloupe of a gut. His brown polyester slacks fell a good two-and-a-half inches short of his shoe tops. He grinned with half his mouth. Canin sensed that the man harbored a suspicion of strangers. Maybe it had something to do with the assault rifle the man had aimed at his head.

"What's your business?" the man asked.

His voice quivered with an edge of fear, though he continued to grin halfway. His accent was not quite the sticks and not quite the city, but somewhere out past the suburbs.

Canin wasn't sure if he should raise his hands. And if he did, how fast?

"We're from ..." Canin started to say, but he was distracted by the snap of a mirror flapping inside a camera body. And the footfall of a photographer who engaged in something of a ceremonial dance while hitting the shutter release.

"Hey!" the skinny man screamed. He wrapped a finger around the trigger. "No goddamn pictures!"

"No problem," Danny said, slowly letting the camera come to rest on the strap around his neck.

"So, who are you? What do you want?" the man asked, his brown eyes jumping from Canin to Danny, and back again. He grinned nonstop, though Canin didn't think the man was amused. It was more of a facial tic.

"I write for a newspaper. We're looking for a man who lives in the river bottom with his dog."

"What man? What kind of dog?"

"Rhino Holloran and his pug."

The man lowered the rifle. The half of his face he still had control over became sympathetic. The other half kept grinning. He moved closer and held out his hand.

"Jim Smith. Glad to have known you."

Canin grinned back, and shook hands. The man's sudden change in demeanor made him wary.

Jim Smith pointed to a break in the line of tamarisks extending up river from the old school bus.

"Rhino Holloran is back there," he said, "in a clearing behind

11

those trees. Him and his pug."

The old man leaned on his rifle like a walking stick. If it went off, he'd blow a hole in his hand, then make a new chest cavity.

"You know," he said, philosophically, "pugs come from ancient China originally, where – if memory serves me – they were treated like gods by the royal family, the emperors and what not. Ordinary folk weren't even supposed to look at a pug, or they'd be executed on the spot. Yeah, some people are very touchy about their pugs.

"You seem to know a lot about pugs," Canin said.

"Oh, it's just a little something I saw on a place mat."

"Place mat?"

"At a little restaurant in Pusan," Jim Smith replied. "You know, in Korea, where I served my tour in the Army."

"A restaurant with placemats about pugs."

"All kinds of dogs, really."

"A restaurant that honored dogs."

"Honored dogs ? …. well, let me put it this way. Back then, when man bit dog in Korea, it wasn't news."

Canin said nothing, thinking what he didn't want to think about. Danny looked for, an instant, as though he might part ways with his breakfast.

"Hey, don't me get wrong," Jim Smith said. "I'm a vegetarian. You know, baked beans, Doritos, stuff like that."

With effort, he forced a frown on one side of his face, which now looked the mask of comedy and tragedy.

He had something serious to say.

"Now, let me give you a word of advice. I worry about your well-being at the hands of Rhino Holloran. He is extra, extra touchy about his dog. I learned quick, never mention dog as a menu item to Rhino Holloran. Never touch his dog without permission. And … "

Jim Smith shook his tragic-comic head.

"And?" Canin prompted.

12

"Well, this is the most important. Never laugh at his dog."

"If I do?"

"I don't know, something bad, though. Maybe pull out your liver, feed it to the dog."

Jim Smith then snapped to attention with his rifle butt down on the ground. He looked like an extra in a Mel Brooks movie.

"OK partner, you can take my picture now."

Canin looked at his watch. The deadline was drawing near, and Jim Smith had stability issues.

"Come on, Danny. I got to file this story by two. For the Web."

He turned to Jim Smith.

"We'll, uh, see you around. We have to, uh, go."

Canin and Danny hopped back in the car. Canin backed up, then turned it around. He inched the Toyota along the silt highway until he saw the break in the tamarisks – and through that -- an expansive ranch-style shack of plywood and two-by-fours.

A dog came running out. It was black and shaped like a big pot roast, carried around on short and spindly legs. It hopped up and down, and barked. Most barking dogs scared Canin, but this one didn't strike him as particularly threatening. It was just too much of an oddity. He got out of the car for a closer look. He couldn't help but notice the tail, curled up like a piggy's. And the eyes, bulging from what appeared to be perpetual shock. The face itself looked like it had been flattened against an anvil. A fold of skin drooped across the muzzle, giving the dog a sad-clown look. *This wasn't a dog. It was a running joke. Just look at that tail ...all curlicue, and that face ...You just have to laugh.*

Canin stifled it. But the more he stared, the harder it was to bottle it up. He made a gurgling sound, as a air began to escape involuntarily. *Shit. So I laugh at an ugly dog. What's the harm in that?*

Something in his peripheral vision moved. Something big. Canin looked up. And up. He stood in the shadow of an expansive mountain

13

of flesh.

The mountain spoke. "Kirby, quiet, boy."

Canin looked back at the pug. He thought: *I value the absence of pain. I shall not laugh. And nothing that dog does now can make me.*

Then the dog hopped in circles and wagged its little piggy tail.

Chapter Two

"Hey, your lip's bleeding," Rhino Holloran said.

Canin smiled through clenched teeth, canines digging into his lower lip. The pain helped to refocus his thoughts – save him from laughing, and its consequences. He dabbed at the blood with a sleeve.

"Mosquito bite."

"Now, what's your business?" Holloran asked.

Canin handed Holloran a business card, told him he worked for a newspaper, assigned to write about the big man and his pug.

"Snooping around for a story, huh?"

Canin nodded.

"Hell, that'd made a good one."

"That's what my editor said."

Holloran extended a hand that looked like hamburger stuffed in a catcher's mitt.

"Rhino's the name. Come on around back. We can sit out on in the patio."

Holloran led them to the patio – a tattered sofa and plastic deck chairs atop a soiled carpet tossed over slabs of warped plywood. It was all shaded by an overgrown tamarisk tree. Canin sat across from Holloran and took out his reporter's notebook. Danny stood, glancing about and sizing up the photo possibilities as Holloran slowly lowered himself to his seat.

Canin noticed the horn right off. More like a doorstop, actually, just above the left eye. The effect was somewhat offset by the sheer enormity of his head, which was slightly pinched in the middle. It spread out into a broad and bearded jaw. Rhino Holloran's eyes were small and set back in sockets a sparrow could nest in. They might have been green, but Canin couldn't really tell.

His hair, a tangled mat of straw, fell down across his forehead, around the protruding horn.

Holloran was shirtless. And like a great pink amoeba, he all but swallowed up the cheap lawn chair. And though well upholstered with flab, his arms and chest bore traces from his time spent pumping iron in prison. But his great beer gut took up half his mass. It ballooned out like a giant lump of expanding bread dough, collapsing around a deep wormhole of a bellybutton.

Below that, the gut settled onto a generous lap, where it now competed for space with the dog. Canin noted the contrast in color. Pink Man versus Black Pug. He hadn't expected to see a black dog, frankly. Going by what little he knew about pugs, he thought they came in beige. But this dog was the color of deep space, except for a small, white marking on its chest. It formed a near-perfect circle.

Holloran had a tattoo on his chest, too – a snarling pug wearing a helmet emblazoned with a swastika. Maybe he went shirtless to show off the art. Maybe he just wanted to keep his shirts fresh and dry for more formal occasions. For he was sweating like an overworked plow horse. Perspiration beading up from every pore. The sweat ran in rivulets down his chest, and over and around the great gut.

He did not leave his stomach's immensity to chance. He filled it with beer nonstop, polishing off a can of Old Milwaukee every twelve minutes. He had a routine. After finishing a beer, he'd toss the can onto a mountain of empties and, without pause, grab a full one from a cooler, pop it open and guzzle.

The dog looked like it could use a drink, too. He panted like a husky in Riyadh. But the pug laid off the beer, content just to rest on the man's big foamy thighs and get his neck massaged by fingers the size of burritos. Rhino Holloran looked quite content as well.

16

Whatever stress he felt in being Rhino Holloran, homeless pug handler, was relieved through the therapy of petting his dog. And muttering words of affection. Then, occasionally – with some effort – he bent down and kissed the dog on the top of his little round head. In return, the dog would lick the sweat off Rhino Holloran's hairy stomach.

The pug's behavior confirmed Canin's already low opinion of dogs. They went after anything that fell under the general category of "organic byproducts."

Well, at least Canin didn't find the animal so funny anymore. He could open his mouth without fear of laughing.

He started off the interview with a few perfunctory questions.

"Rhino – common spelling?"

"Right R-H-I-N-O. Holloran – H-O-L-L-O-R-A-N."

"Age?"

"Hold on, let me think – don't tell me. Uh, forty-three."

Canin was again drawn to the horn. He tried not to stare, but he had to ask.

"About your …"

"Say, don't you know my philosophy of life?"

"Sure, I'd like to hear it."

"See, I'm a dog lover. Been one ever since I was a kid. I love dogs. And if anybody hurts one, I'll kill 'em. Well, been there, done that."

Canin nodded, trying to convey that he, too, was a dog lover.

"But … that's not how I got this." Holloran pointed to the doorstop on his head. "I just had a disagreement – over a dog."

"Is that right?"

On anybody else, a horn like that would have made the person a freak. On Rhino Holloran, it didn't look all that out of place. Still, Canin caught himself staring at it longer than good manners allowed. Danny was staring, too, but through a viewfinder. He had an excuse.

Holloran took note of Canin's interest, tapped the somewhat

17

knobby end with an index finger.

"Yep, that's how people came to call me Rhino, not 'cause of my nose. You know, this animal horn, though some people tell me it looks more like a hat rack."

His voice was deep, but not quite resonant, like a loose string on a bass fiddle.

"Oh, that," Canin said.

"Yeah, that. What you been staring at all this time. Naturally, because I'm big, people said I reminded them of a rhinoceros."

"People?"

"My classmates at Florence, the state's maximum-security pen. I acquired it on my three thousandth eight hundred sixty-second day in the big house. Until then I was known as Michael, or just plain ol' Mike."

Canin scribbled the man's real name in his notebook, just as a drop of sweat hit the page, smearing the ink slightly. He dabbed his forehead with his shirtsleeve.

Holloran continued: "Yeah, It was March third. In retrospection, it never should've happened. I told the warden that this guy was a nut case and I wanted him out of my cell."

"Which guy?"

"My cellmate," Rhino said, with a hint of irritation. "Shouldn't be that hard to figure out."

"Of course."

"Anyway, I was watching an *Ol' Yeller* video – tell me that ain't one of the all-time great classics, eh?"

"One of my favorites," Canin said, not having seen it but knowing it had something to do with a dog.

"And well, it was the sad part, you know, where Ol' Yeller starts gettin' all foamy-mouthed and crazy 'cause he's all full of rabies, and the boy knows he's gotta shoot Ol' Yeller so he don't suffer anymore. I tell you I seen that movie a thousand and two times, but I couldn't

18

help myself, I blubber like a baby every time. So here I am, bawlin' my eyes out, and the next thing you know, this little asshole, Willy Ortega, jumps up and pulls the TV off the stand smashes it on the floor and screams, 'How can you stand this shit?' "

"Now, at this point, knowing how much capacity I have to hurt my fellow man — and he'd done nothing but smash a TV — I say: 'Listen, Ortega, you ought to show a little more understanding when a dog like Ol' Yeller takes ill.' "

"Now, Ortega, like many prisoners, he doesn't take well to constructive criticism. To be honest, he just goes fucking nuts. Little guy, runt of the litter, but for the next half-minute he's like a grizzly bear in a bar fight. He kicks my legs out from under me and down I go, face first. Then he jumps on my back, grabs my hair and begins to bang my head against the concrete — ain't no shag carpets with foam padding in cellblock F. Now he's screaming, 'You've played that damn movie every day for the past three years. No more! No more!' Then starts yelling, 'Fuck, Ol' Yeller!' over and over again. And he kept banging my head on the floor, until it cracked. My head, that is. Doctors said that's what caused all that calcium to build up like it did, into the hat rack. And, after that, everyone knew me as Rhino. Oh ... I can't complain. I came out of prison with a fair amount of money, for an ex-con, that is. The state settled the claim I had against them for $5,000."

"I take it prison officials moved Mr. Ortega after that incident," Canin prompted.

"They had to. When I got up off the floor, I broke every single bone in his body. Well, a good five- or six-hundred of 'em anyway. I didn't mind him poundin' my head on the floor so much, but he had no business talkin' about Ol' Yeller that way. But, since he didn't do the dog any actual harm, I spared his life."

Danny, shooting over Canin's shoulder, muttered, "I'm sure he's grateful."

19

Canin scribbled down Holloran's quotes as fast as he could. Actually kind of interesting, he told himself. He also made a mental note to say something complimentary about the pug at some point during the interview.

Then came the question he already knew the answer to – if vaguely.

"Why did you do time?"

Holloran leaned back, looking almost wistfully behind him, perhaps looking back to his past. A more literal take on it would have had him looking out in the direction of Ninety-first Avenue.

He turned back to Canin.

"I killed a man in Yuma."

Canin swallowed and nodded. "Uh huh."

"Not much to say. I did go into his house for the unlawful purpose of ripping him off. But I happened upon him hitting and kicking his dog, real viciouslike. I mean who's the real animal here, huh? I told him to stop, and, here I was, the criminal element, and he just ignored me and kept beating the poor little dog for pee-peeing on the carpet. Well, he didn't stop, so I intervened and beat the livin' shit of him."

Rhino Holloran's eyes, somewhere back inside their immense fleshy sockets, grew moist. He took a breath.

"The dog died anyway. It was a pug, you know. And the man's own wife, she saw it all. They were wealthy, he was a big, big farmer, which was why I chose their house, but all their money didn't prevent that particular tragedy. Money helps, but it ain't the end-all and the be-all. In fact, the wife didn't take it too well. I guess she needed some counseling after that."

As Canin scribbled away, Danny stalked the perimeter of the dirt-laden rug that defined Rhino's patio. Canin leaned forward on a seat cushion upholstered in half-worn naugahyde. The chair-back was missing altogether. He was seated perhaps four feet from Holloran, who was backed against the outside wall of his canvas and plywood

20

shelter. A rotting wooden frame supported a patio roof of tattered green garbage bags. With the tamarisk trees above, there was plenty of shade. But it was not cool on Rhino Holloran's patio. Just dim and stale and stifling.

"See, I wasn't charged with actual murder – you know, first degree – because I was just reacting to what the man was doin' to his dog. They sent me up for second degree. I got an early release for good behavior."

Canin swallowed. "Of course."

"And how long have you, um, lived here?"

"I'd say goin' on, oh, eight-nine months. It's a good place. Good people … What's up, Kirby?"

He had jumped down from Holloran's lap and was sniffing around Canin's feet. He lifted a right leg.

"What's he doing?" Canin asked.

"Peeing on you."

Canin stood up and jumped back. His palms broke into a sweat, as his breathing became rapid and shallow.

"Hey, relax," Holloran said. He picked up the pug and set him back on his lap. "It means he likes you. You should smell my shoes."

Canin nodded noncommittally. He remained standing. His breathing returned to normal in a minute or two.

Holloran continued: "Like I was saying, we got good people here."

Rhino Holloran paused long enough to crumple an aluminum beer can into a marble-sized ball of scrap metal. He tossed it on the aluminum mountain and fetched a fresh one.

"Now, I'm not saying we fit your average yuppie white man's idea of model citizens. I'd have to tell you that right now. More than half the people here are ex-cons and over fifty percent of the rest have deep-rooted psychological problems. And if it doesn't add up, that's because there's some overlap.

"Now Johnny, the guy in the bus behind the trees, he's harmless,

21

like that crazy lady up the road …"

"Mesquite Suzy."

"Yeah, that's what she calls herself. I guess she's entitled, since she's crazy. But she's had a hard life, her share of misfortune.

"Johnny, he's just nuts. Claims to have X-ray vision and can see right inside a person. I know that every time we meet, he says he can see the demon beer sloshin' around inside my stomach. Maybe he does have a genuine gift there, 'cause he's always right. And then there's that Korean veteran guy, Jim Smith. I did at one time suspect he'd been grillin' more than hamburgers on that campfire of his. Before he moved in, this place used to be jumpin' with stray dogs. I asked him about it once, and he said they must have gone back to the rez. I let it go at that. But, if I ever find he's been puttin' dog on the menu, I'd be obligated to grind him into lunchmeat and feed him to Kirby. However, now I'm thinking the dog catchers might be to blame. They've been on some campaign to pick up sick strays."

"Sick strays," Canin said, scribbling furiously as Rhino Holloran talked.

"They work for a veterinarian who gives free care to sick dogs. Part of a group called Animal Rescue Fund."

"ARF."

"Yep, ARF."

"They even offered to take Kirby in for a free checkup. I told them nobody touches Kirby."

Holloran paused to think. Sweat seeped out of his horn and dripped from tip. The man needed a plumber, Canin thought.

"Now about the dog …" Canin said tentatively.

"What the hell would you like to know?" Holloran said with a big grin as he patted the dog's head. Canin noted Holloran's bad teeth.

"Name's Kirby?"

"That's right, just like the vacuum cleaner."

"You named your dog after a vacuum cleaner?"

"Sure. Watch this."

Rhino Holloran picked Kirby up, placed the dog back on his lap. Then, leaning to his left, he pulled a box of Cheese-Its from a large paper bag. Kirby looked up, apparently expecting a handout. He didn't get one. Instead, Holloran dug out a fistful of little yellow squares and stuffed them into his own mouth. They didn't all quite fit, and as Holloran began chewing, crumbs fell around his bulging, sweaty stomach. *This* was what the dog had anticipated. Kirby stood up, steadied himself with his front legs, and began to devour bits of cracker stuck to the top of this massive outcropping of flesh. The dog moved his head back and forth in neat rows until the stomach was free of crumbs.

Danny hovered a few feet away capturing the action with a wide angle lens.

With a beer, Rhino Holloran washed down what crackers hadn't fallen from his mouth.

"What'd I tell you? The dog's a friggin vacuum cleaner."

Then Holloran excitedly leaped up from his chair. This was something on the scale of a tectonic-plate movement of plywood. Canin steadied himself, to keep from falling off his own chair. Holloran set the dog on the ground.

"Hell, that was nothin'! Now this is just gonna blow you away. You gotta see this!"

Canin looked at his watch. It was nearly 9:30. He wanted to start writing by eleven, have something good to show Sommerfield before lunch. And he still had to ask Holloran about the key element of the story: the local angle, the Scottsdale dog show. If Canin couldn't work Scottsdale into it, he didn't have a story. Maybe he didn't have a job.

"What prompted you to enter Kirby in a dog show?" Canin asked abruptly.

"Hey, don't rush me. Come on, I'll show the greatest dog trick."

"Sure, I'd like to see it," Canin said.

23

"OK, now here's the trick. Two weeks ago, I buried a green-colored Milk-Bone, Kirby's favorite, out past that big row of trees. Now we've had some summer rain – you know, monsoon – and dust storms and all kinds of grass growing, and you can't tell anything was ever buried there. But Kirby here, all he needs is the signal."

"Signal?" Danny jumped in, on pause from shooting for the moment.

"Kirby, *radar* on the Milk-Bone, Kirby," Holloran said.

Kirby barked once, then pressed his nose to the ground and sniffed. He followed a scent that led him from the dirty patio rug to the hard-packed silt, into a thicket of river-bottom tamarisk and mesquite, and out the other side into the bright gray light of gathering clouds. Canin, Danny and Holloran followed.

For another fifty yards or so, Kirby bounded along the dry river bed on legs about the right length for a chicken. He kept close to the bank, where the ground was uneven, rocky and choked with weeds. There were no other distinguishing features. It all looked about the same.

But it apparently didn't all smell the same, at least to the dog. He stopped and began pawing the earth. Dirt, small rocks and tall weeds gave way to his digging, which became more and more frantic until the paws were a blur. Then, abruptly the pug stopped, shoved his head deep into a hole just big enough for it to fit. Reemerging, he had the small green Milk-Bone clenched in his teeth. He gave Canin a hard look with his large, brown eyes. It was a warning: Hands off the Milk-Bone.

Kirby then carried his buried treasure to a soft bit of ground, lay down and ate it.

Danny got pictures.

"Some trick, huh?" Holloran boomed. He was clearly proud of his dog's tracking skills. "He's smart, real smart. He picked up on it real fast. And just wait'll he starts winning big at the shows. I tell you, his day's comin'."

Canin nodded, looked at his watch. Time to get to the point and wrap this up.

"Can you tell me about showing Kirby? How you ended up at the Scottsdale all-pug show?"

"What's your hurry?"

Chapter Three

Back at the patio, Rhino Holloran took two beers to collect his thoughts. He began by telling Canin how an ex-con became a big player in the dog-show circuit. He had last shown Kirby at the Scottsdale and Paradise Valley All-Pug Show. It had been hot outside, easily better than a 105 degrees, Holloran said. But the show took place inside the air-conditioned gymnasium at Scottsdale Community College. Otherwise, the field would have been littered with prostrate pugs.

Kirby got first place, a first step toward his championship, the crowning achievement for any registered purebred, Holloran said.

"It's about time," he said. "You'd think some of those people look down on ex-cons."

Holloran pursed his lips, as if trying to bottle up the thought of finally winning.

Canin didn't know whether to laugh or cry. Better for his health if he did neither. He didn't know what went on at pug shows. He pictured Holloran holding up Kirby like a blue-ribbon pie at the county fair.

"Hey, would you like to see some pictures from the show?" Holloran asked. "He's come a long way."

"Sure." He tried to say it like he meant it.

Holloran got up, and carrying the pug in one arm, disappeared into his shack. Curious, Canin stood and followed as far as the door. He peered inside. This was not *Better Homes and Gardens*. Clothes that looked like car-wash rags were heaped atop dirty dishes. Uncontained garbage was pushed into corner – banana peels, burger wrappers and more beer cans. Against a plywood wall, a heavily stained mattress was half-buried in paperback books.

Holloran stooped over the mattress and dug through the books. Kirby walked about the mattress, sniffing out the various stains. Maybe some were his.

Spotting Canin at the doorway, Holloran said: "Maid was out sick this week."

Canin forced a smile. "Yeah."

As he continued to look about, Canin began to notice things he hadn't noticed before. Individual objects took shape, distinct from the overall clutter. They weren't anything to write home about, but they did catch Canin's attention: A broken picture frame, a rhinestone dog collar and a handful of shiny, ornate silverware: knives, forks, spoons.

"There that SOB is." Canin stepped aside as Holloran came out. He settled his massive body back into his chair. Kirby hopped up on his lap as he propped the leather-bound photo album on his perspiring stomach and flipped it open. The two-dozen pictures had a common theme: Nearly all showed Rhino Holloran with Kirby on a leash. They seemed OK as far as focus and exposure. Most were poorly framed, however. Either the top of Holloran's head was missing. Or his right or left side had been lopped off. Or the pug was half-in, half-out of the picture.

"I asked the pug person next to me to take these, with a little camera I got after prison. It's uses real film. You hardly see those anymore."

"Uh huh. And that's the ...?" Canin pointed to a picture of Rhino Holloran with a leash in one hand and a blue ribbon in the other. Holloran's face was nothing more than a big grin. Everything above his mouth having been cropped out by the camera.

"First place," Holloran continued. "Everybody will tell you, that's a damn good showing third time out. Damn good. Not to brag, but I'd look for Kirby to take Best-of-Show at Westminster. Can't say when. Next year, maybe."

Canin looked skeptical.

"There's a dog show in a London cathedral?"

"No, Westminster, in New York. It's the biggest of them all. I've been reading up on it. Only one pug took it all. Champion Dhandy Favorite Woodchuck, in 1981. Kirby's next, but I got to think of a long fancy name."

Holloran flipped the page. There was one photo left to see. It showed an older woman holding up a pug that looked a bit like Kirby, not just in breed. They had a family resemblance, though the dog in the picture was much fatter. And looked to be half asleep. But, like Kirby, he had a white spot on a coat of black. Then Canin did a double-take on the woman.

"I know her."

"That's Alison Ford," Holloran said. "You know, star of the Alison Ford Comedy Hour back in the days when television meant something."

Canin did indeed remember. "She was great. I loved her show. I watched them all growing up."

"You're a little young aren't you?"

"They used to show them, reruns, when I was kid. And Alison Ford, she just played all these different characters. The bum who always got tossed out of fancy restaurants. The bumbling housemaid. And the kindergarten teacher who hated kids. And the pratfalls. She had great pratfalls. It was almost like ballet, the way she flew across the TV screen on her way to the floor."

"That's her."

"And she shows pugs, huh?"

"Well, there's an interesting story there. Our pugs had the same poppa and momma."

"Oh?"

Holloran tossed an empty on the pile, then opened the cooler and took out another beer. "About time for a beer run, here. Only got fourteen left."

Popping the top, he turned back to Canin.

"See, I learned all about dog shows and pugs in the prison library. I became a pug man the day that poor critter in Yuma died in my arms. Of course, I always liked dogs, but after that, I dedicated myself to the pug breed. And I swore when I got out of prison, I'd own myself the best pug I could lay my hands on, and make a champion out of him. All in the memory of that poor little pup back in Yuma. Sort of like winnin' one for the Gipper. My sister told me I was crazy. Told me pugs were a bad investment. I know, I know, I should listen to my sister. She's close to God.

"But then I got a sign of my own. My first day out of prison, I pick up the newspaper, and what do I see? A charity auction where the biggest items on the block are two beauties from Pugs in the Mist. I thought, 'Hell, that's the best pug kennel in the Southwest.' So I take my $5,000 settlement money, buy an old oil-burning Ford Falcon from the Used Car Bazaar up there on Van Buren, rent a tux and drive myself right into the Phoenician resort, swankiest, gaudiest place in town, whereupon I bid $4,200 -- my life's savings at that point -- for the dog you see sitting on my lap before you."

"Can any dog be worth that much?" Canin asked, speaking his mind and instantly regretting it.

Rhino Holloran, a sweating whale, leaned forward.

"So, you're wonderin' if Kirby is worth anything."

"That's not really what ..."

"How much do you think those teeth of yours are worth, you little shit?"

Canin swallowed. "I'd say it's a buyer's market right now."

Holloran smiled and settled back into his chair. "Hey, I like that."

Thoughts formed in Canin's mind. Involuntary thoughts like: I'd like to kill that fat fascist asshole and his ugly dog. Of course, they went unspoken. Instead, Canin took a few breaths and asked, "What about Alison Ford? Is she as funny in person as she was on TV?"

It wasn't a particularly good question, but it was safe. That's all Canin wanted for the moment: To return to safe ground. Still, he had to admit he was curious about Alison Ford. He was part of a whole new generation of TV viewers who discovered her some twenty years after her show first ran. Besides, here was a whole new angle. The famous, if washed-up, TV star angle.

"Is she as funny in person?"

"Yeah, if you like laughin' at drunks. "

"She was drunk at a dog show?"

"No, she only drinks at home. With her dog."

"How do you know that?"

"I was there. We were friends, for a while. By the time of the Scottsdale show, we'd had a bit of a falling out. But we said hi, and she agreed to be in the picture."

"You were friends with Alison Ford?"

"Yeah, I kinda pushed myself on her, I guess. I wrote her and said maybe our dogs could get together, play know. Of course, what I really wanted was to see what it was like up there in that fancy mansion on North Central Avenue, where the crim-della-crim live, you know? I was interested showing my dog, too, and I thought, being rich and all, Alison might be of some help. A lot of it's not what you know, but who you know, and I thought she could help me with both. Hey, made sense to me.

"Well, hell, as it turned out she remembered me from the charity auction. Invited me up. She is a real lover of pugs, I tell you."

"What was the name of the charity?" Canin asked.

"The Anti-Youth In Asia League."

"Coming out against Asian teens. That's a charity?"

30

"No, you know, anti-killin' dogs. Euthanasia. Anyway, it's got a big shelter in south Scottsdale."

"And Alison Ford is a big contributor? Sits on the Board of Directors?"

"Used to, I understand, but not anymore. Now she's all involved with some do-gooder veterinarian. Look, I don't mean any disrespect, but nowadays she's usually too drunk to step out of the house. On pug matters, really important pug matters, she'll sober up, but otherwise..."

"Did Alison Ford invite you up often?"

"I had an open invitation. Neighbors got used to seeing my '69 Falcon heading up her drive. She never came out here, of course, but she sent a messenger out once in a while. Anyway, Ms. Ford liked to tell all her neighbors how a homeless ex-con outbid her for a pug at the charity auction."

"You outbid her?" Canin asked.

"Well, I think she was joking. She really wanted Captain Nemo anyway. That was the other pug put up for auction. She bid four thousand on him, same as Kirby brought. Bargain at that."

"Uh huh."

"She's very attached to that dog, very attached. But I tell you, the pug had some real health problems. I don't know what it was, but he started lookin' real sickly. Just fat and lazy and sick, and just a god-awful bad breath. I think the dog's illness drove Miss Ford into a state of, um, weirdness."

"Weird? In what way?"

"It was right after ... well, never mind that ... it was just about two months ago. Why, it was right after I ... She offered me ten thousand for my dog. Said she'd arrange payments. And when I told her no way, she just went berserk, screaming at me, saying a low-life like me didn't deserve a champion-line pug. Then she kicked me out. I thought it kinda odd under the circumstances."

31

"What circumstances?"

"Well, the circumstances of our being friends and all. But she showed up at the show – uh, to tell me all was forgiven. She remarked how healthy Kirby still looked. I guess she was glad to see Kirb. I don't know."

Holloran swigged his beer and wiped his chin.

"We worked things out, kinda."

A ray of sunlight, breaking through a gap in the clouds and the tamarisks, found a hole in a tattered green-bag overhead. It created a glare on the knobby end of the horn. Reflexively, Holloran rubbed it. It seemed to help him think. Danny captured the moment on film, as Canin made a point to look some other way.

"My guess is, Miss Ford wanted Kirby as a kind of replacement, on account of hers is headed toward an early grave. But that's the way it goes. Ain't no amount of money's going to separate me from my pug."

Ray Canin closed his notebook and stood up. The interview was concluded. Somewhere in that illegible rambling body of notes was a story. Maybe a good story. Maybe a story with a local angle. Better yet, a story that would save his job. It'd be a better story if he could talk to Alison Ford. The pug angle didn't interest him. But if he could work her into the story … The shelter had a Scottsdale address. That was the last place on the planet he'd want to go, but five minutes on the phone. All he needed was her number, and it was still morning. Maybe he could catch her sober.

Canin extended a hand. "Thanks for your time, uh, Rhino. I got what I needed."

As if lifted by some invisible hoist, Holloran slowly rose up out of his chair. The dog jumped to the ground and stayed close to his beastly master. Kirby panted rapidly as he gazed at Canin with a cool indifference. Canin, in turn, was reminded of his wife, of those halcyon days before she openly despised him.

"Hey, how about a beer before you go, both of you," Holloran said.

Danny said nothing. Canin replied with a slight shake of his head. "I got a deadline."

"Wait, I almost forgot. I got one more thing to show you," Holloran said, again becoming excited. He was far from drunk, but after five beers in a little under an hour, he appeared to be feeling quite sociable. "You got to see Kirby's competition strut, you know, how he shows his stuff when he's in the ring. We practiced this for a friggin' year before we entered our first dog show. I tell you, we got this sucker down. Now we're kicking pug butt."

"Might be worth some pictures," Danny said, opening the camera bag and retrieving the photo gear he had already packed away.

"Now, first, I'll stand Kirby for inspection. We call it stacking."

Rhino Holloran manipulated Kirby's paws, setting them far apart atop the dirt-laden patio rug. Any farther apart and the dog would have collapsed. He took on a squared bull-dog sort of stance. With a light touch, Holloran ran his hands over and under the dog. He felt the dog's head, then parted the lips and inspected the teeth.

"That's just how the judge would do it," Holloran said. "All the while he'd be saying to himself: 'Nice, round head, not too big, not too small. Good teeth. Strong shoulders. Thick, strong torso. Strong, well-proportioned legs.'

"Next, the trot, to see if the dog meets the pug standard for grace and beauty in motion."

Standing on Kirby's right, Holloran held his left arm out. "I'm pretending to hold a leash," he explained. "Me'n Kirby don't really need one, though."

Then Holloran pranced about an imaginary ring. His sandaled feet kicked up a small dust storm off the rug. His enormous gut rose and fell over the top of his blue jeans like a buoy on stormy waters. Kirby scampered to keep up.

33

So that's what it's all about. Man and dog move as one, circling the patio with the precision and grace of synchronized swimmers.

Danny was shooting like crazy, stumbling to keep up.

As Rhino Holloran and his dog, Kirby, took one more run around the rug, something caught Canin's eye. Beyond the line of tamarisks. A trail of dust rose up along the path that followed the river bottom out from Ninety-First Avenue. Through the dust, Canin saw a large truck.

It turned up a narrow rocky drive toward Holloran's, then skidded to a stop alongside the Falcon. More dust billowed up, then scattered in the wind. A sign – stuck to the door with magnets – read ARF.

The truck was a rolling dog dormitory, outfitted with doors that muffled the whining and barking of its captives. At least they weren't complaining about the heat. A small air-conditioning unit provided background noise.

Two ARF dog catchers stepped out of the truck. Holloran went out to greet them.

"I thought I told you goons to stay away from Kirby."

One dog catcher was tall. One was short. The tall one spoke first. "Mr. Michael Holloran, I'm AFR consultant Captain Art Nickerson...."

"You already told me your friggin' name. Now beat it before I grind you into Alpo."

The short man resumed talking where the tall man had left off. He may have been small in stature, but he was big on propriety.

"As my colleague started to say, I am officer Gerald Collick and this is Captain Art Nickerson, of the AFR canine consultation team. We tried to tell you. The pug needs a rabies shot, before he becomes a nuisance to public health. It's for the pug's own good."

He held out a rolled up sheet of paper. The alleged nuisance followed it with eyes big, wet and puzzled.

"See? We have a court order to take your dog into protective

34

custody. It's for the best. The pug, please."

Holloran took a swipe at the outstretched hand – and the paper.

"He's had his rabies shot. Let me see that."

Collick pulled his hand back.

"Sorry, it's under seal. It's a secret court order."

Holloran took a breath, and let it out slowly. Trauma was in the air.

Canin heard the camera shutter. He turned and saw Danny making adjustments, getting ready for action. He thought: *Where the hell's my car?*

Chapter Four

ARF consultant Collick was short, skinny and nervous. He had a thick cap of black hair combed back in shiny, well-oiled waves. His face had a perpetual shadow of facial hair. His khaki uniform was perfectly pressed, with sweat stains in the armpits. He carried a five-foot metal pole. It was hollow at one end, where cable came out and looped around to form a noose. The fetch pole was standard issue for dog catchers. Or as these guys called themselves, consultants.

Collick held it across his chest like a soldier's carbine.

"You're taking Kirby from *me?*" Holloran snarled. "You couldn't wipe a parakeet's ass."

Holloran faced off against the dogcatchers on a rocky oil-stained path midway between the ARF wagon and the patio. Canin backed up against Holloran's aging Ford Falcon, perched on a patch of weeds. At this time of year, despite a few showers, they were brown and seed-bearing. The seeds came in two models – burrs and skin-burrowing darts. Canin gave up trying to pick them out of his socks.

The taller dogcatcher reached down, picked out a burr, tossed it aside, then stepped into the discussion.

"Mr. Holloran, we have the full backing of ARF, a fully accredited charitable organization. We're like the Red Cross of dogs. When we say, 'Hand over your pug,' we're not speaking just for ourselves. We're speaking on behalf of a powerful special-interest group, almost a government unto itself."

"The only government I recognize is the American Kennel Club."

Nickerson answered Holloran with a wry smile. He was as

unruffled as the smaller guy was nervous. His voice carried a slight drawl, suggesting a childhood in Kingman or parts west. His complexion told of a man comfortable outdoors or at a desk – lightly tanned and crisscrossed with lines that could have come from squinting in the sun or thinking about what to write in his next report. He looked to be about six-foot-three with a lanky frame that worked best in casual stances, where the hips were shifted slightly and most of his weight fell on one leg. He had extra-large joints, with elbows the size of croquet mallets. His right elbow was bent just enough to let his right hand rest nonchalantly on the butt of a holstered pistol.

Canin did not want things to get ugly, but he knew that was wishful thinking. He wanted to leave but he couldn't. Danny, for one, would never leave a promising scene. And even Canin felt obligated to see how this played out. He didn't want to miss the lead to his story.

But he remained silent. And he stayed to the side. This wasn't a news conference. Nobody was taking questions.

"Now, go. Or I'll give you nothin' but grief," Holloran said.

The little nervous one piped in.

"You talk big, Mister. But we have the force of law behind us."

Collick looked behind him, perhaps expecting a Marine assault to rescue him. There was just Nickerson, looking passive.

"OK, you leave me no choice."

Collick's voice cracked. Whose wouldn't? To get to the pug, he had to get past Holloran. He took a baby step, the fetch pole shaking in his hands. He took another baby step to go around Holloran. But Rhino Holloran moved to block him. It wasn't hard. He just crossed his arms and glared out from his cavernous sockets.

Kirby, apparently sensing all this had something to do with him, took cover behind his master. Danny Stewart crouched in the grass, getting pictures of a frightened dog. Nickerson closed ranks with Collick and unholstered his pistol. Canin noticed that it had an extraordinarily large bore.

37

"The pug, Mr. Holloran. Hand it over. Please, don't force me to use this on you," Nickerson said.

The gun carried some weight with Holloran. For the first time, he showed a measure of fear.

"Hey, come on, now. Why are you doing this to me? I ain't bothered anybody!"

Nickerson let Holloran's words hang in the air for a moment. He seemed to enjoy the sound of Rhino Holloran caving in. And he seemed to be waiting for Holloran to make things easy on himself – to give up the dog rather than face getting shot with a really big gun.

Holloran, however, didn't budge. He didn't blink. He just waited for an answer.

"We're a charitable organization, Mr. Holloran, dedicated to the welfare of dogs throughout the greater Phoenix area," Nickerson said. His own aw-shucks coolness appeared to be wearing thin. Nickerson swallowed. "Our motto is 'healthy dogs are a good thing.' Now, let's see if your dog is healthy. The ARF clinic is … just a forty-five minute drive. We'll have Kirby back before lunch."

Canin glanced over at Kirby. The dog was shaking. Big deal, Canin thought. Reflexive behavior of a dumb animal. The pug had no capacity for real emotion, outside of recognizing hunger pangs. Kirby quivered at the sight of dogcatchers the way a mouse shook when cornered by a cat. Just a reaction to a stimulus. A threat response.

Still, the dog put on a good act. Canin gave Kirby credit for that. He almost felt sorry for the poor creature.

"I'm not letting this dog out of my sight. I'll…I'll take him in for shots, next week, as soon as I drop a new battery in my old Falcon."

"Sorry, the time for voluntary compliance has passed. Step aside, or I'll have no choice. I'll have to use this." Nickerson held out the large-bore pistol. "It's a tranquilizer gun."

Holloran cocked his head. His moment of appeasement had vanished.

"If you shoot my dog, Nickerson, I'm going to give you a lobotomy with a tire iron."

Rhino Holloran reached into the weeds and came up holding a tire iron. Immense and crazed, he began to resemble his namesake. He no longer drew breaths. He heaved in snorts. He pawed the ground like a half-ton bull. His horn, flushed with rage, was poised for a charge.

Nickerson swallowed, spoke slowly and chose his words carefully. He was, after all, dealing with a wild animal.

"His pistol is not for your dog, sir," Nickerson said. "It's for you. The dart will stop a four-hundred-pound bear. Or you. We figured the dog would be easy catch, once you signed on."

"You're not taking the dog," Holloran answered.

Holloran lumbered toward him, passing the tire from hand to the other. Nickerson did not shoot right away. Canin guessed he only had one dart and had to make it count. Nickerson stepped back, all the while keeping the pistol trained on the great white rolls of flesh. Maybe Nickerson had second thoughts about whether – even at this range – the dart would penetrate the man's hide. Or how quickly the chemical would take him down. For whatever reason, Nickerson hesitated. For too long. His heel caught the discarded car battery. He fell backward. Holloran jumped toward him, tossing aside the tire iron. It was trade-in. He picked up the battery, a large block of rubber and acid. He lifted it over Nickerson's head.

Danny, ever the photojournalist, put the pedal to his digital Nikon. He remained outside the story, an observer through the lens. But Canin couldn't just stand by and watch.

"Rhino, don't do it!" Canin shouted. "It's not worth it!"

Rhino Holloran looked back over his shoulder at Canin, some twenty feet away. He kept a safe distance. He had no plans to go in and break things up.

Turning to Canin, Holloran roared: "The hell it's not!"

OK, the man didn't agree.

Canin had bought Nickerson some time, however. Nickerson had scrambled to his feet, then aimed for the crotch. He squeezed the trigger, and nothing happened. He squeezed it repeatedly, and nothing happened. His expression was three parts fear, one part anger.

"Goddamn it!" he shouted.

Rhino Holloran spun around. He stared momentarily as Nickerson kept making clicking sounds with the trigger. He flung the battery. Nickerson dived for the ground. The battery sailed over his head.

"I need something bigger," Holloran said.

Nickerson covered his head as the battery shattered against a large, smooth stone. Acid sprayed out. A half-dozen drops splattered against his arm and shoulder, burning holes in his khaki uniform and skin. One drop seared the back of neck. But rolling over, he managed to ignore all that. Instead, now flat on his back, he inspected his dart gun.

"What the hell? Did I forget the CO-2 cartridge? The safety? The safety! How could I ... Jesus!" Nickerson screamed to no one in particular.

He fumbled to undo it.

"Got it!"

By then, Holloran was standing over him. He had pulled loose from the streambed a rock no bigger than a modestly priced Chevy. He steadied it over Nickerson's chest. This time he was going to crush the man's lungs. And to make sure Nickerson stayed put this time, Holloran placed his foot on the man's stomach.

"Collick! Help me! Help me, Collick!" Nickerson screamed.

"Help him!" Canin joined in.

He spun around to see Collick run past with the noose. He was trying to snag the pug, but the pug was too quick. Give the dog credit for that, too, Canin thought. He know how to dodge a dogcatcher – although, admittedly, Collick didn't seem hard to fool.

Collick backed Kirby up against beer-can mountain.

"You're mine now."

"Help me! He's going to kill me!" Nickerson cried.

The screams finally caught Collick's attention. He cocked his head, as if to track the noise by echo-location. It was the distraction Kirby needed. The pug bolted for open ground. Collick slapped the pole. "Damn, I had him. This happens every time."

Then he turned and saw the size of the rock Holloran was about to drop on his boss.

"Oh, my G-God!" Collick stammered.

Collick dashed toward Holloran, and – with a two-handed cast – slipped the wide-open noose over the rock and Holloran's upraised arms. He dropped it down below Holloran's chin and tightened it with a twist of the wrist. The big man's arms kept the cable from cinching tight around his neck. But Collick had no time for perfection.

The rock teetered over Nickerson's chest.

Collick jerked the pole and snapped Holloran's head back and twisted his body around as he let go the rock. It landed on Nickerson's left wrist. Canin could hear the bone crack. Nickerson cried out in pain.

Canin ran over and tried to roll the rock off Nickerson's arm. It wouldn't budge. And Nickerson didn't seem to care. He lifted his right hand.

"Get the hell out of my way!" he shouted.

Canin glanced over. He was looking down the barrel of the tranquilizer gun.

He did a swan dive into a clump of burr-baring weeds. His glasses saved his eyes, but burrs stuck to his nose and lips. He picked and scraped them loose and ignored, for the moment, the hundreds of others clinging to him like ticks on a dog.

Holloran, caught in the snare, had managed to bend over and wrap his hand around the pole. He pivoted on one foot, spinning the pole like a hammer throw. Collick, gripping the handle, was at the end. He was in orbit around Holloran.

Nickerson couldn't get a clear shot of Holloran, as Collick kept getting in the way, once every revolution.

Then Collick lost his grip and went flying like a Wallenda. He went some fifteen feet, and might have gone farther had not the ARF truck stopped him. It was a body slam. Collick was down and bruised, but not out. He got to his feet, shook his head, then glanced up at the charging Rhino.

Holloran's great white whale of a gut rose and fell with every step as he closed in on Collick.

His back to the truck, Collick moved to his right, until he felt the latch to a large door. Behind it, Canin heard a large and vicious dog. Canin swallowed. His breathing became shallow and rapid. His palms became sweaty. Nothing to fear but fear itself. And that dog.

"Not another step," Collick said. He fingered the latch. "I'm warning you. This dog will go right for your throat."

Holloran did not stop.

"I'm warning you!"

Nickerson, though still pinned to the ground, could raise his head enough to see what was Collick was up to. His eyes widened.

"No, Collick! That dog hates me!"

"That's the other one! This one likes you."

"No ... please ...."

Collick threw open the door, and out leaped a white chow, baring long white teeth and a muzzle covered in a froth of drool. It flew over the weeds and rocks, headed for Holloran.

But the dog ran past him. And toward Canin.

You've got the wrong guy. It's Nickerson you hate, Canin thought to say.

But what did it matter. The dog wouldn't listen to him. Besides, he was speechless. Frozen with fear. A fear so penetrating he could feel it in his bone marrow. A fear he had usually managed to keep in check, pass off as indifference or at most a dislike for dogs. And now, it was exposed raw, as was the experience that spawned it – an experience long suppressed. Yes, it all came rushing back. He saw it now. He could not remember details like where he was. Or how old he was. Only that it was his first memory. He remembers something white and fluffy. On four legs. *Nice doggy. Oh no, doggy, no! Help, Mommy! It's got my nose! Owwie, Owwie!*

As the memories came rushing back, something clicked in Canin. Something opened up, like a good round of therapy. He had faced his fears. In a brief torrent of emotion, he had come circle. Back to reality.

Now all he had to do was run for his life. He headed toward Holloran's camp, toward beer-can mountain. He'd make noise climbing up it and scare the dog. He'd throw beer cans at it and chase it off. Rationally, Canin knew the plan didn't have a chance. Rationally, he knew he was in for another experience that would call for years of repressed thought – if he happened to live through it.

He didn't make it. His legs simply gave out. He fell and hit the ground hard, picking up more burrs and losing his glasses. He got back up and took off running without them. He'd get them later. Right now, he had a jugular vein to keep intact.

As he ran, he had this urge to look behind him. Without his glasses, with the world a blur, the urge was all the stronger – however ill-advised. He knew – that as he soon he looked over his shoulder – he'd see a dog flying at his throat.

Canin turned. There was no dog. The dog had picked up another scent. The scent of Nickerson.

It was just as Nickerson had feared. The chow sprinted toward him like a greyhound to do the business of a pit bull.

Behind the white blur of dog, Canin thought he saw Nickerson raise his good arm. It jerked slightly. The recoil of the tranquilizer gun.

Nickerson must have figured the dog would jump, and aimed high. He shot too soon, and missed. Canin did not follow the dog's path into Nickerson, but rather the dart. It was a bit of curiosity, really. He saw a blur moving slowly south-southwest, toward beer-can mountain. It had a silver tint, and wobbled a bit. It arched upward, then began to fall. It would not reach the beer cans.

The dart pinned Canin's shirt to his stomach. He cried out. Briefly, it felt like a laser of molten lead. Then a rush of numbness. He gazed down at the dart hanging limply from his midsection. Numbly, he studied it. *So that's what they look like.* He had been impaled by an oversized metal syringe with a shock of yarn for a guidance system. Canin tugged at it, but the needle did not slide out. It pulled at his skin from the inside.

Right. It's barbed.

Dimly, Canin sorted out what would come next. He had enough tranquilizer coursing through him to immobilize a 400-pound bear. At 152 pounds, Canin wasn't sure where he stood.

He fell to his knees, then flopped onto his back.

Danny caught up to him.

"Hang in there, Ray. I already called nine-one-one."

"Everything's out of focus, Danny. I … I lost my glasses."

"They wouldn't help."

"You never know, Danny … *you never know.*"

Canin couldn't tell if he spoke those words. Or just thought them. The world began to dissolve. Molecules separated into atoms. The atoms drifted apart and floated away.

A warm, wet slab of flesh found his hand. Panic. Resignation. Comfort. All came and went as Canin's nervous system recorded his final sensation before everlasting peace. Pug tongue.

Chapter Five

The sensation came back to his hand. He felt a smooth stroke and a velvet touch. This was human. He could see the human in his mind's eye. Renee…she had come back. She was holding his hand.

Canin heard a voice.

"Renee…Renee." It was faint. It was his.

Another person grabbed his whole arm and shook it.

"Ray! Ray! Look, Anna, he's coming out of it."

Canin opened his eyes. Danny – or the blurred form of Danny – was shaking his arm like a maraca. Danny looked from him to woman standing beside him. She was not Renee. She was Indian, like Danny. Through the fog of myopia, she appeared something out of a dream. Beauty. Not Renee runway-model, but natural born-of-earth beauty. Her hair was the color of anthracite and fell halfway down her back. She had an oval face – Canin lifted his head slightly for a better look – and a nose slightly bent near the bridge. Her chin was delicate, but not understated. Without glasses, he couldn't tell if she had good skin. Her body suggested a distance runner. Petite with skinny calves – a turquoise skirt covering everything else above the knees. Her blouse was loose, perhaps too loose. Clearly, she did not sport Renee's continental divide.

Anna dabbed her forehead with a handkerchief.

"It's hot in here."

"Yeah," Danny said, mopping his brow with his shirtsleeve.

Canin sat up. He was sweating.

"It is kind of warm for a hospital room," Canin said.

"It's not the hospital," Danny said. "It's your living room."

Canin took a breath, surveyed his surroundings. The walls had the same Janis Joplin poster he had hung up six years ago. Renee had already carted off anything resembling fine art, including a painting a friend had done and a reproduction of Ansel Adams' *Moonrise, Hernandez, New Mexico*. The walls themselves half-glistened with a patina of grime. The furniture looked like early American rejects.

Tossing off a sheet, Canin sat up on his couch. He felt faint, like all the blood was draining from his head. He took a few slow, deep breaths before he spoke.

"I should be in the hospital."

"That wasn't my call," Danny said. "Thank Healthy Lifeline."

"What are you talking about?"

"Healthy Lifeline. Our health insurance. They said all you needed was a few stitches and you'd be as good as new. In other words, no admission on their dime. Hospital patched you up and asked me to take you home."

Canin lay back down and draped an arm over his face.

"But I feel like a piece of boiled spaghetti."

"Doctor said you're lucky to be alive. That dart scored a direct hit on your stomach, filled up it with trank called Telazol. Stomach pump got most of it. Here's the bill."

Canin sat up again, took the bill. He brought it up to his face, inches from his nose.

"Jesus. One-thousand six hundred dollars."

"Sounds like a lot," Danny said. "But look on the bright side. They didn't take you to the Indian hospital. Doctors would have figured you were drunk and put you in detox."

"What the hell, Healthy Lifeline's going to pick up the tab."

"Well, maybe, maybe not. Hospital payment desk said the Healthy Lifeline had second thoughts, when they heard what happened. Somebody on the other end said your behavior was – what's the word?"

"Negligent," Anna volunteered.

"That's not a reason to deny care!" Canin said, finding the energy to yell, then lowering his head into his hands. Speaking through his knuckles, he added: "Who's your date?"

"No date," Danny said. "Cousin, from the Pima side of the family. Anna meet Ray. Ray meet Anna."

Ray held out his hand. "Nice to meet you."

"I'm over here."

He squinted and shifted slightly left and found her own slender fingers, the same ones that had earlier caressed his hand. As their hands met, a tingle traveled up Canin's fingertips and into his arm. He felt like he had grabbed a high-voltage wire and could not let go.

Anna broke the grip, stepped away.

"Nice to meet you," she said, sounding like she half meant it. He couldn't tell by her expression, though, since he couldn't make it out.

"I drove you back in your car. She's taking me home."

"Thanks," Ray said, gesturing his appreciation with his left hand, then noticing it still held the hospital bill. Something else caught his attention as well. Looking down, he noticed he had no shirt. Taped to his stomach was a square of gauze the size of a dinner napkin. Noticing that, he began to feel the pain, as though somebody bored a hole in him with a power drill.

"Ow, hurts like hell," Canin said. Then he looked toward Anna.

"Sorry, Anna. I didn't mean to swear. Well, I did, but not in front of ..."

"That's OK. Uh, Danny, I need to go. I need to prepare for my graduate seminar."

"Seminar?" Canin asked. "You're taking a class?"

"I teach the class – um, Danny?"

"And what is it you teach?"

"It's a seminar comparing post- and pre-Columbian North

47

American tribal governments."

Canin nodded. Now he understood why he went into journalism. "I see."

"Well, I'll tell you all about it when I have more time."

Anna Stewart smiled. She wasn't giving Canin a brush-off, or didn't sound like she was. She simply wanted to go. That didn't tell Canin much about what she might have thought about him. And maybe he had no business thinking what she thought, having met her five minutes ago.

Anxieties were beginning to creep in. As if the blunt instrument of physical pain weren't enough.

"I need a beer," Canin said. "Anybody else?"

"Anna doesn't drink, and – remember – I'm sober, eight years now."

"Fine."

Neither teetotaler offered to get Ray a beer. He pushed himself up by the couch arm. The sheet fell away and revealed a rather ordinary body covered in a pair of gym shorts. The stomach covered slightly more ground than the chest. And the legs were white and skinny, though serviceable.

Getting to the kitchen was a matter of finding furniture for support along the way. The kitchen table, though wobbly, got him from an end table to the kitchen counter, which led him to the refrigerator. Every move stressed the borehole under the bandage. It pained him to open the door. It pained him to reach for a beer. It pained him to pop the lid on the can and bring it to his lips.

Still, it was beer – worth its weight in trouble.

Stretching and hurting, Canin tipped the beer into his mouth.

"Careful, there," Danny said. "Doctors had to plug that hole in your stomach. Don't drink too fast or the cork'll pop out."

Canin lowered the can. Danny often exaggerated or stretched the truth on the spot. His expression usually gave him away. Danny was not the stoic cigar-store Indian. He did not have a "game face." He gave away what went on behind the mask just about every time. On the other hand, Canin couldn't see the mask in the first place.

"You're joking."

"Half joking," Danny said. "You got some bad-ass stitches, though. Doctors had to cut out the syringe, because of the barbs. So no heavy-lifting and no chugging contests."

Canin chugged half the beer, then took a deep breath.

"What time is it?" he asked.

"Ten O'clock, in the PM, Ray," Danny answered.

"We have to be going, Danny. I'm already swamped," Anna said.

Danny followed Anna to the door, then turned to face Ray. He appeared to smile, somewhat crookedly from what Canin could tell, like he had something more to say. Something painful. But he let it pass.

Ray found his way back to the couch and eased himself into it, as slowly as he could.

"This damn thing's really starting to hurt. I feel like I've been harpooned by a New England whaler. Better tell Sommerfield I won't be in tomorrow."

Danny's smile now looked outright tortured, like someone trying to put the best face on kidney failure.

"No need to," Danny sounded strained, worried. Canin couldn't read his face with that absurd grin, but his voice was a book.

"Why?"

Danny cleared his throat. "He fired you."

49

Chapter Six

Canin stared at the fuzzy image that was his colleague and friend, Danny. He sat silent for about a quarter of a minute.

"He fired me?"

"You missed the deadline. You spoke to him on the phone, right after the doctors patched you up."

"I spoke to him?"

"I guess you don't remember. You laughed and said he was uglier than that dog he told you to write about. You said, and I quote, " 'You're uglier than a pug.'"

"Hmm, Sommerfield's not all that ugly, really. Right at pug ugly, maybe, but not uglier."

"Well, it kind of pissed him off. He screamed louder than usual. I could hear him across the room. He fired you again."

Canin polished off the beer, then working his way to the frig, grabbed another one and popped it open. He drank half of it and returned to the couch for the other half.

"Ray, whatever help you need, just let me know. You're out of a job, but you're not off the reservation – not in my book. And by the way, here's your keys."

"Thanks."

"Uh, nice meeting you, Ray," Anna Stewart said, before seeing herself out. Danny followed. Ray Canin took a moment to reflect on his loneliness, before quickly finishing the second beer and starting on a third. Then he reached for a newspaper. There were plenty of half-read sections scattered about the room. The classifieds. That's what he wanted. He'd find himself a goddamn job. And this time tomorrow, he'd have the last laugh on that asshole of an editor. Canin held up the paper. He couldn't tell whether he had the classifieds or the sports section. Without his glasses, he had the eyesight of a mole.

He finished beer number three. And now he had the clarity of mind to make his next move. He grabbed the car keys and headed for the door. Once he had his glasses, he could read the goddamn newspapers. And get that goddamn job. Whatever it was.

The drive to the river bottom was a blur. A few horn blasts from approaching cars told him to get back in his own lane. He might have run a red light and a few stop signs, but he couldn't quite tell. He might have left the pavement once or twice, but he got lucky. He didn't hit any trees. The full moon made them easy to spot. That advantage would be lost when the clouds returned. The radio weather report assured Canin they would be back tomorrow. And a hundred miles to the east, the rain continued to soak the mountains. And the water ran down them, headed toward the Salt.

Canin turned on Ninety-First Avenue, marking its location by the lights of the sewage treatment plant. They looked like fat, blurry stars. As they slid by on his left, Mesquite Suzy's rug hut went by on the right. Without focus, all the colors had slipped out of place, like a poorly registered photograph. A dog barked. It sounded close. Sound really carries on these hot, humid nights, he thought.

The car dipped into the river bottom as Canin slowed to find the turnoff. He turned onto a rocky surface, relying half on intuition and half on the feel of the road. Driving by Braille. The headlights lit up a collage of bouncing gravelscape. He passed something big and yellow. The school bus. He thought he saw a face in the window, glowing in the moonlight.

Canin parked near Holloran's camp, as far as he could tell.

His glasses must have come off in the weeds somewhere around here. He could remember running toward a line of trees —

51

away from Holloran's shack – before falling down.

Canin grabbed a flashlight out of the glove compartment, and stepped out of the car. He switched it on, but nothing happened. He rattled the flashlight. He pounded it on his open palm. Nothing. Damn. Dead batteries. Well, he couldn't think of everything. Canin tossed the flashlight back into his car through an open window.

He'd have to settle for moonlight. Canin looked around. Everything was gray, in varying shades. He took a deep breath and mopped his brow with a shirtsleeve. The temperature had dropped into the low one hundreds. Well, it was almost midnight.

Canin walked toward Rhino Holloran's shack. In the moonlight, it appeared flat against the trees. Canin hadn't planned to visit the man. The place was just a point of reference – something to line up with while tramping the weeds for his glasses. Then again, Canin thought, maybe it would be best to pay a courtesy call. It was late. Holloran might be asleep. But if he heard a strange noise outside, he might just kill first and wait till morning to see who the hell or what the hell it was. And thanks to his run-in with the dogcatchers, Holloran was probably jumpier than usual.

As Canin neared the shack, he heard pebbles grind underfoot. He heard the weeds brushing up against his ankles, the burrs hitching rides. He heard the plastic-bag ceiling of Holloran's patio flutter in the breeze. But he didn't hear the dog. Odd, Canin thought, that Kirby would bark at a car a half mile away, but not an approaching intruder.

The closer Canin got, the more unwelcome he felt. When he was no more than ten feet from the shack and the patio, he stopped. He heard another sound now. His own rapid breathing. But still no dog. The dog must be sleeping now, along with Holloran. Let sleeping dogs lie. That made sense. And why wake a slumbering giant, especially one on parole for murder? And maybe, he gets lonely at night. And would welcome a companion. Like in prison. And Canin would be the girl. The wimpy guy who …

Canin changed his mind about letting Holloran know he was here. It'd be much simpler, perhaps safer, if he just quietly looked for the glasses, and quietly got the hell out of here when he found them.

Then he had another thought: a bit of self-criticism, if you will. The kind that comes with benefit of sobriety. *What the hell am I doing here in the first place? Out in the middle of this Godforsaken hellhole looking for a goddamn pair of glasses? It's dark. I'm afraid. I have no idea what the hell's out there. Someone could be watching me right now. Yes, I think someone wants to kill me.*

Just run, damn it, run!

And run he would have, had not something on the patio caught his eye. He had been looking right at it, but failed – at least right away – to recognize it as a man who had fallen off a chair. Damn fool Holloran, he thought. He had drunk himself into unconsciousness. The dogcatchers had merely provided a break in the routine. Holloran had chased them away, sat down and polished off his fourteen remaining beers. Then he passed out and fell out of his chair.

The chair had been tipped over backwards. Holloran had followed along, and now was flat on his back. His stomach – lit up by a moonbeam passing through a hole in the plastic – looked like an Air Stream buried in the snow.

For a drunk, Holloran was a very quiet sleeper. Most drunks snored when they slept. Uncle Matt sure had. Canin could remember – back about the time he was eleven or twelve – Uncle Matt drank like a fish, passed out on the couch and snorted like a pig in heat.

But not Rhino Holloran. He slept like a baby. And right next to him, snuggled against his head, his dog did, too.

Rubbing his eyes, Canin looked again. Still blurry. Could sure use those damn glasses, he thought. Well, as long as Holloran was out cold, he could look for them without worrying about disturbing the man's sleep and getting killed for it. Staring at Holloran's blurred, gray

53

figure, Canin thought: The poor man needs a pillow. His generous head rested on the patio rug, which was nothing more than a worn-out mat thrown over a hard, lumpy bit of ground.

Canin scanned the porch until he saw what looked like a bit of cloth, a T-shirt or something. He grabbed the shirt and rolled it up. He stepped lightly across the rug and crouched down. Gently, he lifted Holloran's head with left hand and, with the T-shirt in his right ... that's funny, Canin thought. The hair was sticky to the touch. Perspiration perhaps. But that wasn't all. He could see that Holloran had a spoon in his mouth. He had fallen asleep while eating, and it must have been something with raisins, Canin guessed. Holloran's face seemed to be covered with them. He set the head down on the T-shirt, and stepped back without taking his eye off the man. Then he realized he might have stepped on the dog. Well, the dog *was* here.

Still, the dog didn't complain. Not a peep.

"Sorry, fella," Canin said, just grateful the pug didn't bite him. Slowly, he bent down to give the creature a reassuring pat and stuck his hand in a puddle. The puddle that looked like a pug until now.

Canin withdrew his hand and rubbed the substance between his thumb and forefinger. It was thick and sticky. It smelled a bit like scrap metal. Like blood. Just like the goo in the man's hair. Canin wiped his hand on his trousers.

"Christ," he whispered. "The bastard hurt himself."

Canin reached over the pool of blood and gave Holloran a shake.

"Hey, Rhino, come on, wake up," he said. Holloran's head rolled to the left and fell into a small circle of moonlight. Canin got a better look at all the spots on his face and could tell, even without his glasses, they weren't raisins. A bad skin condition, maybe. Yeah, a severe rash that had left his face pocked with little black craters. Everywhere. His chin. His cheeks. His nose. His forehead, craters everywhere.

Some rash, Canin thought. There had to be a simpler explanation.

He kneeled down, careful not to put his hands in the blood, closer and closer, until he was no more than six inches from Holloran's nose. The sleeping giant's face was almost in focus. Canin could explain the spots now. They were small bullet holes, made by small bullets, a lot of small bullets.

"Shit," Canin muttered.

He was numb. He just stared. Thank God, Rhino Holloran had the courtesy not to stare back. The thoughtful killer had closed his eyes.

Canin leapt to his feet, too quickly. He slipped and his right knee and left hand planted themselves in the sticky mess. He jerked away and stood up. He wiped his hand off on his shirt, then thought better of it – after the fact.

"God damn," he muttered.

He gazed down at Holloran, whose bloated, blurry face, once again, looked covered with raisins. And then, a new detail revealed itself. There was something on the forehead. Or rather something that wasn't. Even half-blind, Canin could see that the horn, the doorknob, whatever you wanted to call it, was gone. Sawed off. All that remained of it was a small, whitish stump.

A tight knot formed in the hollow of Canin's stomach, just behind the incisions. What now? he asked himself. First thing ... first thing, he told himself, is to call the police. No, first thing, is to get the hell out of there.

Ray Canin took off running. He could see the white form that was his car and headed straight for it, taking a shortcut straight across the field of weeds and tall grass. The knot in his stomach began to break up from waves of nausea. Canin tried to fight it off, but it was no use. He had to stop and throw up. Wrong-way beer.

When the worst was over, he took a few steps, then stooped over again – his hands on his knees – to catch his breath. He caught a glint in the moonlight. A bit of glass. He picked it up. It was a lens, intact. A pair of glasses, intact. *Couldn't be!* Canin slipped the glasses on, and in the literal blink of an eye, a vague, moonlit riverbed became the land of a thousand details, each detail coming forward with the utmost clarity. He saw the cars, the buses and the campsites of the bottom dwellers. He saw their rock-strewn paths, choked with weeds that had grown strong and bountiful on sewage effluent. He saw the ghostly outlines of tamarisk trees, oversized and ungainly. He saw fat clouds muscling in on a moon as sharp and round as a tiddlywink.

Canin scrambled to the Toyota, cranked it and spun around toward Ninety-First Avenue. He pushed the pedal, kicking up smaller rocks from the river bottom. And pounding the framework against bigger ones. Tires squealed as they hit the pavement. Canin fishtailed into a right turn. The pickup truck caught him by surprise, the one he had pulled out in front of. But he heard the horn. The sound of rubber laying down skid marks. He saw smoke in his rear view mirror, whitish smoke lit by the moon – rising from the brakes.

Canin thought, "Shit. That was close."

He heard a man yell, "Watch out, asshole!"

Canin shot past the sewage plant, past Mesquite Suzy's. He lost the pickup. Better yet, he had found his glasses. Everything was sharp. Clear. Focused. Everything but the blur of a dead man's face riddled with bullets.

Chapter Seven

Next morning the washing machine in the next room pounded the wall with a repetitive one-two combo. The homicide sergeant at the kitchen table looked up from his coffee, curious.

"Laundry? On Wednesday? Why?"

"I have a favorite shirt. I wash it often," Ray Canin replied.

"So, how'd you get it ... soiled?"

"In the usual way."

Ray Canin hadn't expected that answer to satisfy anyone, but the sergeant dropped the subject, for the moment. If he persisted, perhaps he would have found the bloodied shirt and pants Canin had stuffed in the machine just minutes before the police arrived. It was more coincidence, than planning. If he had expected them this soon, he would have done his dirty laundry last night, just after getting home. Instead of falling in bed.

Not that doing the wash was all about destroying evidence. He really did need the clothes, his blue button-down shirt and his khaki Dockers. And, if he get out the bloodstains, so much the better. He'd have clean clothes for job interviews. And fewer questions from homicide cops, like the sergeant and his colleague.

"You know my name, but I didn't get yours," Canin said.

"Sergeant Gene Sterner. And this is Detective Rick Stern."

"Stern and Sterner?"

"Let's get this straight, Murder Man," Stern said, speaking up for the first time. "Those are just names. See, he's just stern. I'm sterner."

"No, he just said he was Sterner."

"When it comes to questioning witnesses, he is sterner," Sterner said. "But I can be stern."

Canin could feel the pain in his stomach gathering again, a knot forming around badly damaged tissue. He sat down at the kitchen table, at the end – a right angle to the two cops.

"Two cops named Sterner and Stern, who are stern and sterner. The odds must be a million-to-one."

"You're unbalanced," Sterner said.

"What?"

"Your load in the washing machine. It's unbalanced."

"It'll stop," Canin said. Which was true. The spin cycle was nearly completed. Still, Canin didn't want Sterner obsessing about it, like he was.

"More coffee?" Canin asked nervously.

Sterner shrugged. "Why not?"

The sergeant smiled, but the apparent burden of looking at corpses all day kept it minimal. If you had to guess what kind of dog he had, bulldog would come to mind. He was not so stern, despite his claim. He wasn't exactly jovial either. He appeared to have reached the humorless age of forty-seven or forty-eight.

His partner, Stern couldn't have been more than thirty-three, a few years younger than Canin. He had a pale complexion, jet-black hair combed straight back and a mustache that was trimmed to some kind of exact military specifications. Humorless would not describe Stern. He was a man who approached everybody like a verbal punching bag. Jab at them long enough and sooner or later, he'll have them begging: No mas! No mas!

Canin could spend a lifetime thinking about how much he disliked Stern, but he had a few other things on his mind. What little mind he had left. He was still half asleep. His head hurt like the Big Bang. Then there was amalgam of pain in his stomach, from stabbing pain to churning nausea. He felt it every time he shifted his weight. Sitting at

58

the breakfast table, he shifted a lot. It was hard to get comfortable with cops in your kitchen.

The two had showed up at Canin's front door about eight-thirty, pushing their way into the living room as they thanked Canin for inviting them in. And for the next twenty minutes, they did little but flip through their mini-size steno pads, while making small talk about the weather and the stress of being homicide cops – so many bodies, so little time. But mostly they drank coffee from paper mugs and dug into a fifty-count bag of Hostess Donut Gems. Their faces were so caked with powdered sugar it looked like they had dusted their own cheeks for prints.

They didn't offer Canin any doughnuts, so he helped himself to some graham crackers from his pantry.

The washing machine stopped, but the house didn't settle into silence. The air conditioner – old and inefficient – sounded like an old man blowing into balloon. It had long ago stopped making cold air. At least in summer. The hotter the days got, the more the unit huffed and puffed. And the warmer the house got. And the more the humidity rose, the harder the unit struggled to make good. In August, it was a losing struggle. The air moved slowly from vent to intake, carrying the hint of a soft breeze from an active volcano.

Canin's T-shirt, featuring a 10 kilometer race he had once run and almost finished, was drenched in sweat about the armpits and back. Sterner had removed his jacket and draped it over a kitchen chair. He had loosened his tie, but kept on sweating anyway. Stern kept on his jacket, a beige blazer. He didn't sweat much, though every once in a while he dabbed his forehead with a handkerchief.

Sterner dried his face with his shirtsleeve, then licked powdered sugar off his fingers. He appeared to be building toward the real reason for his visit.

"Your friend, Rhino, got pretty shot up," Sterner said. "By the time our guys found him, he was ... pretty dead."

"Only it wasn't so pretty. Head full of lead," Stern snickered. "My guess is he took thirty-one, thirty-two rounds in his fat noggin."

Sterner regarded him skeptically. "Thirty-one? Is that what you took in the pool?"

"Thirty-two, actually," Stern said.

"You're high, way high. His head, fat though it is, couldn't possibly hold that many rounds and still be in one piece."

"Wait till the medical examiner's report comes in. You'll see, thirty-two."

"You're always so damn sure of yourself, Stern," Sterner said. He shook his head as if to say: Young cops these days, what are you gonna do?

"There's already eight-hundred bucks in the pot. I see a new set of Ping irons in my future," Stern said.

Canin looked warily from Stern to Sterner.

"You can't be serious," he said. "You're taking bets on how many bullets that poor bastard has in his head?"

Sterner waved off the question with a good-natured smile.

"Oh, it's just a little something we got started down at headquarters. One of our esteemed colleagues saw the crime-lab photo of the body, and tried to guess how many bullets there were in it. And before you knew it, we had an office pool on our hands."

Sterner mopped around the corners of his mouth with a shirtsleeve. Then he leaned forward.

"But, of course, we're not here to discuss how many bullets Mr. Holloran had in his head. We're here to talk about how they got there. Who put them there. And why. Got any ideas, Ray?"

"Not offhand."

"Somebody saw your car leaving the scene."

"How do you know it was mine?"

"Not hard. He took down your license plate. Said you were driving, um, erratically."

"OK, I was there. Holloran was already dead, and I was going to call after I got home."

"No cell phone?"

"No service. It was cut off."

Stern rose from his chair and swung around behind Canin. He leaned over, his breath rustling the hair on the back of Canin's neck. His cologne drifting around and up Canin's nostrils.

"We got the call this morning, Murder Man," Stern snapped. "His sister found him."

"I was going to call when I got back. I was so damn tired."

"His sister! How do you think she felt!"

"I … I don't….."

"I got a better question, Murder Man. Where's the gun?"

Canin slapped the table.

"Would you stop calling me Murder Man? I didn't murder anybody. I don't own a gun. I didn't kill Rhino Holloran. I went back to the river to look for my glasses. I saw him and … at first I thought he passed out while eating raisins."

"Twenty-two-caliber raisins, huh?" Stern said. "Look, Murder Man …"

Sterner cut in. "Maybe he's right. Maybe 'Murder Man's' a little, uh, you know, inflammatory."

"OK, Ray – don't mind if I call you Ray? Well, now, Ray …" Stern pulled a folded sheet of papers from his coat pocket. "Here, sign here, last page, dotted line – and we'll leave you alone."

Canin took the papers, looking from Stern to Sterner, reading their expressions. Sterner had no expression. He just blinked once. Stern, on the other hand, had a hint of a grin. That and his dull brown eyes remained unchanged as he reached across the table for a Donut Gem.

Powder fell on the papers. Canin brushed it off. In the course of his adult life, Canin had signed dozens of papers without reading them. But for this, he'd make an exception.

61

He skimmed down the first page. It didn't take long to get the idea. "This is a confession!"

"Sure, it is. Just sign the damn thing!" Stern said.

"Why? I'm not confessing to a murder I didn't commit."

"No, you're confessing to a murder you did commit," Stern snapped. "Look, you'll save us all lot of trouble if you sign now. Otherwise, we keep asking you questions. Only now, you don't get bathroom breaks."

Stern chuckled, blowing doughnut chunks and powder into the back of Canin's head.

Canin brushed out the doughnut debris. And took a deep breath. Stern's threats had left him shaken, and a little stirred, too. If life were fair, he'd be allowed one free swing at jerks like Stern. Of course, in the real world, it was the other way around. The cops got the free swings. So Canin took in a deep breath and let it out slowly. Then he bit down hard on a graham cracker.

"That's it, Ray. Just try to relax," Sterner said. "That usually works best."

Sterner's voice had a calm, soothing quality, like a gentle laxative.

"Now, tell us, Ray. About what time did you find the body?"

"A little after eleven," Ray swallowed. "Well, that was when I found my glasses. I couldn't read the time before that ... and that was right after I found the body."

"You found the body without your glasses?" Sterner asked.

"I was looking for my glasses."

Stern picked up the questioning: "You were looking for your glasses in the river bottom, below the sewage treatment plant at eleven p.m.? Why didn't *I* think of that? It's so obvious!"

People like Stern gave sarcasm a bad name, Canin thought. But he kept his mouth shut. *You can't win a debate with cops.* Stern reached over Canin's shoulder and grabbed another little doughnut. He stuffed it in his mouth, as if to shut himself up.

62

Canin took another hard bite off a cracker and washed it down with some coffee.

"I went out there to look for my glasses. I lost them ..."

Stern didn't stay quiet for long. He spun around the table, bent down, until he was practically kissing Canin's ear.

"I'm giving you second chances. And what do I get? The same god-damn story," Stern said. Moist Hostess Gem crumbs blasted the side of Canin's face. "Oh, Mother of Mercy, you are something else, Raymond. First, you pump this guy so full of lead he could anchor the Queen Mary, then you tell us you were just out there looking for your glasses."

Canin dug crumbs out of his ear with a little finger. He didn't look up. He simply stared at the green Formica tabletop. When Stern was quite finished, Canin looked over at Sterner. He pleaded his case.

"Come on, Sergeant, I'm trying to cooperate! But I can't get two words out my mouth, and Sherlock Holmes here pins a murder rap on me!"

Sterner arched his eyebrows as he gazed up at Stern.

"Sometimes he's Sherlock. Sometimes he's Inspector Lestrade. Right now, I'm not sure. But, like Lestrade, he tries hard."

Canin glanced at Stern, who had backed off from blowing empty calories into his ear. The young detective pursed his lips and – with folded arms – leaned against the kitchen counter. The crack about Lestrade – Holmes's bumbling foil – seemed to sting. At least it shut up Stern, for the moment.

"Go on, Ray," Sterner said. "Start at the beginning."

Canin explained how he had gone out to interview Holloran Tuesday morning. What had happened when the dog catchers arrived, and how he had lost his glasses in the confusion. He told Stern everything he could think of. Getting shot with a tranquilizer gun. Getting fired from his job. Going back to Holloran's camp after drinking three beers. He told them about finding Holloran. He told

63

them about everything but the blood. You can't help but look guilty when your clothes are covered in blood. He worked his way up to finding his lost glasses.

"It was the only pair I had."

Sterner's face crumpled up into wrinkles of reflection, a bulldog in thought. "D'you ever consider Lasik surgery? My wife got it, and she can see near-perfect now. Of course, like everything, it has some drawbacks. When she couldn't find her glasses, I could read *Playboy* and tell her it was *National Geographic.* She'd ask: 'What're you reading, Eugene?'

" 'I'm boning up on the local culture,' I'd say."

Canin wasn't amused, but he managed a courtesy smile.

"Hmm," Sterner said. He seemed to be thinking now about how to proceed. He rubbed the tip of his nose with his forefinger. He bit his lip. He picked up a Donut Gem and contemplated it as a gentlemen would contemplate a fine cigar. Canin shifted in his seat and got a stabbing pain for his efforts, like he had attempted hara-kiri with a garden tool. On top of that, Canin harbored a vague uneasiness as he watched Sterner pass the Donut Gem back and forth under his nostrils, like a Havana. Then, stuffing the whole thing into in his mouth, he resumed his questioning.

"Now, Ray, did you notice anything unusual about Rhino Holloran when you found him…"

"He had a spoon in his mouth. A silver spoon."

Stern broke his silence.

"We know he wasn't born with it," he said.

The detective laughed, making a noise like a pig having a troublesome bowel movement. Turning around, Canin saw Stern remove a silver spoon from the pocket of his blazer. It was sealed in a sandwich bag.

"He stole it."

"How do you know?" Canin asked.

"It's Alison Ford's spoon. Rhino Holloran took it without telling her. That's called stealing."

"What's that have to do with me?"

"Everything's connected somehow, Suspect Man."

Stern glanced over at Sterner. The sergeant nodded, signing on to the more neutral term, "Suspect Man."

"See," Stern continued, "About two, three months ago, Alison Ford's house on North Central was broken into. The thief made off with jewelry, silverware and one or two paintings. Burglary detectives knew he had visited Alison Ford a number of times. And they knew he had a record. But they couldn't prove he stole anything, and Alison Ford just bristled at the very notion Rhino Holloran could be involved."

"Anyway," Sterner said, picking up the narrative. "The property-crimes guys told us about their suspicions. But it was too thin for a search warrant. Never mind whether you actually need a search warrant for a lean-to on the river bottom. The guy never threatened Ford. And we didn't see Holloran as the cat burglar type – big, slow giant like that. We couldn't see him slipping past a burglar alarm as sophisticated as Alison Ford's, you know, without some help from the inside. I hear ants can set it off trying to sneak in for cookies. So I hear."

Sterner laughed at the notion.

"Turns out, burglary was right. When we went through Holloran's effects – trying to find the gun, of course – we came across that, and about a hundred other pieces like it."

Sterner pointed a Donut Gem at the silver spoon in Stern's hand.

For Stern, it was his cue.

"See, Suspect Man, it all makes sense now," Stern said. "You knew Holloran did a big job and had some really nice stuff on his hands. And you had money problems. You're a month behind on rent. Your car's a piece of crap. Your wife's leaving you for somebody with a real

65

future. Yeah, we do our homework, Suspect Man. So, here's what you did. Under cover of darkness, you go back to Holloran's camp, sneak up and shoot him in the head. You plan to cart off everything worthwhile, especially all the pawnable silverware. But you hadn't counted on transients with cell phones. The police show up and you got to cut your losses and get the hell out of there."

Canin pounded the table and stood up.

"Jesus Christ, I didn't kill the guy! Isn't that clear to you? Look, it wasn't that dark. There was a full moon out. I couldn't just walk up there, unless he was already dead. And if he wasn't, his dog would have barked and woken him up. Well," Canin paused, "if the dog was there."

"This dog likes to bark?" Stern asked.

"At everybody."

"But this time it didn't?"

"It wasn't there."

"Right."

"Of course, you knew Holloran from earlier that day, I guess," Sterner said, matter of factly. "You wouldn't have to sneak up on him."

"Look, sergeant, if you think I killed Holloran for some fancy forks and spoons, look around. You won't find anything here you couldn't buy at Kmart for six-dollars a setting. And if I thought they were worth killing for, why'd I leave the spoon in his mouth?"

"I think it's some kind of criminal trademark you're trying to establish," Stern said. "You know, 'The Silver Spoon Killer.'"

"Get off it!" Canin shouted, still on his feet. He felt no pain now. He had too much adrenalin pumping through him. He pointed to Stern, while facing Sterner. "Tell him to back off it, Sterner. You know he's barking up the wrong tree."

Sterner sighed, a long low sigh.

"Maybe he's right, Rick. Give the man a little room." Then to

66

Canin. "Just a few more questions. Have a seat."

Canin sat down again, still fuming but settling down enough to feel his stomach splitting.

"What kind of dog did Holloran have?" Stern asked.

"I told you, a pug. I went there to write about the man and his pug." Canin said.

"The kind with the flat snout?" Sterner asked, somewhat absently touching the tip of his flattened nose. "And sort of beige colored, small? "

"This one was black."

"Hmm. I see." Sterner momentarily stared out across empty space. Then he returned his gaze to Canin. "Was there anything special about this dog? Do you think it was worth a lot of money?"

"You're asking the wrong person, Sergeant. What I know about dogs wouldn't fill a three-by-five note card. The dog peed on me. I know that much."

"But I'm wondering if there wasn't something special about that dog. You know, special enough that somebody would kill to get his hands on it? Apparently, the dog catchers thought highly of it."

"You think the dog catchers killed Holloran?" Canin asked.

"I don't know. I haven't eliminated anybody, just yet," Sterner said, glancing at Canin just long enough to get inside his comfort zone. "The dog catchers did strike me as a little overzealous."

"Insane is the word you're looking for," Canin said.

"They were just doing their job, Suspect Man!" Stern snapped.

No surprise there, thought Canin. Who would doubt that Stern would side with sociopaths just doing their job.

"So, was this dog some kind of rare breed or what?" Sterner asked, returning to the question of Kirby's value.

"Maybe," Canin said. "Holloran told me that Kirby — that was the dog's name — was a registered pug, which I guess makes it somewhat valuable. He said the dog came out of one of the best pug kennels in the country, which I guess makes it even more valuable."

"What kennel's that?"

"Pugs in the Mist. In Phoenix."

Sterner made a note of that in the mini steno-pad, now covered with white doughnut ash.

"So what do you think a dog like that's worth?"

"I don't know," Canin said.

"Take a stab at it," Sterner replied.

"Couple a thousand?" Canin guessed, remembering that Holloran himself had actually paid four thousand for the dog. But that was at a charity auction, and the dog probably wouldn't fetch that kind of money on the open market. Particularly a hot dog.

"People have been murdered over a lot less," Sterner said.

"And a lot more," Canin said. "I remember now Alison Ford had offered Holloran ten thousand for the pug. But I don't think that's why he was killed."

"Why not?" Stern said.

"Rhino Holloran wasn't killed for the dog, stolen silverware or anything else. Otherwise, you shoot him once, then you take the dog. I think he was killed because somebody hated him. Somebody hated him enough to shoot him in the head, according to you guys, thirty-two times."

Sterner shook his head, his left eyebrow arched slightly.

"Well, that's Stern's guess. The problem is, it was too clean."

He held up his hand as Canin started to speak. "I know, I know. That's a lot of bullets. But they're too evenly spaced, too calculated for anyone who was doing it out of spite."

Canin took a sip of his coffee. It was cold. Stern wrapped his lips around the last Donut Gem while Sterner flipped his notebook shut and tapped it back into his pocket. He got up and lifted his coat off the chair.

That was the signal they were done, for now. The homicide cops

68

were leaving without making an arrest. A wave of relief washed over Canin. He wouldn't have to prove his innocence. He had Sterner to thank for that. Sterner had the good sense to rein in Detective Stern. It's nice to have a friend on the force, Canin thought.

Sterner gave his sweaty face a last wipe with his hand, then slipped on his jacket.

"Come on, Rick," Sterner said, "let's have a look at Ray's wash before we go. I'm curious."

Chapter Eight

Ray Canin had some explaining to do. So he explained: He slipped in a pool of blood when he bent over to examine to Holloran's body. His clothes got a little blood on them, so – after picking off a few burrs – he threw his shirt and pants in the wash just this morning. The explanation, straight-forward and accurate, seemed to satisfy Sgt. Sterner. Still, he warned Canin to tell police about it next time.

"Sure," Canin said cautiously. He didn't like the sound of *next time*.

And detective Rick Stern was not pleased at all.

The three men stood just inside Canin's front door. The two cops had been on their way out all morning. Einstein must have predicted this, Canin thought: For any observer confronted by homicide detectives, time stands still until they get a confession.

"Canin lied to you, Sterner," Stern said. "He wasn't just doing laundry. He was trying to destroy evidence. You gonna let him get away with that?"

"Easy, Rick. I'm sure he didn't mean anything by it," Sterner said. He turned to Canin. "You weren't trying to get away with murder were you, Ray?"

Sterner looked Canin directly in the eye as he waited for an answer. If Canin lied, Sterner would know it. He was a human lie detector. But even an innocent man gets nervous when he's forced to say he didn't do it. Canin chewed on his lip. He couldn't figure out how to answer Sterner without sounding like a liar.

"No, " Canin finally answered. "I was just ... "

"Good enough for me," Sterner said, putting his hand on the

doorknob. "Come on, Stern, We got some work to do."

But Stern gave it one last shot.

"Look, Sterner, let's just take him downtown and work a confession out of him. He'll talk. He'll tell us where he stashed the murder weapon, and lots more, with a little persuasion."

"Not today, Stern. Just make sure you got the bag."

"Yeah, I got it." Sterner said, Hanging from his fingertips was a plastic grocery bag carrying the shirt and pants Canin had worn last night.

"We do need to hold on to these for a while, " Sterner said. "If you really want to wash out bloodstains, though, you should talk to my wife. Boy, she's the expert. Of course, she has to be, cleaning up after me. Well, I'm not as sloppy I used to be. I try to keep out of all the blood and gore anymore, what with HIV and all."

Canin glanced warily at Sterner.

"HIV?"

"People hate to hear that, " Sterner said. "Ah, you're probably OK. We didn't turn up any anti-viral meds. And, big guy like that – he looked healthy..."

"Are you positive?" Canin asked.

"No, but you might be," Stern snapped.

"I mean are you certain," Canin replied.

"I'm not certain about anything," Sterner said. "But let's face it, Holloran had hung out with a high-risk crowd."

Stern snickered. "You mean Rhino was playing hide the enchilada with his cellmate."

Sterner cut him off. "Stern, there are some things just too awful to contemplate."

But Canin was thinking the unthinkable, and thinking he should have thought of it beforehand. Rhino Holloran, homeless ex-con, was probably in every high-risk group for HIV conceivable, and one or two not conceivable. And along comes Ray Canin, poor innocent Ray

Canin, wallowing around in the man's blood.

A burst of thunder made the three men flinch. Seconds later, rain began to pummel the flat, tar roof. Stern opened the front door to an August storm furiously pounding the desert into submission. Canin could barely see beyond the eaves. Everything was washed out and gray. Fits me to a T, thought Canin. He, too, was washed out. He was a man of mounting failures. True, he hadn't been arrested for murder, yet. But just as true: His wife had left him and sued for divorce. He had lost his job. And now, quite possibly he had a deadly virus, *the* deadly virus.

Sterner faced the downpour through the open door, then turned to face Canin. He studied the troubled man's face a moment.

"Hey, cheer up, Ray. It could be worse."

"How?"

"Well, you could be Rhino Holloran, stretched out on a stainless-steel gurney at the medical examiner's office, with a face full of bullets. Or you could be that poor dog of his. Kidnapped, or wandering the river bottom looking for the master he'll never find."

"My sympathies for Holloran," Canin said. "But he was an ex-con on parole for murder and he made a lot of enemies. He didn't deserve it, but I'm not surprised he got it. As for the dog, well, it's just a dog. I can't bring myself to shed tears over a lost dog. Sorry, Sergeant."

"Hey, don't mind me. I'm the type who cries over *'Ol' Yeller.'*"

"So was Rhino Holloran."

Sterner nodded, then peered into the downpour, as if he could actually see anything.

"Stern, does that bluish blob look like our car?"

"A little."

"Where's your umbrella?"

"Inside the bluish blob."

"Hmm, " said Sterner. "We'll have to make a dash for it."

Sterner bolted for the car. So did Stern, but not before turning to

Canin. "We'll keep in touch," he said. "We'll definitely keep in touch."

Chapter Nine

Canin's anxieties slowly crawled around his stomach like lazy earthworms, deep inside – behind the circle of pain. He rubbed a fingertip over the scar on his nose. It was a nervous habit. Sometimes it calmed him, but not now. Canin found himself approaching a state of near paralysis, incapable of anything beyond getting undressed and climbing into bed. As it turned out, he needed the sleep. Canin slept the rest of Wednesday and awoke late Thursday morning.

His anxieties had abated. Now he was just flat-out depressed.

Fortunately, he still had three beers in the refrigerator.

They wouldn't cheer him up, but they would get him a little drunk. Which was all Canin cared for. A little drunk. Not so drunk he tripped over furniture. Just drunk enough to feel a little better about himself. Or not feel anything at all.

He pried the cap off a Tecate and sat on the couch. He stared idly at the dark amber bottle. It was a form of meditation, driving out the memories of his very recent failures. He sipped his beer. It had an odd taste, but then it was still morning. And he was not a morning drinker, ordinarily. A few sips more, however, and the flavor began to grow on him. He began to feel better inside, and outside – all the way outside. He opened a window. He felt the cool breath of the desert rain, tinged with the bittersweet fragrance of creosote.

He went back to the couch. Canin kept drinking, and the first dull waves of inebriation began to wash over him. He took his dirty white running shoes off and stretched his legs out on the couch.

It was working. He was drinking all his troubles away.

But not for long.

Trouble is not so easily turned away. It was knocking at the door, though Canin didn't hear it right off. Not over the raspy snores of his own sleep.

But trouble did not give up easily.

BAM! BAM! BAM! "In the name of God, answer your door!"

Canin sat bolt upright in the sofa, dropping the beer bottle. It missed the coffee table, shattering against the red-tiled floor.

"What the hell?" he muttered.

The pounding and the shouting continued without pause. Canin cursed the interruption as he stepped over the broken glass and padded in his stocking feet toward the front door. He opened it and found himself facing a big woman with ample bosom. She was nearly Canin's height and must have outweighed him by a good 120 pounds.

The woman pushed her way past Canin, forcing him out of the way with bumpers of flesh.

"Come on in," he said, belatedly.

She was big, very big, and homely. She wore a Kelly green polyester jumpsuit that would have hung loose on an elephant. On her, it was stretched to capacity. Her head ballooned out at the cheeks and chin. A small puffy nose had to fight the cheeks for space and lay under a dense tangle of eyebrows. And housed deep in their sockets, her eyes glowed with a green that matched her jumpsuit. Her dark hair was cut short and set in an old-fashioned wavy perm; she either was nostalgic for the thirties, Canin thought, or some sort of religious fanatic.

It didn't take long to find out which.

"Ray Canin?" she asked. Her voice was low but loud, like Gentle Ben. It could not be ignored.

"Yes," Canin answered.

"Mr. Canin," she repeated. "My name's Martha. I was sent here by

God."

"He sent *you?*"

"God doesn't have to tell us why He does what He does. But I believe I know why He decided to take the life of my brother, aside from the fact he was a vile, lowly sinner who deserved what he got. God gave it to him good."

"Your brother?"

"Mike Holloran. You might have known him as Rhino."

Canin blinked. The family resemblance was uncanny.

Still, he had to ask: "You're his sister?"

"As much as it hurts and shames me to admit it, yes." She held out her hand, bigger and meatier than two pounds of premium hamburger. Canin shook it.

"Martha Holloran," she said. She took a deep breath and exhaled. Canin stepped back. He didn't want to interfere with her breathing.

"I'm so tired," she said. "I got off the Greyhound from Yuma, early this morning. I never sat next to so many sinners, although I saved three of them on the way up. I came out to visit Mike, on a personal matter. I took a cab to his filthy shack and – what did I find? His body and your business card. Jesus sent him to Hell and me to you."

"Really?" Canin said. He swallowed. The Jesus talk didn't exactly put him at ease. He'd have to work at finding his comfort zone around her.

"Can I get you a beer?"

"Of course not. But God wants you to offer me a seat. I have business to discuss."

"Sure, take a load off your ... uh, please, have a seat, over there."

Canin showed her to an easy chair directly across from the couch, near the open window. The cool air had already been chased away by the desert sun, which made a brief appearance. She filled up the space around her like a celestial object. She dabbed at the sweat running off

76

her forehead with a scarf. Canin felt mildly claustrophobic. He wanted to reopen the window and crawl out it, or barring that, get another beer. Thank God, she had declined his offer for one. He had only two left.

Excusing himself, he stepped over the broken glass and went to the kitchen. There he took a few deep breaths, got his beer from the refrigerator and returned.

He popped the cap, set down the bottle opener and took a long, slow drink.

"It's not even ten o'clock, Mr. Canin. If you keep this up, you will be face down on the floor by lunch time."

"Scientists think beer is good for you," Canin said. He meant it as a joke, but Martha Holloran was not amused.

"Scientists aren't God. They can't send people to hell." Holloran's sister raised her voice. Even without trying she could easily be heard over the subtle roar of the AC.

Scientists don't need to, Canin thought. They're quite capable of creating hell right here on earth. He thought it, but he didn't say it. Clearly, there was no debating religion with somebody like Martha Holloran. If she didn't like what you said, she'd just damn you to hell. And she was big enough to send you halfway there herself.

So Canin kept his mouth shut and sipped his beer and waited for Martha Holloran to pick up where she had left off.

"Now, my brother's dead. Clearly, Jesus took my brother for a reason."

"And that is ..."

"Jesus wants the little black dog."

"He does?"

"Yes, Jesus wishes it as a companion for our poor suffering mother, who lives with me in Yuma. Jesus has shed many tears for my poor mother."

"Jesus killed your brother for a dog?"

77

"My mother is a lonely widow in desperate need of companionship, and God, in his infinite compassion, has now found her a friend. He found her a dog raised and trained by her own son's hand. What could be more fitting?"

"Your mother couldn't settle for a pound puppy?"

"Mr. Canin," Martha was indignant. "This is what God wants, and this is what God gets. But, as is so often is the case, we end up having to do his leg work."

Canin nodded and took a sip from the bottle. He looked at Martha Holloran and offered a vague smile. "And?"

"And God did not choose to drop the dog in our laps. If he had, he would left it for me to find when He cast my brother's sinful soul into the searing flames of damnation. We must find the blessed little creature. And we must do this on our own, for God did not tell me where the dog was. But he led me to find your card. He told me a news reporter knows how to follow leads. A news reporter would know how to find a lost dog. He said I should talk to you directly, as – I'm told by police –you were the last person to see Michael alive."

"I think you have me mixed up with the man who killed him."

"I don't know about that, Mr. Canin. I do know the police can't be bothered with lost puppy dogs, no sir. The good Lord ..." She gradually raised her voice, from a whisper to a roar "... has them busy picking up murderers, and rapists, and pornographers, and sl-l-l-uts!" And louder still, like thunder. "And so He looked around, and He saw you – He choose *you*, Ray Canin, to find that dog! He fired you – yes, I know, I called your office – he fired you so you could do my work! And my work is his work! Truly, it is! And fired or not, you have a reporter's total lack of moral compass when it comes to rooting around in the dirt!"

"I'm ... was ... more of a feature writer, really."

"It matters not! In the name of Jesus, you must deliver that dog unto my poor, sick mother!"

Martha Holloran collapsed against the back of her chair, a sweating, heaving mass. Canin was bolt upright on the sofa, in audio shock.

"Why me?" he said.

Martha fanned herself with her flattened hand. She spoke as though all her energy had been spent in a mighty burst of speech, and indeed it had. "Because He *wants* you."

"He told you that."

"Yes."

Canin leaned forward and rubbed his hands over his face, from the nose down.

The answer was no. Canin had no wish to do favors for people who talked like God was a Mafia goon. Cross them up, and God'll rub you out. Looking across the room to Martha Holloran, Canin couldn't really see God having much to say to her anyway. He'd be too intimidated.

Besides, Canin had other business. He had to look for work, something that would pay the rent and impress his wife. The first part wouldn't be too hard. A lot of jobs would pay the rent. He could find one of those in three, four months. But impressing his wife – that would take some job. A job like that probably didn't exist, a fact that depressed him all the more. By the looks of things, Canin would have to spend another week drinking and feeling sorry for himself before he could even consider looking for work.

How would he fit in the time to a find a dog for the big woman and God?

And that wasn't the half of it. The rain that had started yesterday began to let up only early this morning. And when Canin had last bothered to look, he saw dark, massive clouds regrouping for another assault from the southeast. It was part of a mid- to late-summer weather pattern dubbed Arizona monsoons. Sometimes, the monsoons just brought a lot of dust and wind. This one looked to have carried some water with it. Streets would soon be flooded, if they weren't already. Canin did not like driving in high tide. There was also the problem of going to back to the spot the dog was last seen. The river bottom. Bad place to be caught in a flood.

Anyway, if the police could be believed, the dog was probably already dead.

He drank the beer down to the bottom of the label.

"Sorry, I can't help you," he said.

The big woman's head turned red and shook with rage. Canin prayed it wouldn't explode.

"How dare you disobey the word of God!"

"That's not ... "

"You have no choice in the matter, Mr. Canin!" Her voice was loud as ever, but had lost its edge of certitude. "You must find Michael's dog. I know you can. You're a reporter ..."

"...was."

"You can track people down, find them. I'm sure you'd do the same for a dog. Mr. Canin, you must find that dog."

"Sorry."

"You can be slow-roasted in Hell, you know."

Canin said nothing. He finished his beer and warily waited for Martha Holloran to pounce on him and beat him senseless in the name of Jesus. That was much more frightening to him than any abstract notion of Hell.

But Martha Holloran did not assault him. She held her hands to the sky, palms up. She pursed her lips in a quizzical grin, then sighed.

"Well, God," she said to the ceiling. "I guess it's plan B."

Then she gazed on Canin. "God wants you to know that doing His good work has its rewards. You will gain the confidence and trust of Jesus Christ Our Savior. You will walk proudly among the saints, for having done such saintly work yourself. And you will be twenty-five hundred dollars richer. Five hundred up front, and the other two thousand when you find the dog."

Canin set the empty bottle on the coffee table. He would stop drinking now. He had seen the way.

Martha Holloran wrote out a check for $500, and Ray Canin placed the blessed note in his wallet.

"God wants the dog by Sunday."

"Sunday. I don't ... I can't ..."

"There's no such word as can't."

"Yes there is."

Chapter Ten

Ray Canin stared back at the face in the bathroom mirror. This was a detective's face now. He could say goodbye to the shopworn mug of a mere reporter for a suburban daily that was possibly a notch above *The Penny Saver*. Yeah, that face was gone, though Canin had to admit: The new face didn't look much different. There was the nose. Scarred, bent slightly to the right and a half-size too big for its surroundings. Yeah, it was the same nose, though a bit red from Canin's breakfast of beer. The cheeks were a bit fleshy and make him look more jovial than he really was when he smiled. They were flush with beer, too. And his chin, not particularly distinguished. Not a balloon. Not quite square. Back to the eyes, and what he did see? Same eyebrows, wiry and abundant, like a pair of dirty Brillo pads. His eyes were brown and set in whites the color of fresh milk. Must have been the Visine. Five minutes ago, they were bloodshot to hell.

His hair, light-brown, hung halfway over his ears and looked like it had been coiffed in a wind tunnel.

Here was the face of a detective, all right. Canin mocked himself with a sneer. He had the look all right. He was ruggedly ... average.

He brushed his teeth, then headed out the door in search of a small black dog last seen Tuesday August Twelfth.

Clouds continued to drift in from the southeast, riding on warm, moist currents of air starting out in the Gulf of Mexico. If these clouds dropped their load, you didn't get a nice drizzle to last the day. You got raindrops big enough to knock down birds. Sometimes a summer monsoon storm would dump three inches in an hour. Two hours of that and Phoenix would have all the rain it usually gets in a year.

The radio said some two inches of rain already had pounded the place. And that was just the beginning.

Canin splashed through a few shallow puddles to get to his car. It was parked on a gravel drive leading off a narrow, paved road in South Phoenix. There wasn't much flooding here. The drainage was good. His house sat on an acre of desert near the foothills north of South Mountain, a city park. At 17,000 acres, it was more on the order of a national forest. Its seventeen-mile stretch of mountains was a great place for rugged desert hikes or horse rides. You could almost get lost in there. Although, from experience, Canin learned that, if you stood on any one spot for more than five minutes, you'd be run over by an accountant on a mountain bike.

The park mountains overlooked Canin's front yard. And, at one time, he could see the lights of downtown Phoenix from the back. Now, he faced a six-foot block wall and a cluster of look-alike stucco houses. They had gone up about three years ago, as developers gobbled up the land and sold houses like fast-food orders. Now half of them were empty. From Yuppieland to Foreclosureville. Canin's neighbors – on his side of the wall – were of the old order. Deep-rooted and eccentric. To his west lived a retired African-American Air Force colonel – full bird. Colonel Morris retired to his old family home and his old family business. Raising chickens. He still had a half-acre of chicken coops. Canin had long ago gotten used to the cocks crowing. Two years ago, people behind the wall had asked Canin to sign a petition. They demanded the city get rid of the chickens. Canin told them to remain behind the gates, where the chickens couldn't get them.

They weren't amused.

To Canin's east lived a retired plumber. He was a red-neck who hated just about everything from hippies to rap music. That put him on the same page with Colonel Morris.

Canin had nothing against hippies, so he pretty much steered clear of the colonel and the plumber. And that worked out just fine with all parties. In the South Phoenix of old, neighbors got along, in good part, because they were easy to ignore.

On top of that, the rent was doable. OK, he was a month behind, but you can't duck car repairs. Still, it was doable – paycheck to paycheck doable. And until now, he had paychecks. Until now, he could afford a rustic house and an acre of land, for money that wouldn't have landed him a broom closet in Scottsdale, home to his former employer, *The Scottsdale Monument*. That was OK with Canin. Scottsdale had all the diversity of a rice cake.

Here, his neighbors were black, brown and white. Some seemed more fluent in Spanish than English. Many of Canin's neighbors weren't his social peers. They were better. Educators, lawyers, business owners and retirees. If anything, they had demonstrated considerable tolerance for putting up with the likes of Canin. His desert landscaping was an excuse for overgrown weeds. His car was old and ugly and – since he lacked a garage – all too visible. And the chickens were noisy, but at least they weren't his chickens. With one exception. The one he adopted.

Canin started his old, somewhat reliable car and ground the gearshift into reverse. The chicken shot out from underneath the wagon in a wild, screeching panic.

The undercarriage happened to be the chicken's favorite roost. But the chicken had a short memory. That its roost sputtered and moved with daily occurrence always seemed to come as a total surprise to it. Whenever the car started, Canin could count on a chicken fleeing for its life. He never backed out fast, the way his ex-wife did.

The bird wasn't a pet, or even a likely source of protein. It was a gift from the colonel. Like the Colonel's home site, Canin's was still zoned for chickens. And as long as he had one chicken, the grandfather clause held. And Colonel Morris had an ally in what he saw as a fight for liberty – the liberty to keep chickens.

Morris often dropped by to make sure the chicken was alive and well. And if it wasn't, he'd give Canin a new one. The current chicken was the fourth.

Renee had run over the first three, one at a time. She always claimed the chicken ran out in front of the car and she couldn't stop. Canin had his doubts, though he kept them to himself. He recalled the time she hit the second chicken. In a blizzard of feathers, she put the car in reverse and ran it over a second time. He heard her scream something about hating the stupid chickens and the stupid low-class neighborhood.

Canin did his best to comfort Renee by telling her the chicken didn't suffer. He did not want her to feel as though killing the chicken was her fault. He did not want to see her suffer in any way. He worshipped her.

He never complained about the dead chicken. He just informed Colonel Morris and got a replacement.

Of course, as he suspected then and knew now, Renee wanted those chickens to feel as much pain as a chicken could feel.

And he still worshipped her.

How could he not? Her Mediterranean skin was flawless to the last detail, and filled to perfection. Her amber hair fell across her shoulders like threads of fine silk. Her face was cut and polished, like the facets of a gemstone.

Maybe inside she had her flaws, Canin thought. Still, she was perfect to behold and worth having, and maybe he still had a chance to get her back. And keep her. Perhaps that was a flight of fancy for him. But now Canin had a new line of work. He was a detective. He was on a missing-dog case. Maybe that would get her attention. Maybe she'd think twice if she knew he was making a quick twenty-five hundred.

85

Then again, if he found the dog, she'd probably just run over it to spite him.

Canin backed out onto the road, then shifted into first. The road was built in a time before everything was leveled with laserlike precision. The surface rose and fell like waves frozen in time. Fresh from recent rains, water rushed down normally dry washes across the low-points, the troughs. Canin eased the Toyota into the current as the water rose halfway up the tires. The next few dips were not any easier, though the rain had let up – for now. The monsoons had a habit of being brief but furious.

Canin made a left on Broadway, heading west to Ninety-First Avenue. Then south. He would search for the pug where he last saw it: the Salt River bottom. He'd ask around some of the campsites. *Did they see or hear anything the night – or morning – of the murder. Did they see anything of Holloran's pug?* He'd query the man in the broken-down bus. And Jim Smith. Mesquite Suzy? Maybe, though Suzy didn't seem all that close to the murder scene. Or the planet earth, for that matter.

Canin might have a look around Holloran's place, too, if the police weren't turning people away. Perhaps he'd have better luck in broad daylight, and stumble onto something besides a bullet-enhanced body. Something, anything, that would answer the $2,500 question: where'd the pug go?

As he drove past Mesquite Suzy's, he decided on a change in plans. The river bottom now cradled an actual river. Runoff from the heavy rain had the Salt River flowing once again. In a matter of hours, the vagabond village of the late Rhino Holloran had become inundated. The police must have gone from investigating a death to evacuating the living. Maybe they saved the pug as well. Maybe Canin could claim the dog and pocket an easy twenty-five hundred.

Maybe. Maybe it'd be the start of a whole new trend – where everything comes easy. Maybe Renee would waltz back into his life. Maybe Sommerfield would rehire him with a big bonus and a big raise. Maybe pigs would start piloting 747s. *OK. No free lunch. No easy way out.* Canin closed down the fantasy factory in his brain and turned his attention to the reality at hand. Drumming the wheel with his thumbs, he stared across police barricades set up to discourage people from entering a flooded road. Some people, though, couldn't take a hint. They moved the barricades or drove around them. These were the people who ended up on the evening news, standing atop their stranded cars as rescuers hovered over them in a helicopter. You might call them stupid. Danny called them a photo op. Whenever a road flooded, Danny would park and wait. Sooner or later, somebody would take the gamble. And lose. Danny would record it all for the next day's newspaper and – more immediately – for the Web site.

Canin watched the water roar across Ninety-First Avenue, white with foam and churning with eddies. Trying to cross that would be suicide. Canin had to admit, given his current state of affairs, it looked inviting. But he didn't take the bait. He had a purpose now, however marginal. He was a detective, paid to find a pug. Sure, most likely, the dog was dead, carried off by the river. Less likely, but still possible, the dog had fallen into the hands of the roving veterinarian, snatched by his private army of dogcatchers. With Holloran out of the way, kidnapping the pug would be easy enough. And getting Holloran out of the way made a strong motive for murder.

Why the vet wanted the pug was another question, one Canin couldn't answer. If he found the vet, he'd ask him.

Canin swung the Toyota around and climbed back to higher ground. Slowly, he passed Mesquite Suzy's fortress of blankets and plywood. He turned off and parked alongside. Getting out, he stepped into a rivulet that paralleled the road, and ran toward the river. Canin looked down to see both feet submerged in water.

He muttered the second word that came to mind.

"Crap."

He didn't say it loud, but it still brought Mesquite Suzy from behind the now-saturated blanket of a front door. All the same, her place had weathered the storm well enough. It at least was still standing. And it stood on higher ground, which was muddy but not underwater – like Ray Canin's shoes.

"Water runs downhill. You must be downhill," she said.

Canin sloshed his way out of the runoff. With each step, his running shoes shed water like a sponge being wrung out. He ignored Mesquite Suzy's comment. He was a detective now. He couldn't sweat the small stuff, like ruining a ninety-five dollar pair of shoes.

"I'm looking for a pug, Rhino Holloran's pug."

"Do you miss him?"

"Well, he's missing."

"No, he's dead."

"The pug is dead?"

"No! Rhino Holloran is dead! Do you miss him?"

"Uh, well, I hardly knew him."

"Somebody misses him."

"What about the dog?"

"What about Kirby?"

"Kirby?"

"The pug."

"Right, Kirby the pug. Have you seen Kirby? Or anybody with Kirby?"

"From here, I see everybody. I see everybody come and go. Everybody. I know who visits. I see people who should not visit, but they do. People should not steal, but they do."

Canin wiped his forehead with his sleeve. The sun had reclaimed the sky. Puddles were evaporating into hot, wet air. He leaned against a section of Mesquite Suzy's hut, briefly. It shifted another five degrees toward collapse, and he backed off. As for Mesquite Suzy, he still had questions, though he didn't know how many more she could handle. Standing just a few feet away, she looked like she had absorbed a gallon of rainwater. It seemed to have percolated up from the ground, reaching her head and leaking out her eyes.

But the odor – that earlier odor of urine – hung low in the air. It seemed stronger. As though the rain had only forced it to the surface. Canin figured her a candidate for a free box of Depends.

Give her a break, Canin thought. He gave her another look. She sure wasn't a beauty queen. Not anymore. The woman before him had black hair, twisted in random knots and hanging limp with rainwater. She wore a brown sweat suit. It looked like a flood-damaged carpet. Her eyes? Her green eyes hinted at something more. Something deeper. Something hidden. But that was somebody else's business. Canin was no shrink.

"Did you see the dogcatchers? The guys with the van?" he asked.

"I can't say. I'm not allowed to say. But I saw a truck with many doors. And behind the doors, I heard many dogs. Do you know why they call me Mesquite Suzy?"

"I've heard stories."

"So have I."

"Did the dogcatchers have the pug, Kirby?"

"I can't say. I heard many dogs. I am sad Kirby lost his friend. Kirby loved him like few others could."

"Dog's best friend," Canin said. "Do you know where they took these many dogs?"

"Maybe ... They were mean."

"You spoke to them."

"They're always mean. Maybe you can talk to them. Be careful. They're mean. Talk to Funny Lady. She's not so funny now. I'm tired. And wet."

Canin stepped back and took a deep breath. He decided against pursuing questions about "Funny Lady." That was a detour down another road of tortured logic. One road of tortured logic at a time, he told himself.

89

"Where did they take the dogs?"

"To the dogs. The place for sick dogs. Next to the fast dogs."

Chapter Eleven

The ARF mobile veterinary clinic took up three spaces at Park 'n' Swap, 10 acres of pavement and gimcracks. The Greyhound Park dog track rose in the background. Here, ran the "fast dogs." The clinic took in the "sick dogs." It only took Canin twenty minutes of question-and-answer with Mesquite Suzy to get something close to an exact address.

The racetrack was closed for the summer. So he had plenty of free parking. He chose a convenient spot, locked the car and walked a quarter-mile to a booth manned by a girl who was all of fifteen.

He paid his two bucks and entered the flea market.

Navigating an ocean of asphalt, Canin passed booth after booth of cheap clothes, cheap toys, cheap jewelry and cheap car stereos (of questionable provenance). Overhead awnings kept the place somewhat dry. But they trapped the heat and humidity and the smell of half-boiled hotdogs coming from the food court. He spotted the clinic – "ARF" stenciled on the side – as he turned the corner where a bald, pale man in his fifties stood next to racks of puffy jackets. Most were emblazoned with silhouettes of naked women. Apparel inspired by mud flaps.

Near the clinic, Canin paused at a plywood shack, painted black. Behind a counter, three dimly lit walls – painted black – were displayed pictures of apparently satisfied customers. They sported big grins as they bared tattoos on their arms and legs, and faces full of studs and rings and other shiny objects. Canin stopped to stare at them the way a person stops to stare at any horror. Then he realized somebody was staring back.

A dark-haired young man, in front of the booth, leaned on the counter with one elbow. His eyes bored in on Canin like hate on a laser beam, mingled with indifference. It didn't matter that his face was spiked like tires, or that a large brass ring had been implanted in his skull and looped over the top of his head like a UHF antenna. The stare was the killer. Then there was the dog, tethered to the man's free hand with a thick rope. Canin was no expert on dogs, but this appeared to be the kind that specialized in killing things – judging by jaws big enough to bite through redwoods. *Pit bull,* thought Canin. Like its owner, the dog was a metal head. Shiny silver spikes rose from its massive skull, lined up like a Mohawk created in a foundry. Thick brass rings pierced the dog's thicker muzzle, in a line of hoops running from eyes down to the black fleshy nose. The dog's face glistened with an array of polished studs, like somebody had blasted it with buckshot, which stuck to – but couldn't penetrate – the triple-thick skull. Canin rubbed his scarred nose, as his pulse and breathing picked up. The man was frightening. The dog was terrifying. The young man looked down at his pet, then back at Canin.

"Tattoo?" he asked, relaxing his gaze, perhaps in the name of customer relations.

"Maybe some other time, uh, Rod."

"Hey, dude, how'd you know my name."

"It's written on your forehead."

"Cool."

Canin excused himself and made his way toward the clinic, mopping the fear sweat from his brow with a shirtsleeve.

Dropping his arm, he saw an animal rescuer planted outside the ARF clinic's door, accessible by metal ramp. The man stood next to a sandwich board sign that said, "No dogs turned away because their people can't pay." Canin recognized him – Collick, the one who let the chow loose on his own partner. If Collick remembered Canin, he

92

didn't say anything about it.

Canin started up the ramp.

Collick pulled him back.

"I need to see the doctor," Canin said, removing Collick's hand.

"He's a veterinarian. He treats animals. You don't have an animal."

"I'm looking for a dog."

"Have I seen you somewhere?" Collick asked.

"Maybe. But I'm looking for a pug. Last seen on the river bottom near Ninety-first Avenue."

"You're the guy who was with Holloran. Sorry, the pug's gone. If Holloran hadn't interfered, we could have saved it. Anyway, you got no business here. No dog, no business."

Collick stepped in front of Canin, and thumbed a pistol tucked under his belt. It looked like another trank gun, and Canin had no wish to go through that again. But, if Mesquite Suzy was right (even if totally nuts), the pug was here. Or had been here. This was end of the trail, and he knew it. He had no choice, but to get inside.

"I have a dog."

"Sure, you do."

"I just tied it up for a moment. He's real sick. I'll be right back — with my dog."

Canin swallowed a lump the size of an Idaho russet, then went back to the tattoo shack. He thumbed through his wallet, then pulled out a ten.

"Mind if I, um, rent your dog?"

The dark-haired kid squinted. The metal in his head shifted with the moving tide of skin.

"I don't know, man. This dog is like my world. How much?"

Canin held out the ten. The metal-headed kid tapped a stud imbedded in his cheek, in thought.

"Choppers is offended."

"Choppers?" Canin asked.

93

"That's the dog, dude. How much, now?"

Canin bit his lip. This detective work had more out-of-pocket costs than anticipated. He dug out his wallet again and removed another ten-spot. What he had left wouldn't buy a bowl of cold soup a French restaurant.

"Twenty for Choppers, Rod."

"Here."

Rod handed over the rope with one hand, and snatched the two tens with the other. Canin looked down at the dog. Choppers had a slight look of insanity about him, as he panted lightly and appeared to be grinning. He had teeth like stilettos carved from elephant ivory. They glistened from drool, the same drool that fell on Canin's shoe in a steady drip.

I won't panic. I won't freak, Canin thought, as he watched the spittle breach the massive jaws. He looked away, and managed not to run off screaming.

"You OK, man?"

"I'll be, um, fine, fine."

"Oh, yeah, I guess I should ask what you have mind for Choppers. If you're going to fight him, I get a cut."

"No, no. That's illegal."

"So I hear."

"See, I'm a veterinary hospital inspector from the state. I want to Choppers to act as an undercover patient, you know, for a routine inspection."

"Whatever," Rod said. "Just one thing."

"Yeah?"

"Choppers, well, there's some dogs he doesn't like. And if he smells a dog he doesn't like, he takes him out. That's not the whole story, though, man. If he smells a dog he doesn't like on a person, well ..."

Canin swallowed. "He'll try and, uh, kill the person."

94

"There's no trying with Choppers. He's a doer, not a tryer. So far, so good with you, dude."

"So far," Canin said.

"OK, half hour. Excuse me, I got a customer."

Rod greeted a girl, maybe thirteen, looking over a selection of body loops. Canin tugged on Choppers' rope and headed to the ARF clinic. Collick was still on guard. He spotted Canin, gave Choppers a once-over, then moved to block the door.

"Sorry. We're closed now."

Choppers pulled the rope taut. Canin looked down. The dog was not grinning. He had parted his lips and bared his teeth with a growl low and guttural, like a distant earthquake.

"Choppers, behave yourself," Canin said, giving a command in a voice completely lacking authority. He smiled at Collick. "No problem, he doesn't like the smell of other dogs, not all other dogs, but some of them, I guess. You have nothing to ..."

The dog drew his lips back. His face became a freakish façade of teeth and gums – well lubricated with saliva. He was the angel of death, in dog's body. The dog growled again. The sound came from deep within his bowels.

Collick began hyperventilating.

"What the hell are you talking about. I smell of every kind of dog on the planet. I'm a dog catcher, you idiot!"

Collick backed up, pulling his trank gun from under his belt.

"Get that beast out of here!"

Canin pulled hard on the rope, and Choppers didn't' seem to fight it, at first. He backed the dog up a good ten feet. Collick edged toward the clinic door and up the ramp. He grabbed the door knob. The dog, and its many teeth, lunged. Canin tightened his grip, but the rope slid away as it burned his hands. Choppers broke free, and Canin could only watch as Collick lifted the gun. Canin thought about what would happen if Collick missed. He thought about where the dart might end up. He thought: *Not again.* Collick pulled the trigger. His aim was good. The dart hit Choppers square on top of the head, then bounced off like a skipping stone.

Clearly, the dog had a skull of granite and nothing could penetrate it, short of an artillery shell.

The dart flew over Canin. He heard a cry, but couldn't turn away from the scene before him. Blood would be spilled.

"No, Choppers, no!" Canin shouted.

Collick screamed and rattled the door without luck. Then he realized his mistake. He hadn't turned the knob. Now he twisted it with so much force, it broke off in his hand. But the door swung open, just as Choppers leaped like a wolf for Collick's crotch. His jaws snapped shut on the first object they met – the door's edge. White from shock, Collick stumbled forward pushing the door out of his way. He hardly noticed the dog attached to it. The dog didn't notice Collick. Choppers had become fully engaged in crushing the life out of the door. His body was frozen in flight, stiff and parallel to the ground like a well-starched pennant. His jaws tightened, pushing his teeth deeper into the door's thin metal veneer. It sounded like a car being crushed.

Canin stepped around Collick, now on his fours and crying.

"Jesus, that was close," he said, mostly to himself.

The door had begun to swing shut again. Canin slowly pulled it back open, leaning clear of Choppers the dog. He stepped into the clinic. Most of the light came from the doorway, but was intermittent, as the door opened and closed – in apparent response to Choppers's low center of gravity. Otherwise, the few small windows added little to the single industrial-grade fluorescent lamp hanging from the ceiling. The flickering light embraced the room – from the fake pine walls to the yellowed linoleum floor – with a cold glare.

The felt couch – in what passed for a lobby – proved a magnet for animal hair. A sharply dressed, well-jeweled woman sat on one end.

She might have been sixty or so, but it was a rich white woman's sixty, with a good diet, plenty of exercise and extensive cosmetic surgery.

That must have been her Mercedes Canin saw in the parking lot.

She glanced nervously at Canin. She glanced nervously at just about everything. She was either worried about her precious poodle in the operating room, or she was trying to hide her disgust for all the loose hair on the couch.

A small counter divided the waiting area from the narrow passage to the back. Canin figured it led to an exam room and surgery, if all that would fit in an RV. A young woman in a white uniform sat behind the counter, pecking away at a computer keyboard. She appeared to be going over statements. She was Hispanic with short-cropped black hair and a body that was stocky, but not overweight. Her reading glasses gave her rounded face a cherubic look.

She looked up and smiled at Canin, her eyes enlarged by the lenses. "Hello."

Canin read her tag. Penelope Reyes.

"Hi, uh, Penelope. Is, um, Doctor ..." Canin realized he didn't know the man's name. So much for his plan to talk his way into seeing an old acquaintance.

"Mullard?" she offered.

"Yes, um, Mullard. Doctor Mullard." Canin paused, before repeating the name.

"He's just finishing up surgery. Is this an emergency?" the receptionist said. She regarded Canin with a bit of suspicion.

"Do you have a pet?" she asked.

"He's shy. I couldn't get him past the door."

The receptionist leaned over to get a look behind Canin.

"Is that your dog?"

"Yes. He's just ... hanging out. But I wanted to see the doctor about another dog. He ran away, and I'm trying to find him. I'm told Doctor Mullard might help me out."

"Well, like I say, he's busy with a patient now," Penelope said.

With her big eyes, she gestured toward the narrow hall and the two doors that faced it, both closed. Canin acknowledged her gesture with a nod.

"I can wait," he said.

He selected a magazine from the coffee table and took a seat. Then he froze. From down hall and behind a door came a short, but intense yelp. A dog in pain.

Then he heard a muffled voice: "Hold still, damn you."

"Oh, God," the woman on the couch said. She gazed at the white-suited receptionist with a mixture of fear and hope. The receptionist played up the hope.

"There, there, it's going to be OK. Doctor Mullard's the best."

The woman smiled tentatively.

"I know," she said. Hope was winning out.

Then a door swung open. Up the narrow corridor and into the reception area swept Dr. Mullard. He was tall, blond and fair-skinned, Hollywood handsome. But Mullard's fair skin was not well-suited to intensity of the desert sun. A cancerous crater an inch in diameter had been cut out of his right cheek.

The fair doctor had a remarkable amount of energy, and charisma. Wherever he went, the spotlight followed. Even the receptionist seemed entranced by his every move. And the same woman who had moments ago feared for her dog's well-being, now gazed on Mullard as if he were St. Francis of Assisi, Dr. Doolittle and James Herriot all rolled into one.

With the grace of a god, Mullard held out the woman's dog with a single hand. It was a Chihuahua. Funny, Canin thought, how much larger and more vicious they looked in person. Reflexively, he rubbed his once-bit nose.

"Mrs. Richter," Mullard announced, "I present you with Alfonse."

Mrs. Richter looked from Mullard to the dog, and appeared to go into shock. Canin could see why. The dog in Dr. Mullard's hand radiated with a hundred acupuncture needles, like a Chia pet sprouting metal. Needles came out of his nose, his muzzle, his ears, his neck, his back, his sides and all four legs. Everywhere but his stomach, which rested atop Mullard's right hand.

Mrs. Richter managed a half-smile out of a corner of her mouth.

"I thought you said Alfonse had a brain tumor."

"He did," Mullard replied. "But you just can't go cutting on these things, you know. They're very, um, intractable. Yes, quite intractable. With acupuncture, however, anything is possible. If you look closely, you'll notice the needles have not been implanted just willy-nilly. They're all pointing toward the area of the brain housing the tumor. All the energy supplied by your dog's own natural healing processes is picked by the needles, amplified and beamed right to the trouble spot. As you can see, he's doing much better already."

"I must admit, Doctor Mullard," Mrs. Richter said. "He does look like a different dog."

"Yes, he does. And I expect the tumor to be in complete remission within, oh, I'd say, five or six days. Just to be safe, give it seven and bring Alfonse back for a follow-up. I'll remove the needles and order another CAT scan."

"But, but Doctor Mullard, how will he sleep?" Mrs. Richter asked.

"Quite comfortably," Mullard said with a reassuring grin. "As long as you have one of these."

Mullard reached behind the counter and brought out what looked like a small hammock suspended from aluminum tubes.

"The Stand 'N Sleep," he said, "designed especially for the canine acupuncture patient. I invented it myself. It works by supporting the dog's tummy and chin, the needle-free zones, giving your pet hours of painless sleep. It's actually better for the dog."

Mrs. Richter didn't hesitate. "I'll take two of them, one for home and one for travel."

"I was just about to suggest that. You can read my mind, can't you?"

The veterinarian gazed into her eyes. Then, setting the dog and the Stand 'N Sleep on the countertop, he said again, "Oh, how you can read my mind."

Mrs. Richter turned away with an embarrassed giggle.

Pivoting back around, she opened her purse.

"How much do I owe you, doctor?"

"Penelope will make out a statement of services performed. But offhand – and keep in mind alternative medicine requires a knowledge and skill far beyond ordinary veterinary school – but offhand, I'd say about, oh, ten thousand for the procedure and forty-five hundred for the follow-up. And the Stand 'N Sleeps, which are actual medical devices, run two-thousand , two hundred each. Well, there is a one hundred twenty-five dollar assembly charge on the one."

Canin was stunned. He had no idea veterinary practice could be so lucrative.

"You can mail me the statement, doctor. I'll go ahead and pay you now, and don't worry. It will more than cover the bill. I have not seen Alfonse look this good since he was a puppy."

"Rest assured, Alfonse is a whole new dog. Now just remember, the energy created by the acupuncture needles can disrupt brain signals. He may even forget his name temporarily. But just keep calling him 'Alfonse.' He'll understand."

"Thank you so much, Doctor. Mullard. I'm so very grateful Alison recommended you."

"And remember," Mullard replied. "One out of every hundred dollars goes directly to ARF. It's deductible."

"You're so generous."

Mrs. Richter opened her purse and began slapping hundred-dollar bills on the countertop, next to the fully assembled Stand 'N Sling, and a dog too petrified to move.

Canin didn't keep track of how many bills she put down, but her supply seemed endless.

"And worth every penny," Mrs. Richter added.

Mullard returned a million dollar smile, neatly scooping up the money with a single hand and tossing it into a cash drawer without counting it – or even glancing at it, for that matter. He trusted her.

"Please call if you run into any complications, Mrs. Richter. Penelope? Can you help with Alfonse? Thank you."

Penelope carefully picked up Alfonse by the stomach and held him at arm's length. Dr. Mullard handed Mrs. Richter the assembled Stand 'N Sleep and a box containing a second one, unassembled.

He showed Mrs. Richter to the door and noticed the pit bull hanging on it.. Slowly, Mullard turned to Canin.

"Is this your dog?"

"He followed me."

Chapter Twelve

Rod had wandered over from the tattoo hut. Collick stepped in front of him. He had recovered from his near-death experience, once again the gatekeeper to the clinic. Rod looked past him – at Ray, standing at the top of the steps with Dr. Mullard.

"Hey, time's up. I want my dog back," Rod said.

"That's *your* dog?" Collick asked.

"Yeah, he's pretty game, huh?" Rod smiled, and the metal in his head fell in line, tracing a big arc of shiny studs and rings.

"He's a menace. We may have to take him in for observation."

Collick glanced up at Mullard, who pursed his pale lips a moment, then shook his head.

"Well, I guess we don't need … well, I still have to get your dog to let go."

Collick reached in his fanny pack and pulled out the tranquilizer pistol, along with a fistful of darts. He chose one that could bring down a gorilla.

"No need for that," Rod said. He turned to Choppers. "Release!"

The dog unlocked his jaws and dropped the ground, landing on his side. Disoriented, he got up on all fours, looked around, sniffed and focused on Collick.

"Choppers, at ease!"

The pit bull sat down and started scratching his ear, like he had nothing better to do. Rod grabbed the rope tied to Choppers' collar. "Let's go, Choppers. I got a customer waiting. She wants to glam up her armpits."

Mullard turned to Canin.

"You'll have to come back tomorrow. I've got surgery scheduled."

"I'm looking for a dog."

"I can't help you there. Try the dog pound."

"The dog belonged to a man living in the river bottom, near the Ninety-first Avenue sewage-treatment plant."

"If the man's still there, I'd say he's under about fifteen feet of water."

"By tomorrow, he'll be under six feet of dirt."

"Oh?" Mullard replied, raising an eyebrow as white as snow.

"The man was murdered. Your own goon squad had paid him a visit earlier that day."

Collick, at the bottom of the steps, fingered the dart gun. Canin stepped back inside the clinic, away from the door.

"OK," Mullard said. "Let's step inside my office and clear this up."

Mullard led Ray Canin down the narrow hallway behind the counter, two doors down. It opened to an office that had a lot of room for something tucked inside an RV. On one side was a trophy case, with a neat arrangement of trophies and medals. Mullard was good at something athletic. Bookshelves lined the other walls, crammed with textbooks and reference manuals on veterinary medicine. Canin noted titles on veterinary anatomy, pharmacology, diseases of small animals, bovine and equine diseases, surgery on dogs and cats, and the principles of mammalian acupuncture. They looked barely used. Canin figured if the doctor wanted to know something, he looked it up on the Internet.

"Have a seat," Mullard said, taking his own seat behind a large and highly polished desk. Canin sat in a high-backed leather armchair. You didn't want to go cheap with personal one-on-ones with clients like Richter, Canin thought.

"Now, you can see who I am by my diplomas on the wall." Mullard said, leaning forward and frowning. "But who the hell are you?"

103

Canin swallowed. Mullard hit first, putting Canin on the defensive. And off his game. Canin drew a breath, saying nothing. He looked around the office, collecting his thoughts.

"Ray Canin, private investigator."

"Show me your license."

Canin ignored the question. He continued to look around, making a point of just looking around.

"This doesn't look like a place you'd expect to find rich women with Chihuahuas. They got expensive clinics in Scottsdale for that."

The blond animal doctor sat back in his own big leather chair. He smiled. His smile said he was better than the person seated in front of him.

"ARF is a free clinic for pets of the poor. Veterinary medicine is expensive, and pets shouldn't go without proper care just because they're in the hands of someone who's poor." Mullard nodded toward to wall. He appeared to see through it and out across the assorted tables of dollar-store overstock, as though he had x-ray vision. "These are my people. I'm here for them, every Tuesday from noon to one. That's when we have free clinic."

He swallowed. "They need me. Their pets need me. I can't tell you how grateful they are – especially the children – when I show them the melon-sized tumor I cut from little Tommy the poodle. But it takes money, lots of money. And, in these hard times, the grants have all but dried up. So, yes, I do business for a small and very wealthy clientele. For them, I charge a lot. They can afford it, and I'm good. I offer alternatives to traditional veterinary care they can't get anywhere else. It's a regimen that works, when used with large doses of antibiotics."

"The dog I'm looking for – it's a pug," Canin said, satisfied he heard more than he wanted about Mullard's business.

Or maybe he hadn't heard enough. Mullard wanted the pug. That much was clear. And maybe would have killed for it. Why? That

104

wasn't so clear. Medical research perhaps, though not for the money. Anyone getting ten thousand for poking a Chihuahua with needles didn't have to moonlight as a vivisectionist.

"I can't help you." Mullard pointed to his wristwatch. "I have an appointment."

Canin pushed ahead. "I was told your dogcatchers snatched the pug. Took off with it. The sister of the deceased wants it back."

"The deceased?"

"The man who was murdered, Michael Holloran. He went by the nickname Rhino. Did you know him?"

"He's not a golfing buddy, if that's what you mean. But I knew *of* him. My outreach team made contact with him, along with others in what passed as a small village, now washed away."

"Your outreach team? You mean the two jokers who laid me up with a tranquilizer dart?"

"I'm very sorry. I didn't know that. All I know is that they went there to help make sure all the pets in that area received their proper shots. It's a public health matter. And I care for the animals. That's what I do. I care for the poor creatures who belong to poor people. And when it comes to poor, the river bottom is truly the bottom."

"But you singled out Kirby, Holloran's pug."

Mullard stood up, folded his arms. A tinge of red crossed over his pale good looks.

"I was trying to help the man. Last month – it was July, hot as hell – I went to him personally and offered my services. But he was … obstinate. I tried to reason with him – the dog needed a rabies shot. I was simply doing my duty, to make sure every dog gets the care it deserves. Mr. Holloran apparently didn't see it that way. But he's bigger than me, so what could I do?"

"Shoot him?"

Mullard walked around the desk, standing over Canin. He looked like a bleached out statute. A pigeon or two on his shoulder wouldn't

105

look out of place. Canin figured the good doctor's next move was to call in the muscle and have him tossed off the premises.

Instead, he offered to show Canin the rest of the clinic.

"There isn't much more to see – an exam room and an operating room. I'll even show you the utility closet, where we keep all the bandages. After you've had your look around, you'll see there is no pug. And you'll have no reason to come back. If you do, I'll have you arrested for trespassing."

The voice had an edge to it, hostility-light. But the doctor had an ability for which Canin had grudging admiration. He could bite your head off one moment, charm you the next. He smiled.

"Follow me."

He led Canin into the next room up the corridor. It looked like a standard veterinary exam room. A Formica-topped table. A counter with some swabs and a thermometer. A poster showing worms crawling around inside a cutaway picture of a dog's heart.

After a brief glance about the room, Canin asked: "Who's Alison? The woman with needled-up Chihuahua asked about Alison."

"I can't say, for professional reasons, Mr. Canin. My client list is confidential."

Doctor Mullard showed Canin into the operating room. Nickerson, Collick's better half, was wiping down the OR table with his good hand. There wasn't anything good about his face. It was swollen, purple and oozing with infection. As faces went, it was big distraction. But not enough to keep Canin from noticing a small rolled up towel on the floor, pushed into a corner. Nickerson glanced down, following Canin's stare. He spun around, bent over and flipped down an upturned corner of the towel, drawing Canin's attention to whatever it was he was trying to hide. It appeared to be a very tiny paw.

"Poor creature," Mullard said. "A young girl brought him in earlier. He had been hit by a car. There was ..." Mullard choked, then

106

cleared his throat. "There was nothing I could do. I had to euthanize him. Rest in peace, little prince. Uh, Art, please dispose of the little dog's remains properly – now."

Nickerson complied, picking up the little bundle and whisking it away to some kind of proper disposal.

"Don't worry. It's not the pug," Mullard said.

"It didn't look like one. It looked like another Chihuahua."

"Yes, quite a coincidence. I guess today was Chihuahua day at Park and Swap."

Mullard smiled. He reached for the door just as it swung open – almost hitting him.

The receptionist popped her head in, noting her boss's narrowed eyes and clenched jaw. Probably not a good sign. Slowly, she opened the door all the way, revealing a mid-sized dog on a leash. It had a long smooth black and white coat. Some kind of sheepdog, Canin guessed. It was nervous, shaking like a hamster in a wind tunnel.

"Dr. Mullard, um, Bobby Moorehouse said Mandy has a psychological condition."

"Moorehouse?"

"He lives in Sunshine Villa, for low-income seniors. They're allowed a dog, if it's …"

"So, what's this dog's problem? Bad skin? Ears? Limping?"

Mandy responded to the doctor's commanding voice. The dog approached in a groveling, half-crawl. Her tail-wagged excited. She shook. She left a trail of pee across the freshly mopped floor, right up to and on top of Mullard's well-polished shoes.

"Bladder control," Penelope said. Then like a prophesy fulfilled immediately after its utterance, she added: "And diarrhea."

Mullard jumped back and looked down at his feet.

"My God! I'm covered in shit!"

The vet swung around, slid open a drawer and grabbed a scalpel. He turned the blade toward the dog. Canin couldn't tell who was shaking more now – the doctor or Mandy. Mullard's complexion had gone from paste white to blood red. He had entered a state of raw rage. And Canin felt something new – a need to help. He stood poised, ready to throw himself at Mullard and wrestle the scalpel out of his hand. Then kick him in the nuts. Something, anything, to save the dog, whose only crime was being eager to please. All the same, he reminded himself, *It's just a damn dog.*

Frightened, Penelope moved first. She pulled on the leash and dragged away the equally frightened dog, now peeing and pooping like a broken softy dispenser.

Mullard's arm relaxed, falling limp. He scalpel fell to the floor. The blond smile came back. Mullard forced it back, with the subtlety of a street mime. It masked the anger, just barely.

"Nickerson, clean me up."

Nickerson found a roll of papers and a spray bottle.

His shoes cleaned, and even shinier, Mullard took the narrow corridor to the reception area. He stayed wide of Mandy's trail of shame. Canin followed. In the waiting room sat an man who looked to be eighty, maybe older. He had a full of head white hair, and a rock hard face – more chiseled by time than wrinkled. He had aged well. But he was troubled, too. Canin could see it in his eyes and the droop of his shoulders. The old man stood up.

"Doctor Mullard, my dog has problems with self-control."

"I noticed."

"If it's not corrected, I'll have to get rid of her, or move out."

Mullard cocked his head toward Mandy, now sitting and panting lightly. The dog appeared to have already forgotten everything that had happened in the past – even if that was a half-minute ago. The big blond smile came out again. But to Canin, it was all show. There was not a hint of empathy, though the old man stood in jeopardy of losing his only companion.

Canin, on the other hand, felt for the old man. And here he was –

the guy who didn't like dogs.

"Penelope," Mullard said, "let's hold Mandy overnight for observation, shall we?"

"Yes, Dr. Mullard." The receptionist led Mandy down the hallway. Sensing all was not right, the dog quivered and urinated the length of the corridor.

Mullard smiled the fake smile. One thing Mullard couldn't hide was how close he had come to coming unglued and slicing up the dog. It was there. Penelope saw. The dog definitely saw. Mullard had a temper. *Let's face it*, Canin told himself, *a man like that could kill*.

Saying nothing more, the vet disappeared into his office.

Canin stepped outside, just in front of Bobby Moorehouse. Just in case the man needed help, Canin turned to offer a hand getting down the ramp. Moorehouse waved him away. He took his time, easing himself down to the asphalt. All the while, he shook his head and muttered to himself.

"Last time I take advice from Alison. She's never steered me wrong before ... but ..."

Canin leaned toward him.

"Alison?"

"Go away, goddamn it. I don't need your help."

"But who's Alison?"

"Everybody over sixty knows Alison. The queen of variety."

"Alison Ford?"

"Of course, Alison Ford."

"You know her?" Canin asked.

"Why wouldn't I? I was the stage manager for six of the seven years she was on the air. If it wasn't for her, I wouldn't have any pension at all. But, hell, I'll never ask her to recommend a vet again."

"That vet has your dog."

"Well, I'll give him a chance," Moorehouse said. He sighed. "Didn't seem to have a choice. Anyway, I think that girl will watch

109

out for him."

"You know where Alison Ford lives?"

"We keep in touch." Moorehouse scanned Canin like radar. "What do you care? You looking for an autograph?"

"I've been hired to find a dog. She might know something?"

"Got a car?"

"Sure."

"Well, I sure don't want to pay for another goddamn cab. All he did was complain about dog barf on the seats. Give me a ride home, and I'llthink about it."

Chapter Thirteen

North Central Avenue in Phoenix was old wealth. Senators and governors lived here, at one time. The men that owned TV stations and newspapers lived here, at one time. Bankers, surgeons and partners in big-fancy law firms lived here. At one time. Those who lived here now still had big money. But the real money had moved northeast to the desert kingdom of Paradise Valley. The real money – the $20 million-a-year major league pitchers, the oral surgeons, the real estate zillionaires – built 20,000 square-foot behemoths on the site of the 30-year-old houses they had torn down.

The old wealth, the old wheezy wealth of North Central, made up a roster of retired judges, fourth-generation heirs to Standard Oil, long-forgotten TV stars and the 1960s used-car king, Mack Dovey. He built his business on TV ads claiming "I won't bite!" while handling rattlesnakes. Sometimes he got bit. Eventually, he suffered brain damage and now spent his time wandering the large grassy grounds of his North Central estate.

Ray Canin learned all this from Bobby Moorehouse. He filled Canin in on Dovey and his neighbors as they drove up Central, headed toward the Alison Ford estate. Canin even caught a glimpse of the one-time car king through a wrought-iron gate. He appeared to be peeing on one of his stately ash trees. They pulled up at another walled mansion. The gate here was overgrown with vines. They did a good job of protecting Alison Ford's privacy from the few fans who still cared.

Canin buzzed a call box next to the gate.

111

"Yes?" a voice answered. The voice had a distinct edge, a razor-sharp whiny quality about it. Alison Ford was Canin's guess.

"Hi. My name's Ray Canin. I'm an acquaintance of Rhino Holloran. He was mur.. "

"Murdered. I know."

"I've been hired by his family to find his dog. He's disappeared."

"What's make you think I took him?"

"I'm just talking to some people who knew Mr. Holloran, looking for any clues that might help me find Kirby."

"Kirby?"

"That's the dog's name," Canin said.

"I know that. What's your name again?"

"Ray Canin."

"Canin? I don't know any Canin."

"I used to be a reporter for the *Scottsdale Monument*. In fact, Rhino Holloran was the last person I interviewed, before he was killed. Before I became ... "

"I know, haw-haw, now you're a big-shot detective. Haw-haw-haw."

Canin chuckled himself on hearing the patented Alison Ford laugh, a kind of combination goose honk and donkey bray.

Abruptly, she stopped. "Move over a little to the right, please. Thank you." Canin glanced around, spotting the video camera high on a post just inside the gate. "Stop rubbing your nose. I can't see you."

"Habit. I have a scar."

"From what?"

"A dog bit me. A poodle."

"Now you're looking for a pug?"

"Yes," Canin answered.

"And you want me to help you find it."

"I just wanted to talk to you. Anything you can tell me might help."

"And what makes you think I can help?"

Canin couldn't think of an answer, other than that he was fishing for clues.

"Well, Mrs. Ford, you knew Rhino Holloran. I just thought you could ... "

"Oh, forget it. Come on in."

An unseen electric motor tugged at the wrought-iron gate, sliding it back behind a high brick wall. It creaked. A little oil wouldn't hurt, Canin thought, as he freshened up by wiping the sweat off his forehead.

A turnaround driveway cut through green lush ground shaded by ancient, venerable trees. Old Phoenix was more like New England, all thanks to irrigation. The water diverted from the now-dry Salt River ended up here, eight miles and a million light-years to the north. The house was a brick mansion, apparently designed after nineteenth-century college dormitories. Greek columns, too many windows, ivy climbing everywhere – the works.

Bobby Moorehouse stayed in the car. He told Canin to make it short. He just wanted to get home.

Canin rang the bell and was greeted by Alison Ford's maid, an almond-skinned Hispanic woman in her thirties. She was pretty, with a small mouth, cocoa-dark eyes and a figure good enough to be distracting. Cute, however, was only skin deep.

"What? Another Ex-con?" she said, on seeing Canin.

Canin shook his head. "No, " he said, a little puzzled.

"I didn't think so, " she said, indifferently, with a touch of disdain.

"Miss Ford invited me in. I'm a private investigator." Canin said it as though trying it on for the first time. Maybe he needed business cards. Maybe then people would take him seriously. Obviously, the maid did not.

She frowned like Canin forgot to shower, then led him to a room that faced an inner courtyard. The room laid claim to a Southwest

113

ambience, as imagined by an interior designer from Milwaukee or Minneapolis. Clunky red floor tiles, furniture made out of tree trunks and a Navajo rug shaped like Colorado but only half the size. Nice rug, Canin thought, except for the wine stains.

Alison Ford was seated at a sofa of Navajo-patterned cushions. She looked every bit her age, which Canin guessed to be about eighty-five. It was a rarity for a woman in her business: letting time mold your appearance instead of a pricey plastic surgeon from the Mayo Clinic. Her face was a ghostly white, and her lips fixed in a permanent pucker and coated with layers of ruby red lipstick. The lipstick strayed from the lips, and gave Alison Ford the look of one of her old TV characters: Bimpi the Clown. Her hair – frizzed-out, shock-white – added to the effect. The hair had always been Alison Ford's trademark. In younger days, at the pinnacle of her TV career, it had been more of a natural yellow-blond – though it had always been frizzed, as if permed with a bolt of lightning.

She still wore the same self-effacing smile she often had on her old shows. It made her look a slightly goofy, but sympathetic character. Some people, Canin recalled, compared her to Phyllis Diller. Others likened her to Lucille Ball. Sitting here now, Canin could see she was her own person. And right now, that person was drinking heavily.

And so was her dog.

In many ways, the pug looked a lot like Kirby. In many ways, it didn't.

Like Kirby, this pug was coal black. The tail curled over the left hip, just as Kirby's did. And the dog had much the same squatness and shape. Same size head. Same bone structure. Same white circular patch on the chest. Same brown, begging eyes. But the differences were just as striking. This pug was truly fat. Its legs weren't even visible as the dog lay on Alison Ford's lap. Sagging rolls of fat fell over them like a skirt. Fatty tissue bubbled up from the beneath lids of the bulging eyes. And the whites of the eyes weren't white. They were yellow, the color of stale butter.

Canin remembered how he'd had to hold back his laughter on first seeing Kirby. But then, Kirby was laughably cute. This dog was just a mess. This dog did not call for laughter. It called for pity.

Alison Ford held out a bowl-shaped goblet, then pushed the pug's two-dimensional muzzle down in it. She was just priming the pump. Once his nose hit pay dirt, the dog eagerly lapped up what was left of the drink. Alison Ford set the empty glass on the coffee table and picked up a second one. Like the first, it was filled with a slushy frozen drink. Alison Ford took a generous sip and offered some to her dog. He didn't need coaxing this time. He drank like a fish, then came up for air.

"Do you often share margaritas with your dog?" Canin asked.

"Occasionally, but this is a frozen daiquiri," Alison Ford said. "And I must warn you, Captain Nemo just lovvves frozen daiquiris."

She threw back her head and laughed. Her eyes were glazed over and half shut. She caught herself, righted her head and opened her eyes almost all the way. She asked Canin to state his business, without dragging it out. She didn't have all day. She had to attend a board of directors meeting for the Animal Rescue Fund, or ARF, at three o'clock. Ford, as it happened, co-founded the Fund. It ran the state's largest no-kill shelter and donated to Mullard's mobile unit.

"How about a daiquiri for you, uh …"

"Ray. Ray Canin. No, thanks. I stick to beer."

"Beer it is."

Alison Ford raised her voice. "Dominique! A cold one for Mr. Canin!"

While he waited for his drink, Alison Ford broke the ice. Even before she spoke, her eyes grew moist.

"Poor Rhino," she said. As the tears ran, so did her black eyeliner. Alison Ford began to exhibit the classic signs of a grieving drunk. It made Canin uncomfortable, but maybe he was just too sober. Perhaps

115

this was the way a heavy drinker like Rhino Holloran would want to be remembered: with excessive and cloying sentimentality.

"Poor Rhino," she repeated. "I heard from the police yesterday. They called and asked me, oh, so many questions, so many. I had no answers, just that, well, when you choose to live in a high-crime area you risk getting shot."

That's a good one, Canin thought. He wondered how many people lived in high-crime neighborhoods, or in the river bottom, because they chose to. Granted, Holloran probably *was* the exception. He walked out of prison with a few thousand bucks and chose to spend it on a dog. *And what about her?* Canin thought. Take away her money, her name, dump her on the sidewalk, replace her fancy drink with a bottle of cheap wine, and she'd be just another drunk on skid row. She'd never rise above the level of a Dempsey Dumpster.

Just listen to her, Canin thought.

His beer arrived. He took a sip. It was good, something dark and foreign and expensive. And cold. Made in brewery Heaven. He was beginning to think the better of Alison Ford. Let her piss on the underclass, he thought. He'd just sip his beer real slow and pretend to listen.

At some point, of course, he'd have to find out what she knew about Holloran's pug. Or else he'd be out two-thousand dollars, and free to move to a less desirable neighborhood.

"I remember the first time I laid eyes on Rhino Holloran," Alison Ford said. "Haw-haw-haw! What a sight he was. It was three years ago, four maybe, at the annual ARF auction in April, at the Biltmore resort. It's our biggest fund-raiser. Mr. Holloran tried his best to fit in, with his rented tux and sixty-dollar haircut. But it wasn't enough. What could he do? Here were the richest, most powerful people in the city on one side, and an ex-con with a horn sticking out of his head on the other. Nobody said anything to him, of course, because he was so frightening. But when he bid four thousand on a prize pug,

116

I think they thought better of Mr. Holloran. He outbid me for Kirby, but it worked out for the best. Didn't it, Little Nemie, huh? Come to mama, and give her a kissy-face, huh?"

Alison Ford lifted the dog's head and kissed his flat snout. The dog, in turn, licked the tip of her nose. The action left the dog panting heavily. Then Alison Ford squeezed the dog's neck in a drunken half-Nelson of a hug. She let go and the pug fell back to her lap, gasping for air.

"He's such a good boy."

"You have a way with dogs," Canin said.

"Kirby went up for bid first, " Alison Ford said, closing her eyes a moment. She was perhaps taking herself back in time. "And Holloran wanted to make sure he didn't go away empty-handed. He went as high as he could on Kirby. I could have easily outbid him. Ah, the royalty checks were still coming in. But Rhino's four-thousand dollars was a very generous contribution to our cause. We don't believe in killing animals just because they have no homes. The county dog pound, they give up trying to place a dog or cat after a few days, or a week. Then they execute the poor creatures. For what? For not having anybody to love them. Well, we don't give up. We find them homes. We give them free veterinary care. But it takes money. We run our own shelters. We have foster families we supply with dog and cat food and support. And, of course, we have the mobile veterinary unit. That was my idea. We have so many needs. And, like I say, the auction is our biggest fund-raiser. And I certainly wouldn't want to discourage people from pulling out their wallets and handing us all their money, which is just what Rhino Holloran did.

"I bid the same for Captain Nemo, next on the auction block. And do you know what? I got the same dog for the same price. For Captain Nemo and Kirby are identical, genetically speaking! "

"I see," Canin said, peering over the rim of the beer glass.

"They're not just littermates. They're identical twins. They came

117

from the same fertilized eggs. Isn't that something!"

"I see some similarities," Canin said, "but not that much."

"Well, my little Nemie is ill."

"So you wanted to replace him, with an exact replica. His twin. Have I got that right?"

"You mean Kirby? "

"Yes. Rhino Holloran told me you offered him ten thousand for his dog. And demanded he take the money. "

Alison Ford's head recoiled, as if she'd been kneed by a horse.

"That's a lie! I wouldn't do such a thing. Rhino Holloran would no more sell Kirby than Timmy would Lassie!"

Canin had no wish to argue. He backed off, even damping his urge to ask if she would kill Holloran for a dog she couldn't buy.

He wasn't out to get a confession. Just find a dog.

Alison Ford paused until she had caught her breath. Then, her face still flush from liquor, she said, "I have my Nemie. That's all I want. That's all I've really wanted. I love my pug."

"And Rhino Holloran?"

"He loved his pug, too, of course. Granted Kirby didn't have the nicest home, below the sewage plant and all. Oh, it's not the ideal situation for a dog of that caliber, but Rhino Holloran did love his pug, yes. But ... "

"Yes?"

"Well, he wanted more. He wanted to show Kirby, make him a champion. I think he saw the dog as extension of himself, Haw! Haw! Haw! As if *that* was an original idea. But Rhino got serious about showing Kirby, not for the dog, but for his own self-esteem, I'm sure. I think, at first, he saw it as a sort of fun, a hobby. But, after he'd taken a few second- and third-place ribbons, he began to get more serious. And that's when he came to see me."

"How'd he find you?"

"He wrote me in care of ARF," Alison Ford said. "I invited him

118

up. I was very reluctant to ask him up here at first, because he was an ex-convict. And a murderer."

Alison Ford rolled her eyes up into her half-lowered lids and shook her head.

"How did you know that?" Canin asked.

"He told me. God, I just wanted to throw him out, but our mutual love for all things pug overshadowed any misgivings I might have had about Rhino Holloran the murderer. Besides, he killed a dog abuser. Some would say the man had it coming. And, before long, I began to look forward to Rhino's visits, you know, when his car was working. Oh, Rhino and I, we would spend hours discussing the many qualities of the pug. Its loyalty. Its noble bearing. Its winsome pug ways…"

Canin nodded. He tried to picture winsome pug ways.

Alison Ford continued: "Of course, I loved seeing his adorable dog, always at his side. And like I said, the mirror image of my own Nemie, before Nemie got sick. But Rhino didn't come over just to talk pugs."

"Right. He wanted your advice on showing Kirby."

"And on winning. He wanted to win very badly. So I showed him rudimentary pug handling."

"You've shown pugs yourself?" Just then he remembered the picture of her at the Scottsdale dog show.

"Have I shown pugs? … It's been a while, but yes – black pugs, both champions. There was Midnight Queenie, the number one pug in California. That was, oh, over forty years ago. We were all at our peak then. Number one pug, number one TV show.

"Jack Benny gave her to me, you know. We were such friends back then. He introduced me to pugs. Very funny man, although I felt somewhat sorry for his own pug, Puggybark. Jack was too cheap to buy dog food. Benny would sneak around Beverly Hills at night and steal leftovers out of garbage cans. That's how the chicken bones …"

Alison Ford's already leaky eyes grow a bit more moist. Her already shaky voice quivered a little more. "Poor Puggybark."

"You had another champion pug?" Canin asked, looking to get past the tragedy of Puggybark.

"My second, Sir Googly Eyes. He took Best of Breed at Westminster, nearly twenty years ago. I didn't actually enter the ring with him. But I advised his handler."

Canin drained the last of his beer. Alison Ford slurped on her frozen daiquiri, loudly sucking tiny frozen crystals of booze through her puckered lips. She saved some for her dog.

"Captain Nemo is only your third dog in forty years?" Canin asked.

Her goblet came down on an end table with such force, the base snapped off. She took her eyes from the broken glass to Canin. They were anxious. They were pleading.

"Mr. Canin, that's why I can't lose Nemie." Her voice cracked. "Not now. The mourning period is just too long. I know he's only four years old, but I can't wait four years to replace him. If he could just make it to eight or ten – that's not asking much of a small dog. And then, we could go together and both live with Sir Googly Eyes and Queenie."

"You lost me," Canin said.

"I so loved each pug that I agreed to mourn their deaths for as long as they lived."

"I still don't ... "

"I mourn for them – wear black, light candles in their memory, and refuse to have any other pugs – for a time equal to their time on earth."

"Really. I once read you should replace a lost pet right away."

"Who said that?"

"Some English veterinarian. I read the piece in a twenty-year-old Reader's Digest, waiting to see the doctor. It was either that or the five-year-old copy of *Golf Digest*."

"Oh, James Herriot. What did he know about pugs?" Alison Ford said loudly, like a bar-room challenge. "What does he know about pug grief? What does he know about the years of healing I must endure before I assume the burden of pug love all over again!"

Canin looked around for Dominique, the maid. Another beer might help, he thought. Then again, the first beer didn't do much for him – just allowed him to sit passively and take whatever Alison Ford dished out. He had to ask himself: How much closer was he to finding the dog?

"Just how valuable a dog was Kirby?" Canin finally asked. "He came out of a good kennel, right? He must have had an impressive pedigree. Could he have become the Secretariat of pugs?"

"No more than my Nemie."

"Sure, they were twins, but I was wondering what if somebody saw Kirby, the healthier pug, in the show ring? Would they think, 'Now here's a pug. Here is a true champion. Here is a dog worth killing for ...' "

"Haw-haw-haw! Champion pug. Haw!" Alison had thrown her head back laughing. Then she sat up straight, looking as sober as she could, under the circumstances. "No, not as long as Rhino Holloran was in the ring with him, or listed as owner in the show catalogs. Otherwise, sure, Kirby had potential."

"Why not with Rhino? He won a ribbon just a week ago."

"Oh, good lord, that was a fluke. Owners and breeders are a very clannish, insular group. They don't like outsiders, and they like outsiders who have done time even less. And they detest any outsider who has done time for murdering one of their own."

"One of their own?"

"Well, yes, Webster Franklin had a reputation as a gentleman farmer and respected pug supporter."

"Gentleman farmer, the pug killer in Yuma?" Canin asked. "Rhino tried to stop him. I thought you…"

"I approved? No, I understood why Rhino acted, but I never approved. Webster, for all his faults, loved the breed, even if he didn't always show it … I don't know. The world is complicated and it drives one to drink." Alison's voice grew faint, as though it had slid back into the ocean of alcohol surrounding her brain. "I suppose Susan Franklin would know the truth."

"Who?"

"His wife. She was there when Holloran killed Mr. Franklin. I think. Oh, I don't know. Things are never very clear. Her least of all. She just dropped out of sight. Haw!"

Canin took a deep breath. This was getting him nowhere. A half hour with a drunk with her pug, and not a clue to Kirby's whereabouts. Damn dog could be anywhere. Could be in the Petrified Forest right now sniffing some fossilized dinosaur's butt, for all Canin knew.

Come on, Ray, he told himself. *Think positive. Drink more beer. Something will turn up.*

"Oh, God, I don't know if I've been of any help," Alison Ford said, her voice fading, her words slightly slurred. "I want you to find that dog, I really do, Mr. Canin, but it's so hard to think now. Would you be so kind as to slap me a few times, the way my late husband did?"

"No, I can't do that."

"Oh, *please,* Dominique," groaned Alison Ford in very deep and loud voice, "*Please* bring us something to drink. Captain Nemo and I are drier than Prince Charles on a sand dune. Haw! Haw! Dominique! Where the hell are you!" Alison Ford turned to Ray Canin. "She's still learning. Less than a year on the job."

Dominique, so summoned, brought two more drinks – a frozen daiquiri in a large communal cup for Ford and the dog, and another beer for Canin. The maid appeared unruffled by Ford's loud and boorish demands, as though she couldn't care less. Perhaps the maid had other things on her mind.

Still, she did her job, setting Canin's beer down without comment. He gazed a moment too long as she bent over slightly. It was an easy faux pas, as Dominique's olive skin was wrapped around a frame that would give the pope a stroke. She returned the glance, only hers had a different message. *Forget it.*

Ray Canin did just that. Dominique left, and he drank his beer. Alison Ford and Captain Nemo took turns lapping up the daiquiri. Drinking had trumped conversation, as the room went silent. Absently, Canin looked around. The place was nicely appointed, but showed signs of neglect. The Navajo rug, not only stained, but frayed at one edge. The chair he sat on had a loose leg and wobbled when he shifted his weight.

Then there was the wall opposite him, behind Alison. It had a picture hanger, but no picture.

"What went there?" he said, gesturing at the spot with his beer glass.

"A painting," Alison Ford answered without bothering to turn and look. "It was stolen."

"Oh?"

Alison Ford let out deep, weary sigh, as though a stolen painting was a trifle. But Canin was curious. Maybe it had something to do with the dog. He wasn't beneath grasping at straws.

And, though so tired of it all, she never lapsed into a complete disconnect. She paced herself, drinking just enough to remain in a steady state of inebriated awareness. If she drank any faster, however, she would have slumped over into a lump of pickled flesh. For now, she could answer a few more questions.

"When was it stolen?" Canin asked.

"I don't know, May or June or something. I don't see what this has to do with a lost dog."

"It might have some connection to the lost dog's deceased

owner."

"What do you mean?" Alison Ford asked peevishly.

"Rhino Holloran, he stole the picture. Am I right?"

"Most certainly not!" She was indignant, almost to the point of sobriety.

"He knew your house. He was a burglar. That's what he did for a living, until he got caught for murder."

"OK, he had a past. Who doesn't? But he was welcome here. He came through the front door, at my invitation. He did not sneak in and rob me."

With a shrug, Canin added, "I just thought since he had stolen some of your silverware and ... "

"What?"

"He was found dead with a silver spoon in his mouth. A spoon from your house."

"Yes, as matter of fact, thieves took some of my best silverware, but not the silver spoon you're talking about. I gave that to Rhino Holloran, along with a whole set of silver. He always complained about his plastic forks breaking, so I said, 'Here, take these. It's not my good stuff, but at least it won't break.' So ... "

Alison Ford spoke with an edge of indignation. She either couldn't accept a pug pal betraying their friendship or she had a reason to protect him. But Canin was inclined to agree with the police on this one. Holloran was suspect numero uno.

No point in pursuing it, though, so Canin polished off his beer. Alison Ford held out the daiquiri tanker for the pug, settled into her lap like a slug washed up on the shore.

As the dog lapped it up, Alison Ford welled up with tears. She pulled out a handkerchief and wiped her eyes, smearing her eyeliner across her face.

"Right now, life without Nemie would be unbearable. But that's what I'm facing."

"You said he was seriously ill."

"Captain Nemo is *deathly* ill. He's dying, Mr. Canin. But he's not ready. He's not ready to go out back and play with his friends."

" His friends?"

Chapter Fourteen

Alison Ford led Canin down a slate path, crossing a lawn of St. Augustine grass – blades thick as kitchen knives and in need of a good mowing. She showed remarkable balance for an inebriate. Perhaps all that liquor gave her ballast. Perhaps she worked as a circus acrobat before turning to television. Canin had heard that somewhere, or so he thought.

He felt a bit light-headed himself. Stepping out into the bright light of a hot muggy afternoon somehow made him feel more tipsy. Strictly speaking, it wasn't sunny. But the clouds were lit up like fluorescent lamps. And it was hot, three digits hot. An intermittent breeze, however, foretold of a drop in temperature, though it came with a price. Miles away, barely visible through the treetops, the clouds had turned dense and dark. They were building for another downpour.

Captain Nemo sniffed the air. Perhaps he could smell change on the way.

He was standing in a baby stroller, his face to the wind. He needed the stroller. Not because he was drunk, or because he was spoiled. But because he was so ill and weak. He couldn't have made it out the door on his own, Alison Ford told Canin.

Dominique pushed the stroller, making sure it stayed abreast of Alison Ford.

The path took them to a high wall buried under a mass of unkempt vines. Behind the wall, a small stand of pecan trees rose up and formed a seamless canopy. It gave Canin a sense of walking into the woods. A high wrought-iron gate stood at the entry. Dominique unfastened a padlock and swung the gate open. She wheeled in Captain Nemo. Alison Ford and Canin followed. The canopy ended at a clearing some fifty feet inside the wall.

Ray Canin stopped to stare. Sweat trickled down off his eyebrows and down his temples, but he did not bother to wipe it off. He was too wrapped up in his own astonishment. The pecan trees had parted like stage curtains, to reveal a kiddy-scale Pantheon. If not the Pantheon, then something very classical looking. Fluted columns supported a massive roof and guarded a thick masonry wall. There was a dome at the top. A relief circled the base of the dome. It depicted pugs in everyday scenes of life: Pugs at play. Pugs at sleep. Pugs eating their kibbles. Pugs chasing cats. Pugs riding in cars with their heads out the window. Pug puppies nursing at their mother's teats.

"Here lie Queenie and Sir Googly," Alison Ford pointed out.

"A pug mausoleum?"

"A dog house for my departed babies."

Canin turned to see the next baby due to depart. Captain Nemo seemed to harbor, as much as any dog could, a real fear of this pug house for the dead. It showed in his rheumy eyes and his prematurely sagging jowls. He seemed afraid of dying. He seemed to know his time was at hand.

Canin let pass this momentary wave of pathos. This is a dog, he told himself. Dogs don't think about dying, let alone fear it. Canin was just reading these feelings into a very convincing face. The face of a sick pug.

"I think Queenie and Googly were jealous of Captain Nemo at first," Alison Ford said. "For the longest time, they had me all to themselves, and along comes Nemie. A pug in the flesh, a pug I can pet and hug."

And a drinking buddy, Canin thought.

"Oh, they were so jealous," Alison Ford said. "For the longest

127

time, they even refused to come out for their evening walks. But they're warming up to Nemie now. I can tell. Just look at them, will you, scurrying around yapping like little puppies, and trying so hard to wag those obstinate little tails. When Nemie's ready to move in with them, I just know they'll greet him like an old friend."

Canin nodded, but said nothing. There was nothing to say, outside of suggesting Alison Ford be tied down or heavily sedated.

"Oh, just look how impatient they are," she said to Canin. Then speaking to a spot in the clearing, she said. "You two just have to wait." She shook her head and smiled as she delivered her mild admonishment. "Nemie won't be moving in for a while. He's going to be cured."

"A cure?" Canin asked.

"Yes, I've consulted with the ARF veterinarian, Doctor Mullard. He'll fix Nemie."

"With needles, lot of needles."

"Well, he does have a way with alternative medicine. But this goes beyond that."

"How far beyond?"

"That's a matter of doctor-dog confidentiality, Mr. … Canin." Alison Ford cocked her head. Canin could almost hear the frozen daiquiri sloshing to one side. "What a coincidence. You're looking for a dog, and your name sounds like Latin for dog. Canin."

"It's Celtic, or so I've been told. Comes from O'Canin, but without the 'O.'"

Canin scratched his chin, raking a nail over a two-day growth of stubble.

"How'd you happen to hook up with Mullard, anyway?" he asked. "You have money. Connections. You could have gone to the best vets around. Specialists. Anybody but Mullard."

"He's offered hope. And I've seen what he's done for friends. He's not a quack. He actually cures the incurable."

"And where'd you find Mullard? In the Yellow Pages, under miracles?"

"If you must know, it was serendoopitous, haw! haw! Did you hear that? I mean it was sernendip ... a happy accident. Last March, I finally found the nerve to visit Rhino Holloran in the river bottom. I wanted to see what sort of home his Kirby had. I look out for the welfare of pugs everywhere, even Rhino Holloran's. So I had Dominique drive me down there. We stopped and she got out to ask for directions, from somebody living in a house made out old blankets. Dominique said it was a crazy woman."

"Uh huh," Canin said.

"Well, Dominique drove the Town Car, me and Nemie in the back, over these big rocks and right up to Rhino Holloran's little shack. Oh, God, I chickened out. I just couldn't picture myself going inside that filthy rat's nest. And the whole place smelled of sewer gas, even with the windows rolled up and the air conditioning on. So I sent Dominique in. She was there the longest time, but she finally came out, fixing her hair – I'm sure it just wilted in the heat. She told me Kirby lived like a king in there. I didn't believe it, but I told Dominique it was time to go. Then Rhino came out, Kirby scrambling through the weeds behind him. We exchanged a few pleasantries, the dogs barked at each other and on we went. It seems, though, that Dominique paid a lot more attention to Rhino than his dog, but – who knows?"

"That's all very interesting. But what's that have to do with Mullard?"

"I'm getting to that, Mr. Canin. We took off, but Dominique wanted to stop for some nasal spray. We parked at the westside Wal-Mart. And right there, in the middle of an ocean of asphalt, I spotted this animal clinic on wheels. The sign said, 'We cure the incurable.' Well, Nemie was already very sick, very ill, and nobody else had been able to help him out, so I looked down at my little Nemie and said:

'What do we have to lose?'"

Chapter Fifteen

Ray Canin glanced over at Alison Ford. She now had Nemo in her arms, squeezing the dog in an affectionate half-nelson. A tear ran down her cheek. He noted, too, that she was losing her ballast. She was top-heavy and listing, ready to flop face-first into the Japanese privet. She had a toehold on consciousness.

Canin looked back at the pug mausoleum, and nodded.

"So you'd do anything to keep Captain Nemo from the crypt."

He thought she'd reply, "anything." Instead, she nailed him with a cold stare.

"Dominique, show Mr. Canin the way out."

Dominique left Alison Ford standing before the mausoleum. She hustled Canin to the front door and held it open and swallowed. Pausing at the threshold, Canin turned to her. Her eyes were red. She had been crying, too. But for a pug? Maybe Dominique had grown attached to the little alcoholic. Canin looked into her eyes, trying to read her feelings. Maybe he could be of comfort.

Laying a hand on his shoulder, she pushed him outside and slammed the door behind him.

Canin let out a puff of air, then spotted Moorehouse. He had nodded off in the shade of a big maple to escape the heat.

As promised, Canin took him home. Then he made his way back to south Phoenix. With no air conditioning, it was sweat-soaked ride in an easy-bake oven. The cloud cover offered no relief from the steam-bath heat. Canin kept the windows rolled down, as he blew through stop signs and red lights, traffic conditions permitting.

Anything to keep the air flow going, even if it felt like exhaust from a jet engine. It sure beat sitting in traffic as the vinyl upholstery melted to the back of his shirt.

He spun into his gravel driveway, still muddy from the rain. He sped up to the house, then hit the brakes. Water rose in waves from beneath the tires, soaking everything in a three-foot range. That included the chicken, roosting beneath a creosote bush. The bird jumped and ran around the yard in a prolonged rage.

"Jesus, sorry!" Canin shouted. That probably wasn't much comfort to a chicken. He wasn't patently cruel to the bird, like his ex-wife had been. On the other hand, there was no consoling an animal with a brain you could fit in thimble. Besides, he had another issue. Staying dry. The storm clouds were back, and – just like that – the rain began pounding the neighborhood. Lightning ripped open the sky. The thunder shook it.

It took Canin all of ten seconds to get from the car to the house. He got drenched. Once inside, the even tepid draft of bad air conditioning raised goosebumps. He was cold and wet, and he had to admit, it felt good. But he was also exhausted and depressed. He had wasted a day and driven a hundred miles, for nothing. He had no dog. He had no clue to the dog's whereabouts. He had no idea if the dog was even dead or alive. And if he found the dog, it would still be ugly. Pug ugly.

Everything was wrong. All wrong. He could sense it when he found himself apologizing to a chicken. Things were just ugly all round.

The phone rang. Canin went to the kitchen and picked it up.

"Hello?"

"Hi, Raymond."

Ray Canin stiffened. Things just got uglier. It was Renee, his ex-wife. And she didn't sound like she called to give him advance notice that she was running back to him. That she missed his hands sliding down her breasts and up her thighs (which he so thoroughly missed himself.) That she missed sliding her own hand down below his navel and caressing ...

His pulse rate jumped. His breathing grew heavy.

"Raymond? Snap out of it. I don't do phone sex."

Canin swallowed. Neither did he, until now. Really getting ugly, he thought.

"What do you want, Renee?" Too blunt, he chided himself, much too blunt. He didn't want Renee to think of him as harboring a grudge because of the divorce. For not visiting him in the hospital. He wanted her to feel good about him, good enough to come back. He was ever hopeful she would change her mind and love him for just being who he was, and not the heir apparent she mistook him for. He'd seen the same blind optimism in dogs. Always anticipating something good will come out of nowhere, right then and there – food, a walk, a butt to sniff. That analogy did not make him more appreciative of dogs. It lowered his opinion of himself.

But that was all he had left, hope that stoked a longing doomed to failure.

It was ugly. Truly ugly.

"Raymond," Renee said. She sounded nominally pleasant, but her voice was sharp, piercing. "Remember when you got fired? Of course you do. It was just two days ago. Now listen closely, Raymond. This is important. Did you have an IRA account? If you did, you'd better not hide it from me, Raymond. And if you have any hidden assets, Raymond, tell me now. Because what's yours is half mine. And if you try to hide anything from me, Eddie will grab you by your ugly nose and haul you into court, Ray. And then it's going to get ugly, Raymond. Eddie is a spider of the first order. He'll suck you dry. Do you understand? Eddie thinks I'm hot, and he'll go all the way to the United States Supreme Court if he has to keep you from cheating me out of what's mine. You've already cheated me out of three years of

133

my life."

Ugly.

"I'm sorry. I didn't mean to ..."

"Just send me half of what you've got. Now."

"Renee, we need to talk this over, somewhere. We could meet for lunch at the Pink Pony or Garcia's. And talk about it." He hadn't intended to beg. It just came out that way.

"We just talked about it. Goodbye."

Then she hung up, and Canin did too, softly, like he was handling explosives.

Seated on a stool at the kitchen counter, Canin stared at the phone. He had to put a wedge between himself and Renee. Not that it mattered to Renee. She'd found her wedge. But Canin needed something, someone to take his mind off her. Deep down at the core, she was an ugly, ugly person. But he kept thinking about the surface, where the beauty was skin deep, and dazzling. Renee would not just go away. She had to be replaced. And the person for the job was somewhere at the other end of the phone. All he had to do was pick it up and dial the number.

He had looked it up. The Arizona State University department of political science. Here, he would find Danny's cousin, Anna Stewart.

Anna was pretty. Maybe not supermodel gorgeous like Renee, but, yes, pretty. She was pretty, wasn't she? He couldn't recall exactly, really. The only time he had laid eyes on her, he was still tranked out. OK, maybe she wasn't beautiful, but smart. Scholarly. She was writing a paper about – what? Something about .... Indians. What did it matter? It was something academic, something mind-numbing and overrun with footnotes. Not a real good conversation starter.

But Anna did have a sense of humor. He could remember that much. It compensated for her plain appearance, assuming she was plain. Damn, he still couldn't picture her. But it made sense. The really good-looking women, like Renee, had no sense of humor, although he could live with that. He put up with her lack of any semblance of wit just to gaze at her, touch her. Well, in Anna's case, perhaps the reverse could be true.

And Anna was available. Nobody said she wasn't. There she was, waiting in the wings to replace Renee and fill the void. The void of a relationship, however destructive. With Anna, he was willing to approach the whole matter with an open mind. He would look for her inner beauty.

Settling for inner beauty wouldn't be easy, after Renee.

Canin picked up the phone, and his memory came back. He stared into the mouthpiece and – in his mind's eye – could see her now, at the other end. The fog had lifted. He looked in on a slender woman with a delicate oval face. Eyes big and the color of nutmeg. Her skin was like maple, smooth and polished. Her dress, a combination of traditional and modern – well, it just good looked on her.

Canin cursed. She was beautiful, after all. And that meant one thing. She was too good for him.

Why'd you have to be so pretty, Anna Stewart?

He cradled the phone, as his picture of Anna Stewart continued to change. He remembered now her beauty was not skin deep. It seemed to flow out from the inside, from a deep spring of perfection. That clinched it. She was way too good for him. But her inner beauty had a bright side. Anna was not – at her core – mean and calculating. She wouldn't look at Canin and think: *He has no redeeming qualities, unless it's money.* Renee thought he had money – until she realized he wasn't related to the O'Canins of the O'Canin fruit juice fortune. So Renee had thought – or was led to believe in an Internet chat room. God knows who told her that. But she threw herself at Ray Canin until she learned he wasn't living modestly to escape his legacy. He just didn't have any money.

Anna would like him for who he was. He could tell. Maybe she'd agree to coffee. Or a latte. Canin dialed the university political science department. The office was still open. It took two transfers to reach her.

"Anna Stewart speaking."

"Hi, Anna. Ray Canin. Remember, the guy with the dart in his stomach."

She laughed. It *was* a nice laugh. "You were nearly euthanized. How could I forget."

Canin laughed himself. She did have a good sense of humor. He felt better. The tide of despair was waning.

"Yeah, I was hunted down like a dog."

He laughed, but Anna did not laugh with him. She said nothing. Her silence gave way to other sounds. The drone of air conditioner. The rain hitting the roof. The chicken still squawking about getting drenched. Like her cousin, Danny, Anna Stewart apparently felt no compunction to fill dead air with idle chatter.

"Yeah, like a big dog, a big stupid dog," Canin said. There was no response. Just light breathing sounds at the other end. Canin swallowed. "Uh, anyway ... "

"You want to talk to Danny? I can give you his cell phone number. You probably don't want to call him at the newspaper, I'm sure."

"I have his cell phone number. No, actually, I want to talk to you."

"Oh."

Canin cleared his throat. He was nervous. The pregnant pauses had unsettled him.

"I can get you some coffee."

"I've got coffee. Plenty of it, but thanks, anyway."

"No, I meant, let's get some coffee. Just you and me, meet at a Starbucks. Doesn't have to be a Starbucks. Dunkin Donuts or ..."

"Sounds like a date, Ray."

"Jesus, that's what I've been trying to tell you."

She chuckled. "That's what I thought. It sounds nice, Ray, but I don't even have time for coffee. I need to submit a draft of my

136

dissertation Monday. I'll need all weekend to work on it."

"Monday evening, then. That'll work."

"No, I don't think so, Ray. I know it's just coffee …"

"How about latte. I'll treat."

"No, it wouldn't be fair to Ernie."

"Ernie?"

"Ernie Milburn, my boyfriend. He's a state senator, a Navajo from Window Rock."

"Oh?"

"I met him while was I doing some archival research at the Capitol."

"Uh huh. Well, that's really great."

"Ray, are you OK? You sound kind of down all of a sudden."

"Me down? Oh, no. I'm not the kind of guy to beat myself up. Plenty of others will do that for me. Well, I'd better ... go. I have to look over some notes. I'm on a big case, and ... "

"Right, right. Danny told me. You're looking for that funny-looking dog. What's it called?"

"Pug."

"You're looking for a pug, how cute. Ernie will get such laugh out of that."

"I'm sure he will. Well, thanks again. 'Bye, Anna."

"Goodbye, Ray. And cheer up. You'll find that dog."

Canin hung up. She had lots of beauty, very deep and substantial. Like the Navajos say, she walks in beauty. But all the beauty on the planet couldn't reverse the charges on that call. It was ugly. Ugly indeed.

Pug ugly.

The phone rang. Caller ID said "City of Phoenix." Canin couldn't think who that would be, though he was a week late on his water bill. He'd beg for more time. He answered on the third ring.

"Hello?" Canin answered.

137

"Hay-yoo?" the caller was mumbling, like someone stuffing food in his mouth. Canin recognized the voice. It was Sterner, the homicide cop hooked on Hostess Donut Gems.

"Hi, Sergeant Sterner, " Canin said.

The lips on the other end smacked, signaling the successful ingestion of another tiny doughnut.

"Excuse me, Ray. You caught me in the middle of a little snack."

"But you called *me*, Sterner."

"Yeah, that's right. Just a little news from the medical examiner. Couple of things."

"Uh huh."

"First, damn that Stern."

"What about him?" Canin tensed on just hearing the name.

"Son-of-a-bitch won the office pool," Sterner said. "The ME counted twenty-nine separate bullet holes in Holloran's head, and managed to recover twenty-three of them. All .22 caliber. All from the same gun, as far as the ballistics techs could figure it. What do you think, Ray? Did the killer have a thirty-round ammo clip – or did he just stop and reload a lot?"

"I don't know."

Someone standing next to Sterner shouted into the phone, "Come on, Canin! Where'd you hide the gun?"

Sterner answered the voice, "Hey, Stern, knock it off, I'm trying to tell the guy something."

"Hi, Ray, you still there?"

"Still here, Sterner."

"Yeah, about the second thing, which is really why I called."

"Yeah."

"It turned out Holloran wasn't HIV positive."

Thank God, Canin thought. "That's a relief."

"Yeah, it is. But it's only half the story."

"Oh?"

138

"He had hepatitis. The kind you get from dirty needles. I guess Holloran was still shooting a little heroin on the side. How he managed to keep drinking like he did and not fall over dead has gotta be the eighth wonder of the world."

"Should I be concerned?" Canin asked.

"Well, this kind of hepatitis is blood-borne, like AIDS. My wife tells me they got a vaccination for this kind of hepatitis. Have you gotten one, Ray?"

"No."

"Well, probably won't do you any good now. Anyway, I just thought you ought to be apprised of the situation."

"That was ... thoughtful. Thanks, Sterner."

"Anytime, Ray. We'll keep in touch, of course."

"Sure you will."

Infectious Hepatitis, not AIDS. Things were starting to look up already.

Chapter Sixteen

By the time his head had hit the pillow, Ray Canin had given up. He had declared himself off the case.

But that was then. That was last night. Now he was back in the hunt. Now, even in somber light of an overcast morning, he felt better about things. There were no dead ends for a good detective. Only poorly marked trails. He felt confident now he'd pick up this one and find his way to a squat little dog once the property of one Michael R. Holloran, known to his friends as Rhino.

So, why the change of heart? Simple.

Caffeine. A bit of coffee, and Canin had a whole new outlook. Last night, that was a whole different beverage. Four beers before bed. *Renee? Anna? Drunk has-beens and their pugs? Hepatitis?* It all looked pretty hopeless back then, in another day, another state of mind. Everything. His personal life. Crime. Poverty. World hunger. The expanding universe. The collapsing universe. And somewhere in the middle of all that: Lost puppy dogs.

False alarm, it turned out. It was just a little alcohol-induced depression.

Now, Friday morning and into his third cup of coffee, he almost felt chipper. He felt the need to act. To get out and do something, by God. And what else was there to do but find the pug? Not a thing that he could think of.

It wasn't just the coffee, though. Martha Holloran had played a part, too. She had called not twenty minutes ago, halfway into Canin's second cup. She said she had a long talk with God after dinner in her

140

hotel room last night.

"Wouldn't it be easier if He just talked to me directly?" Canin had inquired.

"He only talks to me. Besides ... " Martha Holloran paused, apparently reluctant to finish the thought.

"Besides what?"

"I don't know if I should tell you this."

"Come on, go ahead."

"He doesn't like you."

"God doesn't like me?"

"No, he doesn't."

Canin wasn't too upset. Any God who talked to him wouldn't think much of Martha Holloran either.

Still, he had asked: "If He doesn't like me, why the hell did He single me out for the job?"

"You're just an instrument in His hands. And when you've served your purpose, He'll dispose of you."

"Will He still pay me?"

"Yes, of course. He's an angry God, but He's not a cheapskate."

"I'll take your word for it."

Holloran had ignored the vote of no confidence, telling Canin he had to find Kirby by noon tomorrow.

"What's the rush?" Canin had asked.

"Find the dog by morning and get a five-hundred dollar bonus on top of the agreed-upon finder's fee. It's a lot of money, but I cleared it with God," she had said.

God's got a big wallet, Canin had thought.

Seated at the breakfast table, he sipped his coffee. *Caffeine from Ecuador and dollars from heaven.* Now all he needed was a plan. He mulled it over, as he flipped through the morning Phoenix paper. Scanning the police log, he came across an item that told him there was one less suspect in the dog's disappearance. The man in the old

141

school bus – that slightly crazed face in window – had been swept down the flooded Salt River, along with his bus. Canin took note. If the water could cart off school buses, what chance did a fifteen-pound pug stand? He returned to the entry. Police had evacuated the river bottom, but the man in the bus, identified as thirty-six-year-old Johnny Kingstead, refused to budge. He was feared drowned, though nobody had located the body, or the bus. It'll probably wash up in Gila Bend, Canin thought.

The article said the flood had hindered a murder investigation. Police were quoted saying that what evidence that hadn't been collected earlier was lost, washed away. They never found a small black dog Holloran reportedly kept as a pet. Police had questioned a reporter recently fired from a Scottsdale newspaper, but made no arrests.

Canin folded up the newspaper, rubbed his nose. He refused to believe the dog had drowned. Somebody got a hold of it before the police arrived, or the water washed everything away. Until he saw hard evidence to the contrary, Canin would go on the assumption the pug was alive and well. It was all he could do.

Canin didn't see Jim Smith's name, so Jim Smith must have left when the cops told him to. So what about Jim Smith? Well, Jim Smith knew as much about Holloran and the river bottom as anyone. A good reason to talk to the man, Canin thought. Another good reason was Smith's acquired taste. Good chance he regarded Kirby as much of an entree as a pet. It was motive enough for dognapping, though a bit weak for murder. Besides, Smith had a healthy fear of Holloran, as would any person not locked up in an institution. On the other hand, the guy had a gun. Maybe he had lots of guns. And maybe he had lots of bullets. That's what killed Holloran: lots of bullets.

Canin finished off the cold puddle at the bottom of the cup, then headed out the door. He started the car and waited for chicken to fly out from under it in a protest of feathers and squawks. That done, he backed into the street and focused on saving the pug while there was still time. A good deed and payoff. A win-win. That's what people in sales always said. It's a win-win. Maybe that would work for the Cubs, Canin thought. The more they lost, the more their fans clung to them. It's a win-win.

Whatever happened to lose-lose? Like losing your job and your wife in the same month. Lose-lose. Lose the dog, and the bonus. Lose-lose. Lose the … *OK, that was last night's talk. Today is different. Today it will all work out. Today, I'll break into song even as I'm drenched in a downpour.*

Find Jim Smith. Find Jim Smith, first. Where to start? Well, for one, Jim Smith was truly homeless now. Nature had foreclosed on his little patch of suburbia. So he'd be forced to seek shelter – where all the homeless seek shelter.

The homeless shelter. Canin only hoped he wasn't too late. That he hadn't already built a backyard barbecue in a downtown alley.

Shoving the lever into first gear, Canin forged the small river running across the dip in the road. Water ran through the streets here, there and everywhere, thanks to two afternoons and evenings of a hard Arizona monsoon. It was not raining now, but the clouds had already begun to regroup.

The Central Avenue Bridge connected central Phoenix to South Phoenix, spanning the Salt River. Normally dry, the river now churned with roiling floodwaters, foamy white to solid gray. This was a dirty river, though it could have been worse. Along a three-mile stretch, trees and wetlands had been restored in a multi-million dollar eco-upgrade. Still, there was plenty of debris and rock-quarry waste upstream. Plenty enough to make this one dirty river. Canin glanced once, shook his head, then worried that Smith might be a dead-end, even if he found him. Then what? The dog pound? It made him sick to his stomach just to think about it. All those barking dogs. Not that he'd feel sorry for them. And not that they could hurt them. They

143

were caged. It was those other animals, the ones with the tranquilizer guns that scared the hell out of him. Canin tapped the band aid beneath his shirt and atop his stomach. He wanted to avoid the pound at all cost. Perhaps he wouldn't have a choice. Perhaps he'd have to face up to it sooner or later. OK, later.

Then he came around to Mullard. Something about that guy. He wanted to give the pug a checkup and a rabies shot, and for that, he was willing to steal it. Maybe murder for it. And meanwhile, he was treating – if you could call it that – the dying fat dog that belonged to Alison Ford. The same Alison Ford had offered to buy the fat dog's identical twin, Kirby, for $10,000.

What was it about this pug that somebody would offer that kind of money for it? Kill for it? And why was this dog so important to Rhino Holloran's sister?

And why all the questions? Just find the dog and collect the money.

But he kept coming back to Mullard. Maybe, Canin thought, he should do a little fishing around, starting with the state Veterinary Board. Maybe the good doctor wasn't always so good. Why else would he have been practicing from a beat-up van parked outside a Wal-Mart, before Alison Ford and ARF set him up? There must be something on the guy. Something on record. Who knows? He could have been smuggling pugs into Mexico as pets for drug lords. Or maybe Mullard liked doing experiments on live pugs. Awful disfiguring experiments. Then again, a pug's already pretty disfigured, Canin thought.

Maybe Canin would find nothing on Mullard, but it wouldn't hurt to look. And he wouldn't have to go too far out of his way. The state Capitol complex was a stone's throw from the homeless shelter. And that's where he'd find the veterinary board.

The homeless shelter had a number of parts to it. There was something of a campus where homeless people got help getting their heads straight, achieving sobriety and finding work. If they agreed to all this, they bedded down in the equivalent of the Homeless Hilton, which was air conditioned and had some private rooms. If they didn't, they were cordially invited to sleep in a 350-bed swamp-cooled warehouse across the street. Many ended up in the warehouse anyway, as the Homeless Hilton was usually booked solid.

So Jim Smith would have ended up here, if he didn't sleep in his car. And if he didn't have a pug.

And if he did, well, he'd probably be within walking distance – for the food service. No more care packages from the county welfare department, as he had no forwarding address. And here was another possibility – a possibility being the best Canin had. Jim Smith had brought Kirby here to fatten him up on the starchy, fatty offerings dished out by soup kitchens. Like getting a pig ready for roasting.

Canin parked and stepped out onto Twelfth Avenue, a half block from Madison – homeless central. The Homeless Hilton was one block south, behind a locked gate. It was for the upscale homeless. The overflow shelter, as it was called, was just behind him. A block and a half to the southeast was the Five Loaves soup kitchen.

And, filling in the spaces, the homeless. They came in a much greater variety than Canin imagined. Men, women, young, old, middle-aged, families, singles, pleasant-looking, seedy-looking, making sense, talking gibberish, drunk, sober – they ran the gamut. But they had this in common. None of them knew their sleep-number preference. They had no beds. They had no easy chairs. They had no kitchen tables. They spent their days, from moment to moment, just trying to figure out what to do with their bodies, like so much excess baggage.

A few lined up early outside the Five Loaves soup kitchen for lunch. Others slept on the still damp sidewalks and alleyways, fully dressed and scattered over the landscape like nerve-gas victims. Others sat on the curb and treated themselves to a smoke. The rest leaned against buildings or shuffled off to nowhere in particular.

145

They moved slowly, and for good reason. The air was hot and gooey, like steam rising off a giant unwashed armpit. Some people sought shade under the eaves and trees, but that offered no comfort, no escape from the heat and humidity.

Passing alongside a windowless, dull green building, Canin came to a half-open metal door, the overflow shelter entrance. It had a doorman. He had a white beard thick as a shag carpet and a wrinkled polo shirt with bold stitching that read: "Mr. Goodwrench." He greeted Canin with an air of authority and confidence, though he lacked any outward signs of upward mobility. He wasn't dressed much better than anyone else around here. His teeth weren't any cleaner. And his hair wasn't any shinier. Then Canin realized the difference. This man had a job, and a job carried a lot of weight in this neighborhood. And here he stood, possessed with the authority to make sure no one sneaked in and grabbed a cot during waking hours. This was not a time to sleep. It was a time to seek counseling, attend a 12-step meeting, call your probation officer, find work, make something of yourself. That was the theory. Of course, there was a big gap between theory and practice.

The doorman spotted Canin as an equal. Another man who had a purpose in life beyond the daily quest for core necessities – food, a bed, a place to pee and poop. A man who had risen above all that, if just barely. A man who had social status. Canin wondered, though, just how much status the title "dog detective" conferred on him. So he shortened it by one word.

" Detective Ray Canin." Canin flashed his press pass and moved past the doorman, who simply nodded. Authority respected authority.

Canin entered a dimly lit lobby with a high ceiling and a vinyl floor worn smooth. A little sawdust and you could slide a hockey puck across it. There wasn't much furniture. A handful of plastic lawn chairs and a TV tray for a table. A TV was bolted to a shelf high in the corner. A city cop – off-duty security – stood in another corner, half watching the TV, half watching Canin. A too-skinny woman in her thirties stood behind a counter. An ID on a shoelace hung from her neck. Ray Canin smiled. She didn't smile back.

"I'm looking for Jim Smith," Canin said. "Did anybody by that name sleep here last night?"

"I don't know if I can give out ..." She stopped short, then gave Canin a closer look. "Well, I guess you're OK." He wasn't one of *them*, was what she meant. She opened a register and ran her finger down a list of names, shaking her head as she went. Flipping through several pages, she looked up and said: "No Jim Smith here. Not from last night anyway."

"Thanks," Canin said and slowly headed for the door.

"You're looking for Jim Smith?" It was the cop.

Canin turned. The officer came up to him. His name tag said. "M.D. Smotes."

"You might find him at the cemetery," Smotes said. "He's been sleeping there, when he can get away with it. I chased him out this morning."

"What cemetery?"

"The old city cemetery. It's not used any more. Well, I mean they stopped burying anybody in it years ago. Just go out the door, turn right, go a block, and there you are. Smith parks that big car of his on the street there. That giant station wagon, the kind that went out with disco."

"Yeah, I know it. Thanks."

It was just a stroll to the cemetery, but Canin got in his car and drove. He had no desire to walk back this way once he left. There were just too many eyes on him. Too many eyes treating him like an unwelcome guest, somebody who thinks he's too damn good to sleep on a sidewalk.

The eyes followed Canin as he drove down Madison, then past Thirteenth Avenue and on a road that bisected the cemetery, each

147

side surrounded by a high fence. Canin knew a little about the place. It was now a historic site. Phoenix buried its dead here from late 1800s, sometime into the 1920s. Tuberculosis brought a lot of people here. Its most famous soul was Jacob Waltz, buried here, along with his secret to the Lost Dutchman's Gold Mine.

Some say the gold mine never existed, that Waltz just made the story up. It didn't matter. Canin wasn't looking for nuggets anyway. He was grasping at straws.

Jim Smith's Plymouth wagon was parked curbside across from an ornate concrete tomb, resting place for somebody once important. The car wasn't hard to find. Canin just followed the trail of leaking oil. He pulled his Toyota in front of the wagon and got out.

From the sidewalk, Canin scanned the cemetery. There were a few small mesquite trees, but not much shade. Headstones tilted this way and that, like corks bobbing on a desert sea. There was no grass. Canin looked for something out of place, a live body. He expected to see Jim Smith resting against a tree or headstone.

There was no sign of the man, at first. Then Canin heard a groan. It came from the back of the station wagon. Ray Canin made his way down the sidewalk and spotted a pair of feet hanging out the open window above the tailgate. He peered in. Jim Smith was stretched out, flat on his back, feet elevated.

He groaned again. He licked his lips and the sweaty skin around them with an unconscious swipe of the tongue. Canin shook him by the ankle.

"Hey, Jim. Jim, wake up."

Jim Smith's eyes popped open. He jerked his feet back through window, dropped the tailgate down and jumped out. He angled the assault rifle toward Canin's head.

"Never wake up Jim Smith when he's giving Connie Chung the baby she always wanted."

Jim Smith, smiling by habit, lowered the barrel of the rifle until it pointed to Canin's heart. He only pulled the trigger once. A pop sounded, like the burst of a firecracker. The bullet hit Canin in the sternum and fell to ground.

He took a breath. OK, he wasn't dead. Bullets bounce off him like Superman. Pink bullets. This one lay at his feet.

Canin picked it up. Plastic. Very lightweight plastic.

Jim Smith hopped out of the car. He held up his assault rifle like a private presenting arms. And Canin could see this was no run-of-the-mill assault rifle. It was a toy. A cap gun that shot little plastic bullets.

"Looks almost like the real thing, huh? Looks so real, you can't get them in toy stores anymore. I got this from a friend in Korea. Not cheap, though. Cost me a month's take in aluminum-can money."

Canin stood speechless for fifteen, twenty seconds. He was sorting out his feelings. He was relieved, grateful to be alive, yes. But most of all, he was damn mad. Sure, this was just a toy, but it scared the crap out him. Canin paused for a moment and took stock.

Then he grabbed the rifle and clubbed the sidewalk with it, smashing it.

"You crazy old bastard! One of these days you'll end up pulling that stunt on somebody who doesn't have a sense of humor!"

Canin tossed the small remaining piece across the street.

The half-grinning old man backed up against the car.

"You're kind of jumpy, aren't you?"

"Well, seems like every time I turn around, somebody tries to shoot me with a non-lethal weapon."

"Uh huh." Jim Smith lifted a sweat-stained ball cap with one hand, and ran the other through a thin blanket of hair. "So what is it you want?"

"I want to know what happened to the pug."

"What happened? I don't know."

Canin crossed his arms and waited for an answer. Jim Smith smiled his perpetual smile, though it seemed a bit more of a nervous grin at

149

the moment.

"I can tell you I don't have it," Jim Smith said. "And I sure as hell didn't kill Rhino. I didn't know he was even dead until the police came. They woke me up and asked me questions, asked me if I heard any shots."

"What'd you tell them?"

"I told them sure, I heard gunshots. I hear gunshots all the time around there. People down there like to drink and shoot their guns. I guess, why not? You have wide open spaces down there, and people down there cherish the Second Amendment even more than the New Testament. They cherish the freedom to do whatever the hell they want."

"Even put twenty-nine bullets in a man's head?"

"I guess somebody thought it was OK."

"What about the pug?"

"Don't know …" Jim Smith shook, and his involuntary grin broke into a genuine smile.

"Too bad, though."

"Too bad?"

"Too bad, Holloran's dead, and good dog like that's going to waste."

Over the line, thought Canin. *Over the line.* He grabbed two big handfuls of Smith's T-shirt and yanked the little man's nose toward his chin. Canin was no dog lover, but talk about dogs in the dietary sense repulsed him. He felt like a Hindu listening to a Kansas meat packer go on about butchering cows. It was just culturally repugnant.

Canin pushed Jim Smith away. "Goddamn you! The dog's no good to me digested!"

Jim Smith shook his head emphatically. "No, no, no! You have the wrong idea! I wouldn't eat it. I haven't touched dog since Korea. Honest. Never in America. Well, OK, just one time. Some punks beat me up, took my food stamps. And county workers did not come

150

through with my emergency food package. I was starving. Liked to've starved almost to death when this yellow dog of unknown ancestry came along ..."

"I don't want to hear about it. Just tell me, did you take the pug?"

"No!"

Canin glanced over the man's head and shoulders and into his car.

"Sure you don't have him now? Trying to fatten him up? Sure you didn't already ... Hell, you better be straight with me, because time is running out and I want that damn dog!"

"No, I swear, Ray. I do not have the dog. I never saw the dog after Rhino was murdered. I did not see anything. I only heard the shots ..."

"You heard shots."

"Well, yeah, they sounded kinda close, and I opened my eyes for a second, thinking maybe they were coming from Holloran's direction. And, OK, I heard the dog bark, a couple of times. Then I heard somebody whisper, you know, a kind of scolding whisper. Like a mother. She loves her kid, but you, she's scolding."

"You heard a whisper?"

"Oh, yeah. Cause it was loud."

"And what exactly did you hear, could you make out the words?"

"Something like, 'stop peeing on me.' "

Canin leaned back against Jim Smith's oil tanker and shook his head. "That doesn't make any sense."

"I know. It's just what I heard."

"So maybe Holloran peed on somebody and they shot him."

"That I couldn't say."

"What about Holloran's neighbor to his west – the guy in the bus. Johnny Kingstead."

"Only that he's crazy. Except he's more dead than crazy now."

"Yeah, it was in the paper. Got swept away in the flood. Only police found the bus, but not the body."

151

"Coyotes probably got to him first," Smith said.

"Unless he got out before the flood hit. Maybe he snatched Kirby, too. For me, everything's possible right now. Everything."

Jim Smith smiled the perpetual smile. "That's a possibility I wouldn't count on. Johnny didn't like dogs. He thought they were aliens from a distant planet. He told me this once, and said he thought they were trying to take over his body. He said to me he'd have to take care of the dogs before they took care of him."

"Take care of them, how?"

"Let me put it to you this way. I think *he* was the reason why there were so few strays in the river bottom."

"Let's see, you got a gourmand of dogs, a dognapping veterinarian and his goons, and a paranoid nut job – what chance did any dog have down there?"

"Maybe none, except Kirby. Even crazy Johnny wasn't crazy enough to touch Rhino Holloran's dog," Jim Smith said.

"Now that Rhino's Holloran's dead …"

"I'd say that pug's got a problem."

Chapter Seventeen

It was a short drive from the cemetery to the veterinary board's office. Canin wasn't sure what he'd get out of this. But he might find out something about Mullard he didn't know before. And the more he knew about Mullard, the more he'd know about what Mullard might have done with the pug, if anything. Beside, it would keep Canin occupied until he came up with a real idea.

On the fifth floor of the Capitol tower, he found the board's reception room at the end of the hall, past the metal detectors and the sign-in sheet. Canin scribbled in his name and clipped on his visitor's badge. The place was the archetypal 1970s homage to bureaucracy. No windows and pastel pink walls. Fluorescent lights bleached out what little color there was to begin with. At the reception desk, Canin asked a young woman – she looked fresh out of high school – how he might search public records regarding one Dr. Donald R. Mullard. The receptionist picked up the phone and called a superior.

From a hallway that disappeared into a warren of cubicles emerged a tall wiry woman. She looked fifty. Her hair was black, thick and as stiff as wrought iron. Her skin had a gray tint to it, except around the cheeks, where rouge had been applied with the skill of a brick mason.

She came around to Canin's side of the counter.

"I'm Mrs. Bracken, the chief executive officer for the veterinary board. How can we help you?"

Her voice, combining the most notable qualities of her hair and skin, was stiff and gray.

"I wanted to view a file on a veterinarian."

"Why?"

"Do I need a reason? It's a public record."

"Have you tried searching on the Internet?"

Canin looked down, stared at his feet for a moment, then – looking up – took a brief sightseeing tour of the lighting fixtures.

"No, no. I don't have Internet. There was a mix-up. I thought I had paid three months ahead. The Internet provider said I was three months behind. So they …"

"Have you tried the library? That has free Internet access."

The receptionist – looking puzzled – folded her arms, glanced at Bracken.

"I don't think those records are available online anyway, Ms. Bracken. You know, to protect the privacy of our veterinarians."

Bracken lowered her eyebrows, pursed her lips.

"Hmm, how right you are, Sherry. So … whose record do you want to see?"

"Donald C. Mullard. M-U-L-L-A-R-D"

"Sherry, provide the man with a public-records request form."

A two-page form appeared in the receptionist's hand, popping into existence like some kind of quantum particle. She handed it to Canin. Bracken pointed to a basket on the counter.

"When you finish, place it in the basket, and we'll have those records for you – oh, why don't you try back middle of next week."

Canin stepped back, cocked his head. Then he threw out his arms like he was about to catch a football.

"But I don't *have* until next week!" Canin cried. "I am a detective on a case. It's a missing .. uh…pug case."

"Sir, I don't make the rules here. I just make sure they're rigidly adhered to."

"I have a right to look at that file, and I want to see it now!"

Canin gave the woman a hard stare. She allowed herself one blink, then said, as calmly as if she were asking for the time: "Shall I call security, sir?"

"Don't bother. I'll go back the way I came."

The moment to slam his fist on the counter had come and gone. The anger peaked quickly, then settled into numb resignation. By the time Canin stepped outside, he was beyond depressed. He felt useless.

A little more than an hour ago, he had gone out his front door like the world's most upbeat salesman. He had that can-do attitude. *Damn it. He was going to find that pug.* But that was then. Now, all that coffee-fueled confidence had evaporated. And why wouldn't it have? He had to face facts. And the one overriding irrefutable fact was this: He was a failure. This was not some vague abstract feeling. It was simple math. *Add it up, Canin.* His failed newspaper job. His failed marriage. His failed attempt at dating.

And now, he couldn't find a damn dog.

Briefly, he noted a sky in sync with his despair. The clouds had become darker. They pressed down like the blackened surface of another planet. They bottled up this planet's hot and sticky air.

Enough sky. It was not uplifting. Canin turned to his feet, watching them shuffle toward the car. One foot forward, one foot dropping back. Both wrapped in old running shoes, never run in. They felt like lead weights. He felt like a dead weight. He was a joke. He couldn't even measure up to his current job description. Dog snoop.

It wasn't just the money. Sure, he could always use money. But whatever the amount, his not-yet-ex would want half. Half of what he needed for rent, gas and groceries. Half of what he had already pocketed as a retainer. That thousand-dollar check tucked into his wallet. *Got to make it the bank soon.* Beyond the money, though, was the commitment he had made as a professional – return the pug to Rhino's next of kin. Honoring a commitment? That sounded like he was playing by the rules. But, as far Canin could tell, this was a game without rules. Just a lot of players, each with a reason for getting their

155

hands on a dog that could only be described as laughably ugly. Well, Canin meant the dog no disrespect, but it *was* kind of funny looking, wasn't it? The bug eyes, the nose pushed back into folds of skin, the curly tail, and the – what the hell, he could use a laugh.

Just a quick look.

Stepping off the tree-lined sidewalk, he cut across the parking lot. He removed his wallet from his back pocket and slipped out the photo. The dog's head was cocked in a kind of inquiry, the way dogs do. The pug seemed to ask: Aren't you going to help me? And Canin answered silently, *Yeah, sure. Just hang in there, fella.*

Damn, Canin thought, Stockholm Syndrome with a pug. He was starting to relate to the little son of a bitch.

The horn blast nearly lifted him off his feet. He spun to see what the hell it was – hurling the photo, his wallet and its contents in an explosion of soiled receipts and worthless credit cards. They rained down on a Prius practically parked on his foot.

Pushing his glasses back up, Canin began to pick up the scattered contents of his wallet. He focused on making sure he got everything. So he failed to notice the driver get out, at first. Then he looked up and saw a dark-haired woman, her fingers pressed to her lips. She appeared to be smiling, out of embarrassment. She was pretty. Very pretty. And familiar.

"I'm so sorry," she said. "I … I didn't see you, uh … I think I know you."

The voice gave her away. The voice on the telephone. The voice that told him, thanks, but no thanks.

"Anna?" Canin said. "Anna Stewart?"

"Ray? You're Ray. I'm sorry about … You sounded a bit down on the phone. I guess that's to be expected. Probably going cold turkey from animal tranquilizers."

"Well, I wasn't …" Canin was about to correct her mischaracterization of his drug habit. Then a broad smile broke

156

across her small, oval face.

Canin returned the smile. She was pretty, and funny. That rare combination.

"Next time I'll just say no," he said, then looked around the parking lot. He spotted a few loose cards. He went to pick them up.

"Here, let me help you." Anna joined him. Canin paused to watch her as she bent down to pick up what looked like an old eyeglass prescription. He recalled his first impression of her – a very impressionistic impression, as he was half-conscious – the small round face, the slight bend in the bridge of nose. And the skinny limbs. She stood with the paper in hand. The only change was in the details. She still had all the attributes Canin remembered. Only now, they fit so much more nicely than they did in his mind's eye.

She was pretty. Very pretty. And he scolded himself for thinking she'd be an easy date. That was the internal dialogue. Outwardly, he smiled and took the paper from her hands. He noticed those for the first time. Fingers long, thin and light enough to float in a breeze.

"Thanks." Canin.

"Here's another one," Anna scooped another scrap, an easy motion in tight jeans. She was about to hand it to Canin, then paused. She took a closer look at what she had, a photograph of a pug.

She laughed again, though it was more of a giggle. Canin held out his hand and took the picture. He placed it back in his wallet without comment. Anna stopped laughing. She could read Canin's face. And it said, don't laugh at the dog. Kirby wasn't her dog to laugh at. Maybe it wasn't Canin's either. But he had an interest it. That didn't mean he had to like the dog. It just meant he had more right to laugh at it.

Anna managed a weak grin.

"I'd better park my car."

"What brings you to the Capitol. Um, to see your legislator boyfriend?"

"Not unless I bump into him. He's busy with some committee

157

business, and I'm here to poke through the state archives – for my dissertation. And what brought you out here. The nice statues?" Anna nodded toward requisite statue of a guy on a horse, built three times to scale. This one happened to be Father Kino, a sixteenth-century Spanish priest who went around Arizona turning Indians into Catholics.

"I was under the mistaken impression that state veterinary records were open to the public. Now I know better," Canin said, dejected.

Anna folded her arms. She frowned.

"Hmm. Maybe some records on veterinarians are kept sealed, to protect their privacy."

"Well, these records are public, except I was told to come back in a week, and I haven't got a week. I have to find the pug. And I've got a feeling this veterinarian I'm up against knows something about it. OK, OK, I'm fishing. But I'm hoping there's something in his file that could tell me something I don't know."

"Where's the veterinary board?"

"In the big square tower, behind the old Capitol."

"It's right next to the archives. Maybe I can help. I can be very persuasive," Anna said.

Canin didn't doubt that. Anna parked, and they walked past the big statue of the guy on the horse – and a few others.

Soon enough, Canin was facing the receptionist a second time. Only now, Anna stood next to him. She bent down over the counter and gave the receptionist a look – something between a glare and a question.

"I'd like to see your supervisor."

The receptionist blinked, considering her options. She chose door No. 2 .

"Just a moment." She picked up the phone and asked for Ms. Bracken. The unflappable woman strode up to the reception desk. She cast Canin an exasperated glance, then lowered her gaze to Anna.

"Yes?" she asked, serving the word up ice cold.

It was meant to freeze out further discussion. Anna kept her own cool, and pressed on.

"This man wants to view a public record. And public records are meant to be viewed. What's the difficulty? Why does it takes a week to open a drawer and pull a file?"

"I'll tell you what I told him. Listen carefully. Come back next week. We have channels here. Perhaps you've heard of them. Proper channels."

Anna pursed her lips. And shrugged her shoulder. What more could she do? Canin thought. A wall's a wall.

Then she pulled out her cell phone.

"I have channels, too. I happen to be on very good terms with Ernie Milburn, chairman of the House Appropriations Committee – you know, the state ATM."

"Oh?" Mrs. Bracken said, in two syllables. "Are you threatening me? Is that it? You're threatening to have our funding cut?"

Anna dialed a few numbers, then looked up.

"No, no, no. I'd never do that. I just wanted to ask if a state agency, that's you, should be dragging its heels in releasing a public record. He knows about these things."

She continued dialing.

Mrs. Bracken cleared her throat.

"I'll get the file." In defeat, Mrs. Bracken did not become downcast or deflated. She simply became more rigid.

Five minutes later, she returned with a file folder nearly an inch thick. Files like this weren't stuffed with letters of praise. Canin fanned through the pages. He got the picture – page after page of complaints against Mullard.

Canin wanted a little dirt on the guy. He got hit with the whole dump truck.

159

Chapter Eighteen

He should have been ecstatic, but there was just too much here for one person. Canin had a habit of getting bogged down on any government report longer than half a paragraph. And here was a file that, by the looks of it, ran a hundred pages.

Canin despaired of finding what he wanted, and he wasn't sure what he wanted. A clue. A lead. An ah-hah moment.

Anna must have read his mind. Or maybe his expression.

"Need some help?" she asked.

"Always," Canin replied.

Ray Canin carried the file into an adjoining conference room. Anna Steward followed. They settled across from each other at a large table. Canin opened the folder and separated the stack, picking up the top half for himself and sliding the rest to Anna. Canin begun thumbing through his half.

Twelve years ago, Donald R. Mullard graduated from the Chihuahua University School of Veterinary Medicine and Zoological Sciences. Five years and four tries later, he passed the Arizona veterinary board exam and became licensed to practice.

Then things got interesting.

Mullard opened a strip-mall storefront practice. The file included a full yellow-page advertisement: "Vet Mart. Free lipo for fat puppies with every tooth cleaning." Soon after, the veterinary board investigated a complaint by a Phoenix woman who said her corgi came back fatter than it went in. Mullard, it turned out, had accidentally run the lipo machine backward and plumped the animal with the previous dog's fat. Things got worse when the dog's immune system began rejecting the new fat. Mullard also admitted to the board he didn't really clean the dog's teeth. He just put down a bowl of water for it and later told the woman the dog had been given a full fluoride prophylactic. Translation. The only treatment the dog got was the fluoride the city put in the water.

Later, Mullard opened a non-invasive spay and neuter clinic. He ran cats and dogs through a device that rendered pets sterile with high-intensity rays. As it happened, the device was a tanning machine Mullard had picked up at a yard sale. All this came to the board's attention when pet owners complained their dogs and cats kept having puppies and kittens. The board reprimanded Mullard and told him, this too, was going in his record.

Canin wondered what it took to lose a veterinary license. The board noted, in Mullard's defense, that – having seen photographs – the animals did have a healthy glow about them.

Still the complaints piled up:

Implants to track lost pets turned out to be those chips put in greeting cards. Dogs lifting their legs to pee could be heard singing "Happy Birthday."

An older man brought in a cat to be declawed. Mullard surgically removed its paws.

He cut the tails off the wrong litter of puppies – golden retrievers that been brought in for vaccinations, instead of the Old English sheepdogs. He told the golden retriever owners the tails fell off from stress. He told the sheepdog owners that, once in a while, the tails grow back.

The veterinary board had had enough. It decided Mullard had to work under supervision. He found a position at the All Critters Big and Little Animal Clinic in Scottsdale, working with Dr. Janice Moyer. They ended up getting married, then two years later, divorced – right after his full privileges had been restored.

161

According to the record, the board took into consideration Mullard's charity work for ARF.

"Interesting," Anna Stewart said under her breath.

Canin looked up.

"Oh?"

Anna carried her stack around to Canin's side of the table. She sat down next to him, pointed to the top document. Canin failed to see what she was getting at. Not at the moment. For the moment was taken up by the presence of Anna Stewart. Her breath. Her hair. Her skin. He'd never felt so...contented. He could feel the hair on the back of his neck rise up. He felt a warmth flow through him like a soft light through the ether. He looked up at her face. She raised an eyebrow and tapped a finger on the file.

Right, Canin thought. She's all business.

He turned back to the document.

"See?" she said. "He's been reprimanded for performing transplants on dogs."

"They do it on people," Canin said.

"But doctors don't kidnap donors, then kill them for their hearts and kidneys," Ann replied.

"Or livers."

Canin scanned down the page, but – before he could finish – Anna Stewart turned it over and moved on the next one. She was good at this. He tried to read faster, but he couldn't keep up.

"Not only that," she said. "He botched the transplants. The dogs receiving the organs, they kept dying. Here, see?"

Anna Stewart's finger began moving down the page, faster than Canin could follow.

"Here's a woman who brought in a sheltie. She filed a complaint. Her dog, Maxie, made it as far as the car, then collapsed."

"And the board suspended his license?"

"They gave him one more chance. He agreed to stop doing

162

transplants," Anna Stewart said.

Canin briefly buried his head in his hands, then – rubbing his eyes – he read on. She must have sensed he was slow. Anna let him catch up before turning the page.

Here's what he read: Dr. Donald Mullard had a loyal following, contrary to what his poor skills would lead one to believe. His file wasn't all bad news. Letter after letter cited Mullard's caring professionalism. His expertise. His kind handling of sick animals. This didn't sound like the same Donald Mullard described elsewhere as grossly incompetent and negligent. This was the new Mullard, the practitioner of holistic veterinary medicine. Pet owners said Mullard was nothing short of a miracle worker. A man who gave renewed life to their incurably ill poodles and Shih Tzus.

For Mullard, it was a big turnaround. And, Canin noted, his good fortune started about the time Alison Ford found him practicing veterinary medicine in a Wal-Mart parking lot.

Canin took a deep breath, one meant to convey a serious effort at thought. He got a good bit of the essence of Anna Stewart instead. A slice of heaven. *Let it go,* he told himself. And he did.

"But Mullard's still doing transplants," Canin said. "I saw it. Maybe he's perfected it. At least he's no longer killing the recipient. Yesterday, he handed a lady a … Chihuahua with a new, I don't know, a set of lungs or something. But the donor was very deceased, on the floor of the operating room, wrapped in a blanket. So Mullard had a reason to kill for Kirby."

"A reason to kill, for a dog?" Anna asked.

"Mullard kidnapped Rhino Holloran's pug. The two goons he sent out to do the job – failed. So Mullard took it on himself. He knew Holloran wasn't about to hand over the pug for any amount of money, or any amount of persuasion. So he shot Holloran instead. And now Kirby's a donor-in-waiting."

"You mean an organ donor."

"Right. For a pug with a blown liver. Dog belongs to Alison Ford. She's an alcoholic. So's the dog. Except the dog has a bad liver. It's dying. And she must have arranged a transplant through Mullard. And he's got the perfect match. Kirby, Captain Nemo's littermate twin."

Anna sat silently for a moment. She reflected, it seemed, on a distant memory. And not a happy one. Then she stood, raised her eyebrows and smiled.

"I have to go. The archives call," Anna said. "I have much work and little time."

"Thanks," Canin said.

"I helped?"

"You found what I needed. The pug's current address. This time I'll make sure to overstay my welcome."

Moments later, Ray Canin found himself in the elevator with Anna. As the doors closed, he felt the pull, the attraction. Like gravity. He tightened his grip on the handrail, to keep from flying into her arms. Not that he could have anyway, as she had made a point of crossing them.

The elevator arrived with a modest ding. Ray and Anna stepped out and headed toward a narrow hallway, a 1919 extension of the original Capitol. Halfway down was another elevator, one that led to the third-floor archives. As they neared it, Canin struggled with one question. How would he ask Anna Stewart to see him again? It'd be like a date, well, not a date but a relaxed get-together. For coffee. For lunch. If she got to know him, maybe then.... The elevator doors slid open.

A distinguished man in a smart blue suit stepped out. He was Navajo. He was tall and had a face chiseled from rock. Anna's eye lit up. She smiled like a saint basking in the glow of the son of God.

Ernie Milburn.

Maybe some other time, Canin thought.

"I went looking for you in the reading room, up in the archives"

Ernie said.

"I was helping, Ray Canin – this is Ray – with some ..." Anna Stewart gave Ernie a sidelong glance, and lowered her voice in a mock tone, "with some private detective work."

Milburn smiled, as though he were in on the joke. Though Canin saw it as less of a joke than rent money. Milburn offered his hand.

"Representative Ernie Milburn. Window Rock. Nice meeting you, Ray."

Canin liked firm handshakes, but Milburn's was on par with an auto crusher. Canin held back his tears.

"Bye, Ray," Anna said. The elevator, having gone, arrived again. Anna and Ernie stepped in, and the doors closed.

Canin stood for a moment, lost in self-pity. Then he told himself: *Pug Time.*

He spun around and crossed through the rotunda of the old Capitol, now preserved as a museum. He pushed aside a set of nicely restored double doors and came out onto a large plaza. On either side stood a three-story block building designed with a total lack of imagination. On his left was House of Representatives. On his right, the Senate. Canin picked up the pace. He had to get to Kirby before Kirby became little more than a relocated liver.

Canin hurried past the statue of WWI flying ace Frank Luke, who had earned his Medal of Honor the hard way. Posthumously.

The air was still, and so dense with humidity that Canin felt like he was carrying it around on his shoulders. Then he saw the monsoon storm rolling in, still miles away. It was pushing a dust storm, a wall of dirt rising hundreds of feet and moving in like an airborne tsunami.

This was the big one.

By the time he reached the parking lot, he couldn't see anything – let alone his car. The dust storm had swept over him, a blinding swirl of topsoil. Canin was getting sandblasted by nature. It was relieved by the downpour that followed two minutes later – less a shower than a

165

furious bombardment of raindrops the size of knuckles. Canin still couldn't figure out where his car was. He felt his way along rows of fenders, side-view mirrors and bumpers.

He felt a face and jumped back, against the grill of something big. A lightning bolt lit up the parking lot like a stage, revealing a tall man and a short man. The tall man had his arm in a sling. He held something in his hand. It looked like a gun. The short man held a pole. Canin couldn't tell what it was. In a flash – all the time lightning has to spare – the scene went dark. The silence was broken by a cannon-roar of thunder.

"Grab him!" The tall one, Nickerson, shouted.

Canin turned and ran. He collided with a large SUV and fell to the pavement, face-first into a half-inch of water. The noose on the pole slipped down past his nose and tightened up around his throat.

"Got him!" The short one, Collick, said.

Canin rolled over onto his back and thrashed his arms and legs about the air like a dying bug. He clawed at the noose, but it just got tighter. And tighter. His breathing stopped. His arms and legs relaxed, settling into the puddles.

Chapter Nineteen

Canin stirred and remembered the rain. He remembered it pounding his face and running into his mouth, wide open for a breath of air he couldn't get. Then he coughed. A good sign. He was breathing. A better sign. He rubbed his neck. It was sore but still in one piece. The space he occupied rocked with the movement of the road. The dog he occupied it with was inches away, lapping up some viscous bit of regurgitated breakfast, lit by the gray muted sunlight squeezing through slots in the door. Canin recognized the breakfast. It was his.

"Stop it!" he snarled. But the cocker spaniel snarled back. Ray Canin took a breath, rubbed his nose and backed away – as far as his cramped space would allow.

The dog finished lapping up the congealed assortment of Frosted Flakes and buttered toast. As the van kept rocking, summer heat and humidity began to fill the cage. Canin felt sick again.

The van stopped. Doors opened and shut. Footsteps approached, carrying the voices of two freelance dogcatchers.

"Let's get him out," Nickerson said.

"No funny business, Canin!" Collick snapped. "We've got a noose, a gun and other instruments of discomfort!"

The door opened. The smells of Park 'N' Swap swept over Canin in a fog of boiled hot dogs and nachos simmering in fake cheese. Collick and Nickerson yanked him out of the cage, letting him fall to the ground. It was sticky with the goo of bad dietary habits. Canin lay there, waiting for somebody to end his misery.

167

"Aren't you going to shoot me?"

"Not yet," Nickerson said, pulling him to his feet. The cocker leaped to the ground and took off across the acres of asphalt.

"Hey!" Collick shouted. "He's getting away!" Collick made a move to chase him, but Nickerson grabbed his arm.

"Don't bother. We have to see what Mullard has in mind for him."
He nodded toward Canin.

Nickerson poked Canin in the ribs with the gun, a gesture to 1950s crime dramas.

"Is that a real gun?" Canin asked.

"Of course, .38 special," Nickerson said.

"Good."

Relieved, Canin went in the direction suggested by the prodding muzzle. Relieved, because he'd rather take a bullet than another tranquilizer dart. The gun led him to Mullard's clinic on wheels. Canin stepped inside, followed by Nickerson and his gun. Collick took the rear, gripping the dogcatcher's noose like a lance. They passed the front desk, paraded down the hall and stopped outside the operating room. Nickerson knocked.

"We got him."

"Dead or alive?" Mullard said, through the closed door.

"Alive."

"For now."

"For now."

The door swung inward, opening to a gleaming stainless steel table and a tray of surgical instruments. A pet carrier rested on a countertop along with cotton swabs and an array of hypodermic needles. Two pugs occupied the carrier. Kirby and Captain Nemo, their flat noses pushed up against a wire screen. One curly tail drooped. The other wagged. It was Kirby. Canin smiled at the welcome wag.

"Don't get too attached," Mullard said, stepping from behind the door. The operating-room lit up half his face, giving it the color of

168

pasteurized milk.

"No problem," Canin said. "I don't care for dogs, but Kirby's little tail – it's kind of funny, don't you think?"

Mullard scooped up a scalpel from the tray and whipped it through the air, slicing through an imaginary organ. His bleached-white hair fell across his forehead. He pushed it back.

"Kirby won't be Kirby much longer," Mullard said, in a sing-song voice. Then he lowered his voice, speaking to Canin in a near whisper. "And your own life expectancy will fall far short of actuarial predictions."

"What'd I do?" Canin said.

"Your job, I'm afraid. You learned too much. I had you followed to the state veterinary board. I know what you were looking for."

"Really, I looked, but I didn't find anything. Really, the files were all mixed up. I went to the file clerk and said, 'These are the wrong files. I asked for Mullard, not Ballard.' There you have it. I know everything about a Dr. Ballard, nothing about you and your record of underachieving."

"I can't take that chance."

"So …" Canin looked at the two sets of bulging pug eyes, particularly the bright ones. Kirby's. "You've perfected the transplants. You're putting Kirby's good liver in Captain Nemo, and your main benefactor, Alison Ford, well, she makes sure you and your ARF goons are well-rewarded. Captain Nemo, dog lush, lives. Kirby, moderate beer drinker, dies."

"Close, but no cigar, Snoopy. My organ donors are perfect matches."

"Sure, or they'll reject the organ."

"It's not the organ I fear will be rejected. It's the donor dog."

Mullard lifted the pet carrier, as if to give Canin a better look at its contents.

"They're twins. Identical pug twins. I couldn't ask for a better

169

match. Ah, if only Rhino Holloran had taken my generous offer. He'd probably still be dead, but richer."

"You'd kill him anyway?"

"I didn't kill him. Somebody beat me to it."

"OK. That's a technicality. Your goons did."

"Did not!" Collick said from just outside the door.

Canin nodded toward the carrier.

"What do you mean you fear the donor will be rejected?"

"Kirby will undergo training. He will be taught that his name is Captain Nemo. If he responds to 'Captain Nemo,' he gets a snack. If he responds to 'Kirby,' he gets twelve volts from a shock collar. And if all goes well, we bring Alison Ford a brand-new Captain Nemo, the same dog in every way. Except the all-new Captain Nemo is in the peak of condition. He has a new liver and much, much more. New heart, new lungs. New, new, new, new! No sign whatsoever of the toll token by that poor dog's heavy drinking."

"Alison Ford will probably get Kirby ... "

"Nemo! From now on he's Captain Nemo!" Mullard grabbed Canin by the collar and greeted his throat with the scalpel's edge.

"Nemo then," Canin said.

Mullard let go. Canin took a half step away. He finished his thought.

"I was just going to say Alison Ford will turn this poor pug into a lush, too."

"I don't think so. This dog doesn't drink the hard stuff. And if he does, he'll be starting fresh. He'll be able to abuse himself for years and years. Three or four anyway."

"Uh huh."

"And the real Captain Nemo?"

"He's dying anyway," Mullard said. "We'll just make it a little more conclusive."

"You don't think Alison Ford will get a little suspicious, when she gets her dog and finds no surgical scar?"

"Oh, that's the easy part. I simply make a superficial incision with a scalpel and sew it back up. When Mrs. Ford comes in tomorrow, and sees her dog in post-op, the new Captain Nemo will be so doped up, he'll look just like any dog recovering from major surgery. Of course, being in very critical condition following an organ transplant, the dog won't be able to return home for at least a week. We'll use that time to coach Kirby on the finer points of being Captain Nemo."

"What if the new Captain Nemo doesn't drink? That'll be a dead giveaway," Canin said.

"We thought of that, Mr. Canin. We'll tell her the medication has created an aversion to alcohol."

"Medication?"

"Cyclosporine, the anti-rejection drug. It's very expensive, and we expect to make a sizeable profit on that, I tell you."

"The dog won't need cyclosporine."

"Well, Alison Ford doesn't know that."

Mullard turned to Nickerson. "Art, remove the guest. And this time, do it without making a mess of everything."

"What mess?"

"The mess both of you made at the river bottom, at Holloran's camp. You didn't get the pug, but you had a vicious dog running wild, Holloran running wild, tranquilizer darts flying everywhere and, eventually, bringing in police to investigate a murder."

"We didn't murder anybody!" Collick shouted from the hallway, behind Nickerson.

"Well, you might as well have!" Mullard snapped, reaching past Nickerson and dragging Collick in by the lapel of his white overcoat. He placed the scalpel point up against Collick's cheek.

"It was all his fault!" Collick protested, closing his eyes in a hard squint. He pointed to Nickerson. "Just look at him. He's all bit up and bandaged."

Nickerson kept his composure. He waved his bandaged arm in the air.

"That's what I get for working with an idiot."

"Just do your jobs right this time," Mullard said. "I have a, um, transplant to perform. Gerald, you stay and help out. Art, take Dick Tracy to my office and keep an eye on him. When I'm finished, both of you … deal with him."

Mullard slipped on a pair of surgical rubber gloves, then a mask.

Canin spoke up. "I have – if not an attachment – something of a personal investment in the pug. I'd like to say goodbye before he goes under the knife."

"Just don't call him Kirby. Gerald, take the future Captain Nemo out of the carrier."

Nickerson took out Kirby, then relatched the door. The pug, seeing Canin, wagged his curly tail and lifted his leg – in Canin's direction. He let loose a stream, soaking a shirt already saturated with rainwater.

"Jesus!" Collick handed off the pug to Mullard, who reflexively handed the dog over to Canin. He didn't mind the hand-off. He now had the dog that would pay his rent. And he knew the dog meant well.

"You got it all wrong," he said. "It's a sign of affection."

"Well, a little negative reinforcement will take care of that," Mullard said.

"I got splashed, too! By dog pee!" Collick said, almost in tears.

"Well, go wash up and get back," Mullard snapped.

As Collick ran out the room, Mullard glared at Nickerson – his disembodied eyes peering over the mask.

"No more fuck ups. Get him out of here."

Nickerson raised the gun, but too late. Canin's foot was already in his stomach pushing him out the door and throwing him against the wall in the narrow hallway. Nickerson said: "OOOF!" Canin slammed the door shut and, holding the pug like a pigskin, snatched a

172

hypodermic needle from the table and aimed for Mullard's throat.

He hit the target and pushed the plunger. Mullard stood for a moment, marshaling nothing more than blank stare.

"That was for Captain Nemo," Mullard said.

"You only delivered half the dose. I'll be ..."

He collapsed to the floor. Canin threw open the door, grabbed the carrier and – stepping over a groaning Nickerson – sprinted for the exit. A bullet flew past his head and punched a hole in the mobile unit's skin.

"He's getting away!" Nickerson shouted.

"No, he ain't!" Collick answered. Canin flew out the door and jumped to the pavement. And he ran. As he sprinted past the tattoo parlor, Choppers the pit bull sprang over the counter to give chase. Collick collided with the dog, and both went down. Canin heard screams. And snarls and more screams. Stopping next to a rack of leather jackets, he turned to see dog and man rolling around the gooey asphalt. Dog was winning. Man needed help, and Canin thought about it until he saw Nickerson fly out the door, waving the gun. Rod leaped the counter, just avoiding another collision with a wild dogcatcher.

"Hey, leave my dog alone," he shouted and began pulling Collick away.

Nickerson, sidestepping Rod, was gaining on Canin. He was almost in target-practice range. Much closer and Canin would get powder burns.

Rounding the cotton-candy court, Canin spotted an old pickup pulling away. It was an off-brown amber and well-dented, like it had been in a meteor shower. Canin decided not to wait for a newer model. Running alongside, he set the case with Captain Nemo in the bed, then lowered Kirby – into a space between a shifting load of unmarked boxes. The truck pulled out from the shade of the big tents and onto a parking lot the size of Manhattan. Canin, his legs pumping

173

as fast they could, did a running alley-oop for the truck bed. He fell short, tumbling face-first onto the asphalt. Palms out, Canin skidded to a stop, drew a breath and realized his skin was on fire. Even on a cloudy day, the asphalt in August could cook a buffalo.

A hand reached out, and pulled Canin up by his belt.

"I wouldn't loiter facedown on the pavement. It's bad for your complexion." It was Mullard, rubbing his neck. He must have been out for all of fifteen seconds. Nickerson ran past. He shot at the truck's tire. He missed. A pair of eyes, wide and surprised, filled the rearview mirror. The driver hit the gas and the truck roared off across the parking lot.

Canin spotted a black pug, peering over the top of the tailgate. His eyes bugged out more than usual. The pug was scared.

Chapter Twenty

The pickup slowed at the parking lot's far end, some one hundred-fifty yards away. It began to turn, a full one-eighty. Canin knew it. And Mullard knew it. Traffic had to come back along a driveway that paralleled the parking lot to reach the exit. The driver knew it. He gunned the truck, apparently anxious to be a tougher target than a duck in a shooting gallery. He kept to an inside lane. Canin pushed Mullard away and leaped over a guardrail. He ran between two cars – a horn blared but he got through unscathed. He headed to the last car on the inside lane, where the truck would have to stop. It slowed. With a foothold on the bumper, Canin scrambled up and over the tailgate. He flung himself atop the boxes. He felt a tongue slip across his cheek. A pug tongue.

Collick fired three shots. In a split-second, three bullets hit the pickup bed – making a noise like a drum riff on tin. Canin threw a protective arm over his reward money. In appreciation, Kirby tried to lift his leg. Canin pushed back on it.

"Not now!" he said in a loud whisper.

Then the detective, the pug, the pug carrier – compete with pug – and the boxes were shoved into the tailgate. The driver had put the metal to the pedal. The acceleration pressed Canin's face and hands into the hot sheet metal. He thought: Feel the burn. Tires screeched as the pickup spun into a left turn, throwing all the contents of the bed against the side. Then the truck hit the straightaway, and Canin had more face time with hot metal. As the truck's speed leveled off, Canin managed to grab the tailgate's edge and peer out over the top. Judging by the blur of otherwise stationary objects, like utility poles, they had leveled off at eighty miles an hour.

After a few miles and horns blaring from all sides, the pickup slowed to a prudent sixty-five. It turned off Washington and headed south to Buckeye Road, then west. And west. And west. Canin had a bad feeling about this. Sitting in the truck bed, he faced the eastern horizon. The pickup slowed, and the northern horizon swung into view. They were headed south on Ninety-First Avenue. A few blocks later Mesquite Suzy's and the sewage plant came and went. The truck stopped. The sound of rushing water replaced the sound of rushing air.

Canin turned to the front. The pickup had come to stop just before the police barriers. Past them, the ribbon of asphalt dipped under the now-flowing river. The road-bed – what was left of it – was likely higher than the streambed. It was still impassable. Or so it looked to Canin.

The driver stepped out. Canin took an extra big breath. *Why would he bring me back to the scene of the crime? Something was up. Something that involved pain or end-of-life care.*

But the man looked more puzzled than intent on harm. He was about five-nine, wide, round and had silky black hair tied into a ponytail. He wore jeans and a t-shirt that read: "Forty-Third Native American Art Festival."

He placed one hand on the tailgate. With the other, he lifted his ball cap and scratched his head.

"I thought all those bullets were for me, until I saw you back there. You must have pissed somebody off real good."

Canin said nothing as the man walked around and examined the right side of the truck bed. He poked around with his fingers.

"Double-walled. Bullets got through the first one, got stopped by

176

the second," the man said. "You're lucky."

"Why are we here?" Canin asked.

"I live here. Well, across the river. On the rez. In case you hadn't noticed, I'm an Indian. The Maricopa part of the Gila River Pima-Maricopa Indian Community. I left my booth early. Things were slow today. I silkscreen these."

The Maricopa Indian pinched the shoulders of his t-shirt and pulled the shirt forward for viewing. Behind the lettering, Canin could make out the faint picture of an old warrior. It was likely meant to be faint. The fading warrior.

"I'm Herman. What's your name?"

"Ray."

"And your dogs?"

Canin pointed to the pug standing on the box, then to the pug in the crate.

"That's Kirby, and that's Captain Nemo."

"They're kind of ugly."

"They grow on you."

"Hmmm," Herman said, not quite convinced.

Herman walked up to toward the front of the pickup and, folding his arms, gazed out across the now-flowing Salt River. It looked to be twenty feet from one side the other. Herman turned to Canin, still seated in the truck bed.

"What you think?"

"About what?"

"Whether I can make it. It'd be close, but this truck sits up pretty high."

"I'd call it suicidal. Your obit would read, 'self-inflicted drowning.' "

"Well, I didn't plan on coming this way. But when people are shooting at you, I guess you forget things, you know, like the way my home is flooded. But I've driven through worse. I'm good," Herman said.

"Hmm. Do you have a cell phone?"

Sure. Who doesn't?"

"Can I borrow it? I'm staying behind. I'm going to call a friend to pick me up."

"OK, Ray. But take your dogs. I don't want the elders laughing at me."

"Sure," Canin said.

Herman lowered the tailgate. Canin stood on the edge, ready to jump to the pavement – until he looked up. Behind Herman's wide frame, Canin made out the front grill of the ARF dogcatchers' truck, approaching without regard to posted speed limits.

"I think we've been followed," Canin said.

Herman spun around, scratched under his ball cap.

"Holy Gila Monster!" he shouted, then made it to the cab in two long strides. Before Canin could remind him the tailgate was still open, Herman cranked the engine and jammed the stick into "Drive." The truck lurched forward, crashing through two barriers and onto the flooded roadbed. The water rose a third of the way up the tires. Kirby slipped out from under Canin's arm and stepped out onto the tailgate. He peered out at the ARF van. Looming larger. He barked, a warning bark.

The pug had moxie, Canin thought.

"Hold on!" Herman screamed. "I gotta punch it through!"

He punched it, and the tailgate slid out from under Kirby. He plunged into the river and sank.

"Kirby!" Ray Canin yelled. "Come back!"

Not rational, but instinctive.

The pug bobbed back to the surface and began paddling upstream toward the truck. He had a ways to go. The current had carried him from midfield to the ten-yard line. And, he was still going backward.

"Come on, Kirby, swim!" Canin yelled, as the pickup pulled onto dry land and slowed.

178

"You lose!" The voice came from across the river. It was Mullard. Standing at the floodwater's edge, he stripped off his white coat and jumped in. He swam furiously for the black pug, now almost lost in the shadows of overhanging trees.

Canin bit his lip. *Why didn't I think of that.* But he knew why. Mullard knew why. The currents didn't look like much. But they were deadly. They were enough to drive a man into a rock, a loose tree root or right into the bottom. And hold him there. Of course, Mullard would have nothing to worry about, if he happened to be an Olympic swimmer. And he was. It was in his file.

Easing himself down from the tailgate, Canin leaped onto the pavement.

"The pug's down! I'm going in!" Canin shouted, without much enthusiasm. He was not an Olympic swimmer. He was more of a shallow-end kind of guy. Herman draped an arm on the backrest and looked back at Canin.

"Take care of Captain Nemo!" Ray said over the water's roar. He waded in until the river pulled his feet out from under him and took him away. Leaving the roadbed, he couldn't touch bottom.

Calm waters would have made for an easy swim. But the swirling eddies and foam made it hard to keep his head above water. Canin took big breaths every chance he got and swam as hard as he could, with the current as his back. He could see Kirby, still bobbing, but no longer swimming upstream. He just slowly rotated like a boat with a stuck rudder. Canin made some headway, but Mullard was closer. And closing in. The veterinarian reached out, thrusting a hand through a swirl of foam and grabbing the pug by the scruff, clutching folds of skin.

"Ha! Got him!" Mullard cried.

Then he hit the major appliance. Something had held the refrigerator down on the streambed, likely an overgrown mesquite. Whatever it was, it had given way. The refrigerator surfaced and

Mullard met it face-first, losing the dog as he tried to remain conscious and push away from what appeared to be a vintage Kelvinator. The unit neared the bank and got caught in a tangle of roots and branches, along with Mullard. As Canin surged past, Mullard reached out for help.

"I'll be back for you!" Canin said, slapping Mullard's hand away.

How would he manage that? He'd have to work out the details later.

Kirby came first. But even as Canin got closer, the river churned up more solid waste – a table, plumbing parts, pieces of buildings, car tires and a small bathtub. Canin pushed his way through it as he caught up to Kirby and, turning over on his back, cradled the pug in one arm. The roiling surface lapped over his mouth and nose, and made breathing a matter of timing, and luck. The pug didn't have it any better.

Now to get out of here. Canin angled toward the bank. Or where he guessed the bank to be, judging by the current. But he couldn't seem to reach it. The sheer force of the water made it all but impossible. And the river rose. And the junk multiplied. Metal, wood, mineral, vegetable, animal and one body, stripped bare and unrecognizable. The unknown drowning victim.

Maybe it was Johnny the busman. Canin pushed his glasses back up his nose for a better look. But by then, the body was gone, consumed by the flood. Other things came into view. Canin could see his feet. He could see Kirby. He could see the discarded volleyball net, just as his head slipped through a tear. The current carried him downstream, feet first as the netting caught his neck and held on. He went down, only by a few inches. But a few inches, a few feet. Either way, there was no air. Nothing but water for the lungs. And Kirby – Kirby squirmed for air, desperately kicking to be let go.

Canin thrust the pug upward, holding him aloft. He could see the dog balanced on his palm, at the end of an arm that broke the surface

180

right at the elbow. Holding his breath, he could see the dog breathing – a wavering image filtered through the prism of rushing water.

That'll work, for maybe a minute. The dog – a good twelve-to-fifteen pounds – weighted Canin down. And to complicate matters, Canin's head was still stuck in the netting. Not that he wasn't clawing at it like a maniac with his other hand, desperately trying to free himself. But the current showed no mercy, pushing and pulling to carry Canin downstream, while the netting held tight and grew tighter still. Jesus, Canin just wanted some air.

OK, this is the time. Time to panic. I have to breathe, I have to breathe ... even if it's just two quarts of contaminated river water. Sorry, it didn't work out, Kirby.

He observed the dog above him, in the fresh air. The sun was out, and the water lit up here and there like a chandelier in the wind. A rose-colored solution mixed with the current and drifted downstream. Canin felt a tinge in his shoulder. The tinge became burning pain. He twisted around, losing the dog – Kirby hit the surface, bobbed and drifted out of view. The blade slashed again, as Canin grabbed at the hand wielding the scalpel. He missed, but so did the scalpel. It sliced away enough volleyball netting to let Canin slip out, and push his way to the surface – gasping for all the air he could get. The pain hit his thigh. More blood spurted into the water.

Mullard broke the surface and sucked in air like a vacuum. His skin had begun to glow with sunburn. His eyes were just as red. They glowed with hatred. His land broke free of the water and made a lateral slice at Canin's throat. He blocked Mullard's arm with his own. He raised a foot and pushed Mullard away. All the while, they moved with the flow of the river. It was not an even flow. It was twisting, turning flow against, in and around banks of mesquite roots and submerged creosote. And debris and other major appliances.

And sediment, mixing with blood and giving the water the look of thin tomato soup. And the garbage, from years of dumping in dry

181

river beds. Now rushing water picked it up and hauled it off. Nature's garbage collection. No, this was not a clean, sparkling river as seen on Coors beer commercials. This was practically an open sewer.

The washing machine had apparently found the Gulf Stream. The appliance shot past Canin, shot past the pug – *Kirby!* – and smashed against a midstream boulder. Knobs and bolts spewed out and darted off like minnows.

Mullard found the passing lane, but grabbed Canin's shirt on the way by.

He slipped a forearm around Canin's neck, working it into the crook of his elbow.

"If I'd known were this much trouble, you'd be dead already. So first things first. Kill you, then rescue Captain Nemo."

"You mean Kirby," Canin managed to say.

Mullard squeezed tighter, choking off Canin's air supply.

"First, I'll take some of the fight out of you. I hate it when patients struggle under the knife."

Mullard grabbed Canin by the hair and pulled his head backward and down. Water rushed into his nostrils and filled his sinus cavities. It burned like battery acid. Canin thrashed, reaching for anything he could grasp. All he got was more water. And all he could see through churning water was the arm pulling him down. And Kirby swimming by overhead, a fish-eye view of the mechanics of pug swimming. It looked like a large yam propelled by toothpicks.

Hang in there, Kirby!

Canin accepted that as his last thought, as he waited to drown. Or for the scalpel to open up the contents of his throat. It was Mullard's choice.

Drowning it was, as he slipped toward unconsciousness.

He heard a cry of pain. The scalpel hit the water, and Mullard let go. Canin fought his way to the surface, and noted the pug clamped on Mullard's right arm just below the shoulder. With his left hand, he pried off the dog. There was a flow of blood and a bite mark like a pit bull's dental chart.

The river grew calmer yet and settled into a murmur. It had widened. But it was moving as fast as ever. And it was just as dangerous, maybe more. It had entered a lowland mesquite stand. Trees once at the riverbank's edge were now underwater. But never far under. Their tangled, thorn-tipped branches occasionally clawed their way to the surface.

Canin tried to swim clear of them, the ones he could see. The ones he couldn't tore his pants and scratched his legs as he passed over them. Then a pair of branches, where they joined, caught his heel. The river carried him forward, but his foot remained wedged tight until his shoe was torn away. His foot came loose. The shoe drifted out of reach, and joined the rest of the river's debris.

Something brilliant caught his eye, riding the surface just a few feet away. It glinted. Sharp, shiny, metallic.

Mullard was right behind it. He caught up to it and grabbed it, even as Kirby continued to circle him and snarl in ways seldom heard in a pug.

Kirby was looking for an opening to Mullard's neck. He was looking for the kill. But Mullard lashed out first, lunging at Kirby with the newfound weapon. As it twisted in his hand, the glare fell away. It was, Canin saw, a washing-machine knob. It bounced off the pug's side with little effect. Mullard didn't stop, though. He hit the pug again and again, even as the dog tore at his wrist and fingers, and bloodied them.

Canin doubled back and fought the current to reach Mullard. He grabbed veterinarian's right wrist, holding the hand out for Kirby. The dog took it with his teeth, and hung on. But Mullard ignored the pug. He brought his open left hand down on Canin's face and forced him underwater, and Canin – with nothing else to hold onto – took a fistful of Mullard's shirt and pulled Mullard down with him.

Overhead, he saw the branches ... they appeared joined. Canin thrust his hands into Mullard's face and pushed – just high enough for two adjoining mesquite branches to snare his head.

Canin slipped his fingers free.

But the current carried Mullard's feet forward and secured his neck tightly in the joint. Mullard squirmed to get loose, but he was stuck fast.

Canin crashed through the remaining branches and treetops, managing a last submerged look at Mullard's feet. Canin couldn't see his face, but he could imagine the panic. Well, there was no helping him now. The river made that impossible.

Mullard passed out of view, slipping into the broth of dirt soup.

Canin broke the surface. The pug floated by like a small marine mammal.

Both were beat. Too beat to swim. Canin did the geography. The Salt entered the Gila. The Gila entered the Colorado. They were headed for the Gulf of California. Of course, they'd be dead by the time they got there.

Chapter Twenty-One

The pug got ashore unscathed. Canin's clothes were in shreds. He was covered with scratches. And he had one shoe.

The sun sat just atop the horizon. The rain had passed, for today anyway. The heat and humidity hung around. Canin's clothes, what were left of them, stuck to his skin, as his sweat mingled with river water.

No glasses. Everything was a blur. He was somewhere in the desert, of course. The land was flat. The tall skinny blurs were saguaro and broad green blurs were mesquite and paloverde. So he guessed. He could make out some lights faintly glowing in the twilight. He set out toward them, going at a one-shoe, one-sock pace across the desert.

The pug kept up. He had a determined stride, chin up like a bulldog. Or Canin guessed. He just saw a jaunty black mass. The pug stopped in front of Canin, lifted its leg and let loose on the unshoed sock.

"Thanks, Kirby," Canin smiled. The pug didn't stop there, though. He began to push his nose up against Canin's tattered pants.

"OK, OK, I really mean it."

Canin bent down to pet the dog, and got close enough to see Kirby had a surprise for him. His glasses. The pug had plucked them from the river. And now the pug was giving them back.

"Wow – good boy!" Canin said, as he took the glasses and patted the pug's head.

He slipped the glasses on and the world once again became a panorama of stark detail. The cactus had needles. The distant clouds had edges. The ground had a path. It led to a dirt road, that in turn led toward the lights. Canin and Kirby did what came naturally on dirt roads. They walked down the middle of it. They did not sink in mud. The rainwater had largely run off the higher ground of the center. Canin walked with purpose, with as much purpose and pace as one shoe allowed. The pug kept up. He, too, had a determined stride. Occasionally, he glanced up at Canin, as if to make sure the water-logged private investigator was all right. Yeah, Canin thought, they had found their comfort level around each other. Together, they had survived the river together. Conversely, had they not been together, they would have both been dead.

Canin guessed that made them buddies.

Just yesterday, he had regarded dogs with indifference at best, and fear and suspicion at worst. Now, here he was bonding with a pug.

Canin had to laugh. If he had liked dogs when he was younger, he would never have gone pug. He would have regarded the breed as too odd. What with the buggy eyes, the nose flattened into folds of flesh, the knobby head, and those skinny little legs poking out of a well-plumped body.

Well, so much for idle speculation. However he might have regarded pugs in the past, he held them in high esteem now. *Pug ugly no more.* Canin saw beauty in the breed. Inside and out. Perhaps pugs were not big. Nor particularly aggressive. But neither would they back down. Certainly, the pug now at his side was more game than any pit bull. Kirby had proved it in saving Canin's life.

"Going to miss you, boy," Canin said, forcing a smile.

Dusk was settling in, as the sun felt its way to the horizon. Canin and Kirby, headed the other way, edging toward the lights. With each step, the lights grew farther apart – like stars repulsed by dark energy.

"Pretty soon we'll need radar to find our way out."

Kirby leaped. He spun around, then scampered into the desert. In a panic, Canin followed. The pug crashed through a ring of creosote bushes, then paused and sniffed the air. Then he scurried off in a wide arc, as his pug-flat nose alternated between sampling the air and surveying the soil. Like a rocket with a tailfin missing, he sped along an inward spiral, his excitement growing as he closed in on the center. Hitting the bull's-eye, the pug dug furiously into a small muddy mound between a pair of discarded tires.

"Come on, Kirby," Canin said. "It's getting dark."

Kirby wasn't listening. The mud flew, as he uncovered old bottles, styrofoam cartons, crumbled wrappers. They flew out between his legs with the dirt. Mud splattered Canin's pants. Pausing, Kirby sniffed to check his bearings, then began to dig again. Out popped a box the size of a dictionary. It landed near Canin's feet. Kirby chased after it, but Ray Canin scooped it up first. The writing on the box was faded, but he could still make it out. *Milk-Bone brand dog biscuits.* It was open at the top. Canin tipped the box, and a small dog biscuit rattled down the side and dropped into his hand. It looked like a well-preserved lump of crust. Kirby was now on his two hind feet, begging for it.

Canin shook his head. Amazing, he thought. He recalled how Kirby had uncovered the Milk-Bone in the riverbed. It was no mere parlor trick. This pug had a nose for dog treats.

He tossed the lump to Kirby, who snagged it on the fly.

They backtracked, then headed on down the road. Ten minutes later, they approached a floodlight over a small porch. It was nearly dark. From what Canin could tell, the place looked like standard government housing built for the reservation. Under the bright light, the lime-green exterior glowed like a radium watch dial.

The man answering the door was a few inches short of six feet and built wide and sturdy. A Maricopa Indian in his sixties. He stared at

Canin for the longest time, not quite believing what he saw.

"I didn't expect to see you again," he finally said.

"I didn't expect you to see me again either, Herman," Ray Canin replied.

Herman looked down at the dog and laughed.

"You, too, huh?"

Opening the door to his home, Herman waved an arm toward living room.

"Come on in. Me, Hoover and the kids were just watching TV."

"Hoover?"

"Yeah, they're all on the couch."

Kirby at his heels, Canin followed Herman inside. It was dark, the only light coming from the television. An old Looney Tunes cartoon flickered across the faces of a small boy, a small girl and the rump of a pug. They sat on an old, overstuffed couch. The pug lay stretched across the girl's lap, sleeping. Foghorn Leghorn strutted across the TV screen, loudly announcing his intention to marry the widow hen.

"I say ... I say ..."

Canin interrupted.

"Hoover?"

Herman laughed again. "Yeah, since your dog was named after a vacuum cleaner, I'd thought it'd be a good fit for his brother."

"Hmm. Hoover."

The pug once named Captain Nemo lifted his head, responding to his new name. The dog gazed at Ray Canin with bright, moist eyes. The girl, perhaps seven or eight, patted the pug on the head. His little curly tail acknowledged the favor. The boy, he looked to be about six, reached over and scratched the dog behind the ear. Hoover licked his hand. The boy giggled.

"Gotta tell you, Seth and Margie just love Hoover. Two hours and the dog's right at home."

"I can see."

And, truth be told, the affection of a good family looked like the miracle cure that all of Alison Ford's money couldn't buy. The dog didn't need a new liver. Corny as it sounds, he needed love. As far as Canin was concerned, Hoover had found a home. He glanced down at the pug now at his feet, Kirby. He and this dog could bond all they wanted, it wouldn't do any good. Kirby was property of Rhino Holloran's sister. And once he delivered the pug, he'd get rent money. Enough to tide him over until the next case.

"Could I use your phone?" Canin asked. "I need to call a friend for a ride."

"I can give you one, no problem," Herman said. "I owe you for the dog."

"That's OK. You saved my life back at Park 'N' Swap. That's not how I wanted to go, lying in a pool of mustard on the food court."

Herman nodded. "In the kitchen."

Canin called Danny, and asked for a ride from a corner of the Gila River Reservation, south of the Salt and west of Ninety-First Avenue.

"Why don't you put the guy on the phone," Danny said. "Maybe he can tell me how to get there."

Herman turned out to be Danny's second cousin, and they had a long talk about family, about acquaintances and old times. The old Maricopa Indian had gone to Phoenix Indian School with Danny's late father. They talked about the now-closed boarding school and how Danny's father was the best trumpet player in the school band. Those who'd heard him said he was every bit as good as the late Russell "Big Chief" Moore, who went on to play with Louis Armstrong. But, when Danny's father got out of high school, he became a carpenter, framing houses. Among the Pima and Maricopa on the Salt and Gila reservations, many had drinking problems. And many drove when they shouldn't have.

But the drunk driver who killed Danny's father was a white certified public accountant from Mesa.

189

"Go figure," Herman said. "White guy with ledgers. It doesn't add up."

He laughed, and Canin guessed Danny must have done the same.

Herman and Danny kept it up for about thirty, forty minutes.

Canin and Kirby meanwhile joined the others on the couch. The dogs sniffed each other in the appropriate parts, then settled down. On the television, Roadrunner watched Coyote plunge down a mile-high canyon, then went "beep-beep" and sped off.

After Herman finished his chat with Danny, Canin called Martha Holloran at her hotel. He woke her up.

"Hello?" she asked.

"Hi, it's Ray Canin."

"Oh, I hope you have good news, Mr. Canin. Or I will call upon God to smite thee senseless for waking me up."

"I have the dog."

"Bring him in the morning."

"But I can bring him tonight, as soon as ..."

"Mr. Canin, God has a plan for everyone and everything. His plan for me is to get a good night's sleep, and for you to bring the dog in the morning."

"Plan?" Canin heard himself say. He was tired, and given to say what crossed his mind rather than opting for discretion. Testily, he said: "You call that a plan?"

"Don't question God's plan, Mr. Canin. You'll go straight to Hell. You know that."

"What time tomorrow?" Canin asked.

"It's God wish that we meet in the lobby of the downtown Hyatt-Regency at seven."

"How can you be so damn sure?" Canin asked.

Martha Holloran hung up.

Danny arrived about an hour later, in his new GMC pickup. Carrying Kirby, Canin hopped in. He took in the new-car smell.

190

Better yet, he took in the air-conditioning. The arctic blast felt good. Danny didn't get his nice truck on a newspaper photographer's salary. And he didn't pay for the gas from his share of the tribe's casino revenue, though that helped. No, he made his fortune in real estate. He sold his family's land allotments so the state could build a freeway. It wasn't an outright sale, but a ninety-nine year lease was close enough. And the state had given him one big, fat check.

Danny seemed quite comfortable digging into the coffers of white man's government.

"What could be more fair," he said, "than an Indian getting rich off real estate?"

Canin couldn't argue with that. He had heard, however, that some members of the tribe didn't care to have a freeway slicing through the reservation. He suspected one of them was Anna Stewart.

In the truck, Canin was lolled to sleep by the tires slapping mud. Kirby slept on his lap.

Sometime later, well after dark, Canin awoke to the sound of a chicken fleeing for its life. He was home. He carried the dog inside and Danny followed, toting a six-pack of Tecate beer in bottles.

"You've had a rough day. You could use a cold one,"

Danny said.

Canin didn't think he had the strength to open the bottle, let alone hold it up to his mouth.

"You've got a long drive home," Canin said, nodding toward the beer.

"I'm gonna watch TV, watch you drink and crash on your couch."

Canin looked at him blankly. God's plan?

"Anna, my cousin, told me she ran into you. She said you were nicer than she remembered the first time. And less despondent than you sounded on the phone."

"Animal tranks. They mess with your mind."

"Anyway, she thinks you're nice, like a brother," Danny said.

191

"That's a far cry from eligible bachelor. Maybe, I need a make-over. Muscles, bronze tan, stronger chin, Mensa-member credit card."

"You know, you remind me of the story of Coyote and Little Redbird."

"Yeah? What's that's about?"

"Well, one day Coyote looked up and saw Redbird in the tree, singing away while pulling out all his old feathers. When Redbird was finished, Coyote was amazed by what he saw. Redbird had a new coat of feathers, even redder and more brilliant than before. So Coyote thought: 'I can do that.' He sang and pulled out all his fur. But he didn't have a dazzling new coat to show for it. Just bare-ass nakedness. He froze to death."

"What are you telling me, Danny?"

"Just drink your beer and forget about Anna. She likes you, but …let's face it, Ray, you just don't measure up, and you never will."

Blunt words, but Canin smiled. Danny, if unintentionally, had given him hope – hope he realized he didn't have any right to. Hope he shouldn't entertain. Hope that only led to anxieties. And now, just thinking about anxieties, overwhelmed him with even more anxieties – all fed by a confluence of emotional and physical exhaustion. … *Jesus Christ, I need help. I'm a complete wreck. I need help.*

Then he spotted it, standing right next to him, down by his feet. Stooping, Canin patted the pug. Blood pressure dropped. Pulse rate fell. Outlook improved. *Much better,* Canin thought. *Much better.*

Relaxed, he stood up. "He's hungry," he said. Then he found some old, but untainted, hot dogs in the refrigerator and offered Kirby two. It was the closest thing he had to dog food.

Danny found a Diet Pepsi in the fridge, popped the lid and flopped down on the couch. He began digging around in the cushions.

"Where's the remote?" he asked.

"Renee ran it down the garbage disposal."

192

"I thought she ran your glasses through the disposal," Danny said.

"Yeah, you're right. She took a hammer to the remote."

"Got fed up with your channel surfing, huh?"

"I don't know," Canin said. "She was mad, and I think she wanted to break something useful."

Danny pursed his lips together and nodded. He got up and switched the channel manually to David Letterman, then settled back into the couch.

"You're still staying then?" Canin asked.

"Hey, I thought I'd help deliver the dog tomorrow, in case you run into more trouble."

"Right, and there's one other detail."

"What's that?"

"Yeah. My car's still down at the Capitol."

For Canin, the idea of a little added protection began to sound like a good one. Especially now, as he had second thoughts about Donald Mullard's role in Rhino Holloran's death. That is, that he didn't kill Holloran after all. You've got to believe a man who's about to kill you. Mullard had nothing to lose by fessing up. And he had no reason to admit to a murder he didn't commit.

Of course, that begged the obvious. If Mullard didn't kill Holloran, then the murderer was still alive. And at large. And perhaps still willing to kill for a pug. And who would that be? Maybe Martha Holloran herself. Maybe she killed her own brother, but didn't get the pug. And maybe she'd kill again.

Maybe killing just ran in the family.

Canin felt the anxiety meter inch back up. He reached down, once again, for a pug pet. Then he thought where this was all leading. After tomorrow, he'd have no pug.

Pugless in a world full of anxieties.

Chapter Twenty-Two

Martha Holloran came out of the coffee shop just as Ray Canin and Danny Stewart entered the hotel lobby. She wasn't hard to spot. She was only person around in excess of 250 pounds wearing a muumuu. It was ocean-green, and if you stared too long as she bobbed across the room, you were bound to get seasick.

She had her hair pulled back in a tight bun. Her complexion was ruddy and her head was big and doughy, like a lump of child's clay.

The three of them stood near the hotel entry, about where they bumped into each other. Canin had Kirby in his arms. Martha Holloran carried a small portable pet kennel by the handle.

"You're right on time, Mr. Canin. Right on time, just as God would have it."

"Does he ever *not* get his way?"

"Mr. Canin, please, don't make your stay in Hell any more unpleasant than necessary. Now just allow me to ..."

Martha Holloran set the carrier down and gave the pug a four-point inspection. She ran her hand over his neck and chest, nodding slightly. She felt his paws. She pushed back his lips and examined his teeth.

"Yes, there is it. The chipped molar."

Chipped molar? Canin wondered if Alison Ford would have caught that.

As Martha Holloran checked the ears, something caught the pug's

194

attention. Something in a big loose pocket stitched to the muumuu at the hip. Kirby stretched his nose out over the pocket and sniffed. The aroma worked its way to his tail, which thumped against Canin's rib cage. Martha Holloran grinned, then slid a big puffy hand into the pocket. She came up with a small green Milk-Bone and offered it to Kirby. The pug was ready for it, mashing it up in a slurry of teeth and drool.

"God is with me today," Martha Holloran said, patting the pug on the head. Then she picked up the kennel.

"Go on, boy," she said, urging Kirby to come on board. The dog sniffed around the edges, but declined the offer.

That was far as the coaxing went. Martha Holloran set the carrier on the hotel counter, and snatched Kirby from Canin's grasp. She shoved the dog inside, swung the door shut and latched it. The door, like a cage, offered a view. The rest of the carrier was like a cave ventilated by a row of dime-sized holes. Kirby did not have a view. His black tail curled around a bar in the door, with his head hidden deep in the cave.

"Welcome home, Kirby," Martha Holloran said to the tail. "You'll be such a comfort to Mother."

"It's all Mother has left – of Michael," she said to Canin. "And I'm sure she will love this little dog as she loved Michael himself. She loved her son deeply, as only a mother could. Of course, in the eyes of God, he was an abomination."

"He's probably uncomfortable," Canin said.

"He's in Hell. He's supposed to be uncomfortable," Martha snapped.

"I meant the dog."

"Oh." She held up the kennel and inspected the tail.

Canin opened the door and pulled out Kirby. He swung the dog around and loaded him rump-first. There, Canin thought. Now all he had to do was avoid eye contact. Otherwise, the morose face now looking out from behind those bars might drive him to regret what he'd done: Given up the pug to an uncertain fate in return for some rent money.

Uncertain fate? Come on, Canin. The dog will be treated like a long, lost son. He'll be just fine. Pay no attention to that face in the cage. All pugs look like condemned prisoners.

"I thank you, Mr. Canin. You've done God's work," Martha Holloran said. Then she glanced pointedly at her watch. "The bus to Yuma leaves in forty minutes. Ah, there's a taxi now."

For once, she seemed upbeat. Almost personable. "Good luck," Canin said, managing a smile as Martha Holloran turned and headed out the door.

"God's speed!" Danny Stewart shouted to her back. Canin couldn't tell if Danny was mocking her or not. With Danny, it was often hard to tell.

They watched from the lobby as Martha Holloran found a place in the cab's back seat for the carrier. Then she squeezed in next to the dog. It was a very tight fit, like twelve clowns in a ten-clown Volkswagen.

Canin was about to suggest coffee at the breakfast bar, but – as he watched the cab leave – he realized something was wrong. He turned to Danny, about to tell him, but Danny looked puzzled himself.

Danny snapped his fingers.

"Hey, you notice she didn't have any luggage?" Danny asked. "Just the kennel. Why no luggage? She's going back home to Yuma, isn't she?"

Canin, it happened, was struck by a different thought.

"Hey, my money!" he screamed. "She didn't pay me. Jesus Christ, she didn't pay me! She owes me! Two thousand dollars, on delivery! That was the deal. Damn!"

At first, twenty-five hundred for delivering a pug sounded over the top. Now, after what he had been through, it hardly seemed like a fair

196

day's wage. Still, Holloran owed him.

"Man, you forgot to collect," Danny said matter-of-factly. "Well, send her a bill."

Canin shook his head. And his fist.

"I'm broke, God Damn it! And I had too many near-death experiences to get stiffed."

He ran outside as the cab pulled away. Danny followed.

"She didn't take her luggage," Danny said. "She'll be back."

"Forget the luggage! She's got the dog, and my money. Come on!"

Canin scrambled down the sidewalk toward the truck. Danny jogged behind, reluctant but resigned. As Danny stepped from the curb, he noticed the parking ticket pinned under the wiper. He removed it and tore it up, letting the pieces flutter to the pavement.

He slid into the cab, alongside Canin.

"I'm from the sovereign state of the Salt River Pima- Maricopa Indian Community. I have diplomatic immunity."

With that, Danny cranked over the engine and headed west on Adams, then left on First Avenue, a one-way street going south. Canin spotted the cab. He expected it to make a left on Jefferson, for the bus depot.

The cab, Martha Holloran and the pug kept going south.

"They didn't turn," Canin said.

"Maybe they'll take Buckeye Road. That goes to the Greyhound depot."

"Yeah, eventually," Canin said.

"And we're going to catch them, eventually," Danny said.

He hit the accelerator and slipped through the intersection at Jefferson just as the light went from yellow to red. Legal, if barely. When it came to beating the lights, Canin thought, Danny had a talent. Or perhaps a skill common to newspaper photographers rushing to a disaster scene.

They kept the cab in view, as First Avenue merged with a parallel street and took that street's name, Central Avenue. Where Central crossed Buckeye, the cab sped on through.

"They're not going to any bus depot," Danny noted.

He gassed the truck through another close yellow and closed in on the cab. Canin peered through the windshield, into the cab, looking for the pug. Instead, he made eye contact with Martha Holloran, who had turned to look behind her.

Canin froze. Martha Holloran did a double-take, eyes wide as nacho platters. The very religious woman mouthed the word, "fuck." She turned back around and – as far as Canin could make out – began to slap the cab driver repeatedly across the back of his head. Apparently, she got through to him.

The cab practically left the pavement as it jerked forward and sped off south on Central.

"They spotted us," Danny said.

"What's going on?" Canin asked.

"We'll find out."

Canin braced for death. The taxi ahead ignored common courtesy, like traffic lights and speed limits. It went around other cars by speeding down the middle "suicide" lane, meant for left turns. It had to be doing seventy-five. Canin knew this, because that's how fast Danny was going – and he just barely kept pace.

"The suicide lane – that's crazy," Danny said.

He chose instead to weave through traffic in the two lanes open to him, though open was a relative term. The right lane still had large pools of standing water, compliments of yesterday's monsoon downpour. Storm drains were made for average annual rainfall, which wouldn't fill a toilet. This was a summer deluge, infrequent – and way above average. Danny passed a big Ford pickup on the right. A wall of water rose and shot through the cab's open window.

Canin glanced back as the Danny sped ahead. He saw the hand emerge, gripping a pistol. The gun recoiled in sync with four pops.

198

"Shit!" Canin ducked.

Three shots missed. One hit the back window, then – with a slight change in direction – exited through the windshield.

"Hey," Danny said. "Don't piss off Anglos in pickups. They don't just salute with their middle fingers."

"God damn that Second Amendment," Canin said, waiting for bullet number five.

But Danny deftly lurched into the left lane, and sped ahead, losing the Ford. The distraction, however, had allowed Holloran's cab to pull ahead. Ray and Danny crossed the still-flooded Salt River on the Central Avenue Bridge. They had entered Ray Canin's ZIP code, South Phoenix. Here, Central Avenue was a mix of industrial warehouses, thrift stores, bodegas, fish-and-chips takeouts and a welfare office.

The cab came into view. Danny hit the gas again, just as a Mayflower moving van pulled out of a storage lot. There was no time to brake. Just time to think, "Can't be."

Danny and Ray screamed. There was a difference, Canin kept his eyes open. He glanced over at Danny, who had his eyes shut tight. Ray screamed louder.

Danny spun the wheel left, then right. He opened his eyes. There was no moving van. They had gone around it. Or perhaps passed through it. They spotted the cab, some two blocks ahead. Danny sped up on a BMW about to pass a slower car. As the BMW made a move into Danny's lane, Danny leaned on his horn and knocked off a fender on the way by.

Canin turned toward the BMW. The driver fit the type. Thirties, sculpted hair and a white, open-collar shirt. He was also easily offended in traffic. And getting cut off was the greatest offense of all.

The driver gunned it, overtaking the GMC. He swerved in and out of Danny's lane. Braking and speeding up. This was road-rage, Yuppie-style. The BMW dropped back and sidled up to the GMC.

199

The driver rolled down his window.

"Hey, assholes, you ain't seen nothing yet."

The BMW sped up toward the intersection at Southern Avenue, not heeding the yellow signal, or the color that came after. The motorcycle cop was half hidden behind a hedge. He probably couldn't believe his luck when, right in front of him, a Beamer ran a red light going eighty. On green, Danny eased the GMC through the intersection and crept past the offending BMW driver, pulled over a half mile ahead. The cop had just dismounted his motorcycle. Canin thought he detected a hint of a smile behind the sun-glasses and poker face. He seemed to be thinking he had made his week's quota, all in one stop.

The cab driver, an old pro, must have spotted the cop. He had slowed down. The cab was within sight.

"Maybe stay back," Canin said. "They might think they've lost us."

Danny sighed. He punched a button on his CD player. It picked up where it left off … "the girl with kaleidoscope eyes …" followed by a thumping drum rift.

Danny continued on Central, cautiously.

"That was scary," he said. "I almost got killed by a Mayflower moving van. Think about it, Ray. I'm an Indian. And that cowboy in the Ford nearly picked me off."

Canin held up his hand. It was shaking.

"That bullet nearly gave me a third eye socket."

"Damn, the things I do for my white Anglo-Saxon Protestant friends."

"I'm not Protestant. I'm agnostic."

"So you're a WASA."

"It's a small demographic."

Two miles later, traffic had thinned out. Central had gone from mom-and-pop strip malls to empty lots and houses. Then the houses gave way to desert as the road bent sharply around a low butte. Odd place for a cab, Canin thought, as he watched it disappear in the bend. South Mountain Park. A few hundred feet ahead, the cab was stopped at the park entrance. The cabby leaned his head out the window, tilting it toward a guardhouse built of smooth river stone held in place by fat slabs of mortar. The park ranger, visible through a plate of glass, indifferently waved the cabby through. He had better things to do.

Canin expected admission on the same indifferent wave as Danny pulled up. But the ranger eyed Danny and grew suspicious.

He signaled Danny to stop. The ranger was tanned, with a gritty complexion. He had a head of slick, black hair. He stepped out of his personal fortress and gestured Danny to roll down his window. Danny complied. Canin watched the taxi roll out of view, behind a small hump in the road.

"Nice truck, except for the bullet holes," the ranger said, smiling. He leaned against a post, arms crossed. "Bet you had to sell a lot of beads to come up with a down payment for this baby."

Danny shook his head. "Real estate," he said. A simple truth spoken like a wisecrack.

The ranger nodded. He took it as a joke.

"Well, if you're selling jewelry, you need a license. Rangers have been checking lately."

"I'm not selling," Danny said nonchalantly.

Looking past Danny to Canin, the ranger added, "What happened to your friend? He looks half-drowned."

"That was yesterday," Canin answered. "Today, I'm sober."

"That's right," Danny affirmed.

The ranger raised an eyebrow, and with a slight and practiced nod of the head, he let Danny go.

Another quarter mile up the road, a cyclist entered from a half-hidden trail. Danny didn't see her. He had his head turned, watching a family of quail run around the desert without an agenda.

"Stop!" Canin yelled. Danny braked hard.

Ray Canin jumped from the pickup and ran back down the road. Danny was right behind him. Before they reached her, the cyclist picked herself off the asphalt. Her mountain bike lay at her feet like titanium road kill.

"You OK?" Canin lightly took her by the elbow. She pulled it away.

She took off her helmet and revealed a perky neck-length cut of blond hair. She was attractive, perhaps early thirties. But for the hair, she wasn't perky just now. She was beyond annoyed, halfway to pissed off, as she brushed off the dirt and pebbles embedded in her knees.

Canin gestured toward Danny.

"He was driving."

"You OK?" Danny took her lightly by the elbow.

She pulled away from him, too.

"Is this the only way you can get a date?"

"It was an accident. I was distracted," Danny said.

"I bet you were. Anyway, I'm fine. You missed me, mostly."

She picked her bike off the roadway, adjusted the handlebars. Then she held up a loose brake cable.

"Snapped."

"Anything we can to do help?" Danny asked.

Canin gave Danny an elbow to the ribs.

"She's getting away, with my money and the pug."

"Don't worry," Danny said, "We'll…"

"Please," the cyclist said. "Go get your pug. I'll be OK. I'm meeting a friend in a minute. We're tossing our bikes in the car and taking up them up mountain. Then we're riding down the trail – flying down, I should say. The gravity's intense this time of day."

She waved the brake cable about.

"First, I have to fix this."

Danny and Canin stared at each other for a second. Canin knew they both had the same thought. Was her friend man or woman?

It would be rude to ask, and they couldn't wait around to find out.

"Right," Danny said, as he and Canin scrambled back to the truck. "There's a pug and money involved."

Up a narrow and twisting road, Danny took the corners just under what the laws of physics allowed. Canin looked anxiously for the taxi. He caught sight of it as they came out of a hairpin turn. Danny slowed, but kept a pace that continued to close the gap. The road forked. One branch led to a picnic ground. The other snaked its way further up the mountaintop, which rose up like a piece of jagged glass. Up and down the steep slope, boulders as big as living rooms held their ground, somehow. And Saguaro cacti, twenty-five and thirty-feet tall, stood with arms raised in perpetual surrender, like some abstract rendering of the Italian army.

Through tight turns and around blind curves, Danny put the taxi in striking distance. That is, until the Cadillac from Michigan got in the way. From a roadside pullout, it swung out in front of the pickup and maintained a nice leisurely pace of twelve miles per hour. The four people inside were treating themselves to a self-guided tour. Each took turns pointing. And wherever one finger pointed, the other three heads swiveled to follow. They were thorough and showed an interest in every plant, bird and rock along the road.

The taxi, several hundred yards ahead, slipped out of sight. Danny didn't seem to mind. He was concentrating on *A Day in the Life*. The song was not a toe-tapper. It asked for concentration, but Canin had none to give. He was chewing on his lip, rubbing his nose – anxious to get around these refugees from the Midwest. He didn't want to lose Martha Holloran now.

He no longer worried about the money. He wondered where the hell she was taking the dog.

Canin kicked the floorboard.

"Come on, run 'em off the god-damned road!"

Danny gave him a sidelong glance, shrugged his shoulders.

"Can't do that, Ray. They're from Michigan." Another joke, possibly.

"Yeah." Canin took a deep breath and let it out slow.

Ten minutes later, the Cadillac pulled off into a scenic view. Two minutes after that, the GMC came to a side road leading to a village of towering antennas. Here, all the major TV and radio stations broadcast their shows. A road led into it, but it was heavily gated. They kept to the main road, ending up at a scenic lookout, a collection of stone ramadas offering shade and the best free view of downtown Phoenix. Despite the heat, a few enterprising Native Americans had their jewelry on display. Silver and turquoise necklaces, earrings and bracelets – all in neat rows, taped to sheets and blankets spread out on the parking lot.

"Cuts down on the shoplifting, huh?" Canin asked about the tape.

"No, that's not it," Danny replied. "They do it so they can roll everything up and toss it in the car when the day's done."

"Looks like some pretty nice stuff."

"It is, it is. Hopi, Navajo silver-work. It's all good."

Nice jewelry, but no taxicab. They headed back to TV Tower Road. As they rounded a curve, the towers slid into view. Still high up the ridge, they looked like movie props set up for Godzilla.

Danny followed the road up toward the towers.

"They couldn't have gotten past the gate," Canin said.

As they closed in, the gate rose up. It was about ten feet and was secured by a padlock the size of third base. Danny slowed, then saw another road branching off. It was marked: South Lookout.

He followed it to a small parking lot. Out his window, Canin caught the view. The Gila River Valley lay in the distance. Closer up, at the mountain's base, was suburbia. Thousands of houses, each one the same as the one next to it – red-tiled roofs, pink stucco exteriors and a swimming pool in the backyard. Monotony and conformity enforced by homeowner's associations. Communism for

Republicans, Canin thought.

"Over there," Danny said.

"Hmm?" Canin said, freeing himself from the spell of endless repetition. He turned and spotted the taxicab, parked at the east end of the lot.

Danny pulled up next to it.

The motor was running. The windows were closed. Inside, the cabby was reading a newspaper. The air-conditioning, blowing full blast, didn't budge his curly well-lacquered hair. He looked up, startled to see a pair of faces peering back at him.

Canin knocked on his window. The cab driver turned his fan to low, but kept the window rolled up.

"What do you want?" he said, loud enough to be heard.

"The woman who was riding in the back ... Where'd she go? What'd she do with the dog?" Canin asked.

The cabby shrugged. Twisting the fan back to high, he returned to his paper.

"Son of a bitch ..." Canin muttered.

He kicked the tire, and regretted it, as it hurt like hell. It was an act of pure frustration. After getting tranked, shot at, nearly drowned and almost crushed by a moving van – to come all the way up this damn mountain to get the brush off – Canin had every right to be frustrated. But that didn't matter to the cabbie. He could have cared less what Canin had to endure to get here.

He left Canin with no choice. A pug was about to be abandoned to the desert. He had to act now. He reached into his pocket.

Chapter Twenty-Three

Canin pulled out his last ten and waved it in front of windshield. The cabbie rolled down his window.

"How can I be of service?" he said, extending his hand and making it clear his service wasn't free. In fact, it called for another ten, which Canin had to borrow from Danny. With money in hand, the cabbie pointed toward a post halfway across the parking lot. A trail marker. Just as another car pulled up, Ray and Danny were already half-running down the trail in pursuit of a pug.

They spotted Martha Holloran and Kirby within two minutes. Kirby's nose glided just above the trail like a hovercraft. He was onto something. Ray Canin could tell. Then Kirby paused, looking up at Martha Holloran.

"In the name of Jesus, don't stop now! Use your radar!" Martha shouted out. The pug continued.

Ray and Danny followed from a discreet distance. The trail followed a ridge that curved northeast into the heart of the mountain preserve.

The dog kept a brisk pace, driven by the distant scent. In the oppressive heat and humidity, it was an uncomfortable pace for all parties: men, woman and beast. Canin, minutes into the hike, was soaked in sweat. Danny, descendant of desert dwellers, was holding up a little better. It helped he didn't wake up with a liver full of beer. Still, every few steps, he paused to mop up a wet forehead with a shirtsleeve.

Martha Holloran must have worked up a bit of a sweat herself. But she had thought ahead. She had brought a canteen. Every so often, Canin would see her stop and bring it out of that massive pocket sewn onto her muumuu. She'd take a drink and offer a little to the pug, but the pug wouldn't bother. He kept his nose to the trail. He kept on the scent.

Body of a pug. Soul of a bloodhound.

The trail split. Kirby took the left fork. It dropped into a narrow, isolated valley.

The pug broke into a trot, then a run – his nose pulled by a force stronger than magnetism. The farther he descended into the valley, the faster he ran – toward a scent that must have grown with every step. Canin and Danny were doing all they could to keep up. Soon they were running full speed, through the sweat, the heat and the exhaustion. Ahead, Martha Holloran pursued the pug at a full run, stomping down the steep trail on booted feet.

Kirby came to a rise, where the trail leveled off, made a brief ascent and then dropped off again toward the valley. The pug stopped, and sniffed around, as if to check his bearings. Martha Holloran slowed to a halt, keeping a wary eye on the dog. Not far behind, Ray and Danny froze and crouched down. Martha Holloran pulled out the canteen and took a long, sloppy drink. She next took a long sweeping look around as the water dribbled off her cheek.

Ray and Danny pushed each other into a hiding spot behind a boulder. If Martha Holloran saw them, she didn't let on.

After a silent ten-count, Canin peered out over the rock. Holloran slipped the canteen back into her pocket. Kirby picked up the scent again and dropped out of sight, down the other side of the rise. Martha Holloran, sliding the canteen in her pocket, followed. She, too, disappeared from view, like the setting of a giant sun.

Ray and Danny came out from hiding and clambered up the rise.

They spotted Martha Holloran and the dog heading down the trail. They moved in and took cover, again, behind a creosote bush. Through its tangled and blackened branches, Canin saw that Martha Holloran was not adapting well to the desert heat. She likely didn't get out much in Yuma, a place often hotter than Phoenix. She was a creature of air-conditioned habitats, and she was panting harder than the pug. Her face appeared swollen and mottled. Her muumuu clung to the puddled contours of her very large and perspiring body.

But she didn't care. The pug was all that mattered. The pug and his nose.

The nose led the dog to a big rock at the base of a saguaro cactus, just off the trail. The saguaro, a good twenty feet in stature, had a single arm curving up from the main trunk. It looked like it was giving a friendly wave.

The pug didn't wave back. He couldn't be bothered. He was running around the rock, his wagging tail telegraphing the exciting news – something good was here. Once more around the rock and Kirby stopped. After a couple sniffs to confirm the location, he began to dig. The rain had softened the usually hard desert topsoil. Dirt flew up from beneath his squat, pug rump. As he dug, the ground around the rock settled. And the rock, the size of a rough-hewn medicine ball, began to settle. The more the pug dug, the more rock sank.

Somebody had dug here before. And somebody had placed the boulder atop a loose covering of dirt. Somebody big enough to move boulders. Somebody the size of Rhino Holloran.

The bottom fell out of the dirt, and the boulder dropped, maybe a foot. The ground around Kirby collapsed and the pug fell with it – yelping in terror.

"Jesus!" Martha Holloran yelled, her hands raised to the air. She seemed ecstatic.

"Jesus," Canin whispered. He feared for the pug.

He scrambled around the hillside until he could see down into the hole. It had a gaping entry, five feet from side to side. And it was deep, plunging into darkness, well beyond sight. Kirby had fallen as far as the boulder, coming to rest on a latticework of steel rebar. The boulder laid atop. The pug was on his stomach, legs dangling over the endless shaft.

Well, perhaps there was an end – but it could have been hundreds of feet down.

The pug had dug up an abandoned mine. Maybe a gold mine, from years past. Arizona had tens of thousands more just like this, all over the map. Sometimes people fell to their death. Kirby got lucky. This one had been sealed up, with a bit of dirt shoveled on top.

Martha Holloran crawled up to the yawning hole. She reached out and got hold of Kirby. The dog had something clenched in his teeth – a line or rope.

"Good boy. Just like Michael said and God ordained."

She sat down on the hole's edge, reached out and lifted Kirby from the rebar. Moving like a crane on a barge, she swung around and set the pug on the ground. He held fast to the rope. Holloran turned back and began pulling the rope herself, one hand over the other. Until it caught on the steel bar.

Looking into the hole, she saw the hang-up. And seeing it, she appeared euphoric. She raised her face to the heavens. She cried in triumph.

"Oh, God Almighty!" she shouted, squinting into the still-bright sky. "You have led the pug here and so this is the place! In Jesus' name, I have found it. Aaamen! Aaaamen, Jesus!"

The pug, too, sensed he had found the treasure. He began running around the hole, yapping in a pitch of pure excitement. Holloran turned and swatted at him, missing.

"Shut up! I don't have time for that. I've got buyers waiting in California."

Martha Holloran pulled the rope this way and that, fighting it, like

209

an angler hauling in a tuna. Finally, with a yank, out came a small box suspended inside a net. Holloran excitedly ripped up the netting and pulled out the box. Then she cursed God's name soundly.

"Dog biscuits?" she asked. "Green and red dog biscuits? God did not bring me to the mountain in one hundred degrees to dig up dog biscuits! Where is it? You pug bastard! These are no good to me!"

She flung the box one-handedly across the desert. Kirby, tail pulsing with joy, ran it down and began tearing at the cardboard. Martha Holloran, sat there, deflated. With a sigh, she shook her head. Somebody up there had let her down. She shifted her weight in preparation for standing, knocking more dirt into the shaft. Standing up on the edge, she stared down and cocked her head. She saw something. She stared at a pile of dirt still resting on the steel bars – in the middle of the shaft entry.

Slowly, Martha Holloran got on her hands and knees and crawled. As she left solid earth and moved her full mass onto the mine enclosure, the steel bars warped with the strain. They looked like the graph lines that show how gravity bends space. The metal creaked, sounding like nails being pulled from old wood. Fearing a collapse, Holloran moved with more caution. Slowly, she made it to the dirt pile.

And she dug at it, with more fury than the pug. The dirt flew down the shaft, carrying with it the occasional stone. Canin could hear each one descend, hitting the sides of the shaft, the sound growing fainter and fainter. Then silence. There was no bottom. Or so it seemed. Holloran paid no attention to the sound of falling rocks. She just kept digging, until her fingernails scraped a surface smooth and hard. She brushed off the remaining dirt. She clasped her hands in prayer.

"Tell me this is it, God! Don't let me down, dammit!"

Canin duck-walked up to the next creosote for a closer look. Martha Holloran had struck a shiny disk, perhaps four inches across. Martha Holloran pried at the disk with her fingers, trying to dislodge it. Maybe it was valuable. Gold or … well, gold was all Canin could think of.

The disk popped loose. Martha Holloran tossed it into the desert, then reached down again. Now, into a round hole – a top of a tube secured to the crossbars with straps. The woman carefully coaxed out a tightly rolled canvas. She brought the furled up canvas to her lips. She kissed it.

Then, holding it aloft in one hand, she spoke yet again to the sky.

"Oh, Lord, Jesus, Praise thee. Now everyone can hear my message of Jesus' love and eternal damnation!"

She stood, and knowing she was in God's hands all the way, she walked back across the rebar sealing the shaft. She did not step gingerly. She walked casually, confidently, like Jesus on water. Back on solid ground, she stood beneath the saguaro. She unrolled the canvas. Canin could not see what it contained, only Martha Holloran's eyes – visible above the edge – scanning it from side to side.

The pug came up behind her. Then he stopped and sniffed the air. Kirby picked up something new – something no longer masked by the overwhelming aroma of a well-placed Milk Bone. Kirby trotted around the mineshaft and up to the bush Canin was hiding behind. The dog lifted his leg and peed, splashing Canin's shoes.

"Kirby! Bad dog!" Canin said in a whisper.

Whispers carry well in a canyon. Canin could hear his voice echo off the hillside.

Martha Holloran lowered the canvas so Canin could see her face. It was flush from a circulatory system working overtime to prevent heat stroke. And streaked with dirt and mud. But the eyes revealed her indignation. Canin stood. His location was no longer a secret. There was the booming whisper, and the puddle of pee at his feet.

"How did you get here?" Holloran said angrily.

"Mass transit."

"You know what? There are no wise-asses in heaven."

"How many chiselers are there? You stiffed me."

"And what are you talking about? I paid you."

"Just a retainer. You still owe me two grand."

"The Lord has spoken. That's all you're getting."

"I went through hell to get that dog."

"That wasn't Hell. That was the Lord's guiding hand." She smiled. "He led to you the dog. And He led me to this."

She turned the canvas around and showed it to Canin. He had expected something biblical. Sermon on the Mount. David and Goliath. Noah and the Ark.

"Pug on the Moor," she said. "A little-known Edwin Landseer, 1855. It's English."

And Canin saw a painting of ... well, a pug, a black pug in noble pose – a pug doing an impression of the Hartford Insurance deer. The background was a vast expanse of grassy marshland. The pug itself, though recognizably a pug, looked a little less extreme in pugness. The muzzle was not so flat. The eyes – though dark, glossy and attentive – did not bug out half so much. The body was not as square – more like thick Italian sausage than an engine block.

"Nice painting," Canin said. "And it's not hard to figure where it came from. Your brother stole from it Alison Ford and hid it here with Milk-Bones – knowing the pug would find them. All he needed was a buyer, and he had to be very selective, because most people shy away from buying hot paintings. Alison Ford probably gave him a head start, however. She must have given your brother a list of buyers – possible buyers, anyway. He'd take his time vetting them. I don't think he was all that keen on stealing the painting in the first place, any more than he was the silverware. But I think Ford begged your brother to take the painting off her hands. She had a nice house but it was mortgaged to the hilt – probably to pay for her backyard pug mausoleum, not to mention the money she wasted on that charlatan of a vet. Anyway, she had no cash on hand, and it was cash she desperately needed to bankroll a liver transplant for her pug. She probably expected a freebie, after all she had done for him. But no deal from Mullard. He was going to squeeze her for every nickel she had, then squeeze some more."

"How you do know all that?"

"Just putting two-and-two together. And here's where the murder comes in. Your brother told you about the deal, and you killed him, after he told you how to find the stolen painting. With the pug."

Martha Holloran snickered through a smug, pouty smile, then asked, "The Lord does work in mysterious ways, does He not?"

"Well, things didn't go too smoothly on your end," Canin pointed out. "After you killed your brother, the pug ran off. And you needed somebody naive enough to find him for you. You found my card, called the newspaper and learned that I had been fired. You conned my address out of the receptionist."

Kirby sat down next to Ray Canin, panting softly. Danny came out of hiding and stood next to them.

"There's one big problem with your story. I didn't kill my brother. He was dead when I got there. Anyway, I didn't have to kill him. No need to, praise the Lord. Michael had already agreed I should have the painting and profit from it. But I couldn't wait any longer to secure it. I got off the Greyhound early Wednesday. God told me to rouse Michael and the pug right then, to take me to my fortune. And my mission. Ah, but He decided to test me, by losing the pug.

"That's where you came in. See, without the pug, I didn't have the painting. And imagine my surprise when I learned what somebody would pay for a stolen painting of an ugly dog? Three hundred thousand, and up! I had no idea!"

"Hey, easy on the ugly stuff," Canin said, bent over and patted Kirby's head. "Pugs have feelings."

"They're dogs. They mean no more to Jesus than a pimple inside your nose. Anyway, Michael promised to recover the painting when

213

things cooled down – weatherwise and otherwise. I couldn't wait. God couldn't wait. I had to start production, and I needed the money. And for that, I had to have the painting. The good Lord went and smote him with bullets. But Michael had already told me enough to find the painting on my own, as long as I had the pug."

"Alison Ford made it easy for Rhino to steal the Landseer," Canin said, "but Rhino must have been wary of getting caught and sent back to prison. But he went ahead and stole it as a favor to Alison Ford. Still, he was paranoid enough about it that he buried the Landseer at the entrance to a mine shaft. But I don't think he planned to sell it, list or no list. But then you found out about it …"

"He didn't like to keep things from me," Martha said.

"And no sooner does he tell you about it, he offers to give it to you. He must have thought the world of you."

"I was his worst nightmare. My brother feared me more than anything alive."

"Your brother wasn't afraid of anything alive."

"He was afraid of me, because I always had God's ear, and God had mine. Ever since Michael was the baby, and I was the big sister, I let him know about the power of God. And Jesus. And that the power worked only through me. He found that out when he told me I couldn't ride his tricycle. I tried to take it him from. He was big even then, and he grabbed it away and pushed me face-first into the sidewalk. Did you know he had a pet bunny? He always loved animals. And he loved that bunny. Poor bunny. Jesus crushed that little bunny under the tires of my brother's own bicycle. I told my brother Jesus did it, and that Jesus took that little bunny and cast it into Hell."

"You ran over a bunny rabbit," Canin said. "That is cold."

"You're not listening!" Martha Holloran snapped. "Jesus did it, and I let my brother know that I had the power of God and Jesus to kill everything he loved and cast their wicked souls into the fires of Hell."

214

"I take it he let you borrow his bicycle after that."

"He gave it to me, along with all his savings, maybe two bucks. Anyway, I never stopped following in the path of the Lord and preaching his message of love and eternal damnation. I grew up and started my own church. Many sinners came through the doors of my church, and many left feeling the hot flames of hell on their fannies. Of course, I had wired the pews with heating elements to help convey the message. As many sinners as I saved, though, I knew the Lord had bigger plans for me. He wanted me to reach out across the land. And so He asked me: 'What do sinners like most?' And I said, 'reality shows.' And there I had it, the idea for a reality show where contestants save sinners. And I told my brother if he could help me in any way, especially with money, his dog would grow old and prosper, and sit in the kingdom of Heaven."

"And if he didn't?"

"His dog would not grow so old and prosperous."

"You told him God would get his dog if he didn't help."

"Of course, he loved that dog."

"And all this for a TV show?"

"It's much more than that. It's a reality show with real sinners. I'm calling it *There'll Be Hell To Pay!* Each week, contestants will compete to save the worst sinners, in different situations. We'll book them on a gay cruise ship, say. Whoever saves the most sinners gets ten thousand dollars and a certificate of salvation."

"A ticket to heaven," Canin said.

"Yes," Martha Holloran said. "The losers will get an autographed copy of my four-page pamphlet, 'Hell Is For Losers.' The winners go on to compete in ever-more difficult scenarios. Maybe they'll be asked to save the pope, you know, sneak into the pope's bedroom and make him shake all over with Jesus. I'm still working on the camera angle."

"You're going to convert the pope in a game show?"

"A reality show. We leave it up to the contestants to figure out

215

how. When you have the spirit of Jesus, anything goes," she said.

"I don't know," Danny said. "It sounds kind of loopy."

"What?" Martha Holloran said with a sneer. "It's not loopy to save sinners. We're just doing God's will before a cable audience of .. of … many."

"Sounds, uh, like a winner," Canin said.

At this point, he had given up on collecting his fee. He certainly didn't want it from the profits of a stolen painting. He just wanted to take the dog, get away from Martha Holloran and go have a beer. A cold beer in an air-conditioned bar. There he could reflect on paying one month's rent with a half month of money. That's if the check was still good.

Canin wiped the sweat from brow.

Time to leave the lady Holloran to her own delusions. He picked up Kirby. Martha Holloran reached into her bottomless pocket and pulled out a handgun. As a detective on his first assignment, Canin was not yet expert on guns. As best he could tell, though, this one met the minimum standards. It would make holes in his vital organs.

"Put the dog down," she said.

"I'm taking the dog as my fee. Besides, I like it."

"The dog knows secrets. It goes with me. You know secrets. You're staying here, both of you."

Canin and Danny Stewart shook their heads in sync.

"Secrets?" Canin said. "We don't know any secrets. I didn't see anything. Really."

Danny chimed in. "Right. Right. You know many of my ancestors died in these mountains. They never could keep a secret. But me, well, I can. Stolen painting? Hey! What stolen painting?"

"Quiet, God has it all planned out. You shot each other struggling for the gun."

Squinting into to the mid-morning sun, Martha Holloran aimed the gun at Ray Canin's heart.

216

She said: "To hell with you."

Canin swallowed. Maybe he could rush her. No, no, he couldn't. His could not lift his feet. Fear had bonded them to the earth. Fear had frozen him down the cellular level. Fear had frozen time. Real detectives were not scared by guns, he told himself. He'd have to work on that one, maybe later. For now, he could only stare at the big fleshy finger wrapped around the trigger, pulling it back. And he heard only one sound, the final beats of his heart ... *boom, boom, boom* ..."

"No brakes!"

Canin glanced back up the trail. Her blond hair streaming out from her helmet, the mountain biker flew over the rise like a jet launched from an aircraft carrier. She landed hard on the trail below, then she picked up speed. Canin swore he could see the eyes behind the dark lenses, filled with terror. He jerked his head toward Martha Holloran. She was no longer aiming the gun. She was staring back up the trail. In disbelief.

The trail turned left. The bike went straight. A knobby tire cut a path between Martha Holloran's legs. The handlebars followed and, catching her across the pelvis, freed her from the earth and slammed her against the cactus. And its neat vertical rows of hardened, tempered spines.

The bike and its rider fell away, sliding past the saguaro, and on down hill.

Martha Holloran remained standing at attention, her back nailed to the cactus. Her face was twisted in agony.

"Oh, Jesus!" she cried.

The cactus remained standing. But Martha stumbled away, toward the edge of the mine entrance. She lost her footing and fell forward onto the steel crossbars that guarded the shaft. Reflexively, she thrust her hands out to break the fall. By some miracle, she caught two of the bars, easing the body slam into the latticework. Her back had a thousand pinholes of blood.

She muttered through her armpit.

"God is testing me."

Then, the steel bars – unable to hold any longer – tore away from the concrete support ringing the shaft entrance. And everything fell, like Alice into the rabbit hole. Down down down. Martha Holloran screamed for Jesus, but like the falling rock, she grew fainter and fainter. Until, silence.

The mountain biker got stiffly to her feet. She glanced briefly at the hole that swallowed Martha Holloran, then walked up to Ray. She pointed to her bicycle, now mangled into a kind of abstract sculpture.

"That's your fault."

Chapter Twenty-Four

Ray Canin had narrowed down the suspects in Rhino Holloran's murder to one. Part process of elimination. Part dog pee. Alison Ford might have had a falling out with Holloran, but she had an alibi. The night of his murder, she was at home sleeping off a bender, as her maid, Dominique, would testify. Ford herself did recall waking up about midnight and demanding room service. Dominique, still up, brought her a wine cooler. And Mullard, well, his confession in the river had the ring to truth to it. He expected Canin would soon be dead, from an overdose of water in the lungs. He had no reason to lie to a man soon to be at the bottom of a river bed. And Mullard's goons, Collick and Nickerson? They simply were no match for Holloran.

Then Canin combed through Holloran's past. And out came Rhino Holloran's old cellmate, Ernie Ortega. The man Holloran had crippled for insulting Ol' Yeller. Canin came across a story in an online search of *The Arizona Herald.* Ortega, it seemed, had succumbed to an invasive procedure at the penitentiary. He was stabbed to death with a serving fork smuggled out of the kitchen.

Ernie Ortega was not well-liked by his colleagues.

So now Canin sat before the only remaining suspect. Holloran's murderer, or so he believed.

Canin didn't care to stay too long. It was hot and miserably humid under the shell of blankets and rugs. He was seated on a short stool

219

with stubby legs. Across from him, Mesquite Suzy fanned herself with a flattened cereal box. She was sitting on a heap of clothes. Every so often, she'd force a smile, but mostly she was sullen, unexpressive.

Canin had been here for two, three minutes. He hadn't said much except hi and how's the weather. Mesquite Suzy had said nothing. She wasn't going to make it easy for him. Accusing her of murder was going to be hard enough as it was. Getting her to admit it ... well, he told himself, good luck.

"You, ah, killed him, didn't you?" A little direct for his taste, but he wanted to move things along.

"Who?"

"Rhino Holloran."

"Oh, him. Yes, I killed Rhino Holloran. He meant everything to me."

Canin paused, took a breath, then he took four more. He didn't know what slapped him harder. The non sequitur or the easy confession. He glanced behind him, toward the entry. Nobody came charging in to arrest Mesquite Suzy. So he pressed on.

"Your real name is Susan Pamela Franklin," he said. She didn't say yes, no or change her expression. But he knew he had the right person. The county social service agency had released information it earlier said it couldn't. A court order will do that.

Canin continued: "You were married to Frederick Franklin, an agri-businessman in the Colorado River valley near Yuma. He grew a lot of lettuce, made a lot of money, and he lived in a big house – along with you – until fifteen, sixteen years ago. Until Rhino Holloran killed him, allegedly for abusing his own dog ..."

"He didn't just abuse the dog," the woman said, looking up. She looked engaged. At first, she spoke slowly. But the pieces of shell fell away. And Susan Franklin began to emerge out from under the cover of Mesquite Suzy. "He beat it to death. That's not abuse. That's murder." She spoke harshly. She had dropped, for the moment, the dialect of the street, the dialect of Mesquite Suzy. Her voice carried the ring of the well-heeled.

"OK, Mr. Franklin murdered the dog," Canin said. "Holloran had broken into your house, he was a thief, and caught your husband mistreating the dog ..."

"Please, Mr. Canin, don't sugarcoat it with words like 'mistreating' and 'abuse.' Frederick was kicking and hitting the poor creature with all his might, just for soiling the new carpet. I was screaming for him to stop. Michael, he was in our bedroom – he had broken in through a window – he was back there stuffing my jewelry into his pockets. It was fairly late. Anyway, he was drawn to the kitchen by the noise."

"So," Canin cut in, "Holloran became enraged with your husband and killed him with his bare hands. And you – wait, let me finish this time – and you, you wouldn't forget, you couldn't forget the horrible crime you had witnessed. You withdrew, you had become almost catatonic. You couldn't even be brought to the witness stand during the trial. You had to be hospitalized, then you were farmed out to a residential psychiatric clinic. It's all in the county report. Well, while you were busy making baskets and key chains, you were also nursing a grudge. You made up your mind to track down Rhino Holloran and kill him for what he did to your husband. You were released from the hospital a year or so after he got out of prison, and then you dropped out of sight. You disappeared, and nobody – except maybe a handful of social workers – connected the crazy bag lady known as Mesquite Suzy with the crazy wealthy widow known as Susan Franklin.

"Everybody had all but forgotten about Susan Franklin, but you did not forget about Rhino Holloran. You hated Rhino Holloran. You traced him to Phoenix. You followed him to the river bottom. He never suspected who you really were – no more than anybody else. And you were regular river-bottom neighbors. You visited often. But on your last visit, you shot him. The sound of gunshots didn't alarm anybody. Everybody shoots off guns in the river bottom. And maybe

221

Kirby barked. Maybe he didn't. He barks a lot, doesn't matter who's around. But when it comes to people he knows and likes, the pug has his own way of showing his affection. He pees on them."

"That's Kirby, all right," Franklin said, with a slight smile.

"And Kirby peed on you that night, soaking your boots and socks. That was the smell that hit me when I dropped by your tent. It wasn't you. It was the dog."

"Yes, I was one of Kirby's favorites," Franklin said.

"And you showed your affection by shooting Rhino Holloran twenty-nine times in the face."

"Twenty-eight."

"The coroner put it at twenty-nine."

Susan Franklin stuck her hand into the pile of clothes beneath her. She pulled out a small object wrapped in cloth. Removing the cloth, she held out a steely blue revolver. It looked old, though well-kept.

"Ladysmith .22, made in, oh, in 1905, I believe. Gift from my late husband. It has a seven-round cylinder. Never been fired, before Tuesday night. Then I emptied it, four times, into Michael's head. Not because I hated him. But because I loved him."

Canin blinked. He hadn't thought of that one. He hadn't thought of Rhino Holloran as a lady's man.

He had been overweight, hairy and covered with tattoos. And then there was the little matter of that doorstop on his forehead. That took him beyond ugly. It made him a freak.

Pointing out Holloran's obvious defects to Susan Franklin had crossed Canin's mind. But she had a gun. And, if she had indeed loved the man, well, there was no point in insulting her taste just now.

Susan accepted his silence as an invitation to continue.

"The dog my husband killed was *my* dog, Prince of Darkness. Prince was a black pug, like Kirby. I loved that dog. And Michael...."

"You mean Rhino."

"I mean Michael. I never liked that horrid nickname he acquired

222

in prison. Well, Michael came to love the dog as I did, because of my letters. I wrote to him while he was in prison, whenever I could, and told him just how special Prince was. The poor dog was just a puppy when he was killed, less than a year old. From Michael's replies, I could tell the letters touched him deeply, even beyond his own remorse. He swore when he got out he would get a pug of his own and treat it with dignity. He thought it would restore a balance, a happy life to make up for a tragic death.

"He was, in many ways, a sensitive and beautiful man ..."

Canin cleared his throat.

"What does that mean?" Susan asked irritably.

"Nothing."

"I'll tell you one thing, when Michael killed my husband, he showed me what real justice is all about. Real justice is swift. And irrevocable. Real justice is death."

Canin nodded his head slightly. "That's true, in thirty-seven states."

"What Michael got was real justice, Mr. Canin. He has no cause to complain."

"Why? Why'd you do it, if it wasn't for killing your husband?"

"I'll get to that. But first, now, when I was released from the clinic I wanted nothing to do with Yuma. Nothing. And so I moved to Phoenix and, well, I lost it. I still hadn't worked everything out with the loss of Prince and here I was in a new place, trying to be someone else. I had an identity crisis, you might say. That was a hard time for me. I lost all touch with Michael, as I couldn't even remember where he was living. In prison, of course, but it just didn't occur to me."

"Losing your dog must have hit you pretty hard."

"Yes, very hard. That and the fact that mental illness runs through my family."

"Oh, uh huh."

"Yes, well, anyway, here I was, a bag lady in downtown Phoenix.

There was no place to go, nothing to do. I just baked in the sun ten to fourteen hours a day. As you can see, it did wonders for my complexion. And then, it happened."

"What?" Canin asked.

"I ran into Michael at the shelter for the homeless. He went there on occasion to meet old friends and get a hot meal. I was so excited, well, that I remembered who he was, for one thing. And that he remembered me. And I was so glad I could thank him personally for killing that monster I'd had the misfortune to marry. We soon became friends – me, him and Kirby. He'd come up from the river bottom, and we'd wander the streets, sleeping on sidewalks and under bridges together. We were free, totally, free. Nobody owned us. Michael had spent all his money on a dog and eventually a car. And my husband's estate had been picked apart by his brothers and their lawyers – along with my hospitalization.

"A few months later anyway, Michael invited me to spend a new life with him, a new life in the river bottom. Suburbia for homeless. We each fixed up our own place. That was my idea. I didn't want to commit, just yet. Still, by then, we were more than friends. We'd become lovers. I became a whole new person."

Susan Franklin pursed her lips and raised her eyebrows in a sort of facial shrug.

"Something wrong, Mr. Canin?"

Canin smiled weakly. "No, no."

Susan Franklin then closed her eyes. With a deep breath, she opened them again and let them wander dreamily about the rugs that served as ceilings.

"He was so much more than you can imagine."

Canin tried not to imagine.

"And, oh, that little knob on his head, the things ..."

"But, Susan, why did you kill him?"

Susan Franklin lowered her gaze and, upset, worked all those sun-

224

dried wrinkles toward her lips into a sort of puckered frown. Canin noted she had also set down the gun.

"I'm getting to that," she mumbled, picking at her bare and very calloused feet. "Everything was perfect for Michael and me. We were down in the river bottom, and on top of the world, until, until ..."

A deep shadow seemed to fall across Susan Franklin. Her voice became a whisper, a conspiratorial whisper.

" ... He began seeing more of that washed up relic from television. He had fancied himself a dog-show person. Well, I tried to tell him those snobs would never accept him into their clique. But he wouldn't listen. Alison Ford was supposed to be his ticket to the inner circle, and so he had to see her."

"He had an affair going with Alison Ford?"

"No! It was that slutty maid of hers."

Canin cocked his head, like a dog asking a question. "The maid?"

"Yes, just as I had suspected. Kirby always let me know when she showed up. He barked. He barked a different bark, because he did not like her. And she always came away smelling clean, because Kirby did not show his affection. Why should he? She did nothing, nothing for the dog. She was only there for the ... well, let's put it this way. He'd always tell me she was doing errands for Mrs. Ford. But I wasn't fooled. I watched it all from behind a tangle of salt cedar. I'd watch her go inside his hut and not come out for an hour, maybe more. And I heard noises. Filthy grunting noises."

Susan Franklin shook as she tried to choke back the tears. It did no good. They flowed anyway. She sobbed, then after a minute, she caught her breath and continued.

"Several times, I hid and watched, but I never really got close enough to what was going on inside. I only heard the noises, and put two and two together. But then, I began to wonder if maybe I'm just paranoid. Doctors told me that could be a problem. Maybe she and Michael were just playing some of kind a mind game on me. *That's it!* I told myself. *They're playing mind games on me. I'm just paranoid, that's all.* Well, having put that behind me, I could take the next step and face my fears head-on. I would go right up to the hut and have a look for myself, and so I did. I crawled out of my hiding place and crept closer. There was a space between the boards and I peeked in, and, I saw them together, and oh, God, his horn, the things he was doing ..."

With a long shuddering moan, she broke off the sentence – much to Canin's relief – and began to cry again.

"You couldn't have just shot them just them on the spot?"

Mesquite Suzy lifted her face off the long skirt draped over her knees. Her hair was pulled back tight. Her eyes were red and puddled. She sniffed.

"I didn't have my gun," she said. "Besides, I had no reason to shoot the maid. I hated her, but she wasn't the one who violated my trust. But Michael, he needed the swift, well-armed hand of justice. He had a right to a fair trial, though, didn't he? So I gave him one. It was all played out in my head. I know what you're thinking: *How could it possibly be fair?* Well, the trial lasted three days, you know. All the time I was out there by the road, sitting on my rocker, I wasn't just soaking up the rays. I was calling on witnesses and examining them and cross examining them. But when Mesquite Suzy took the stand, well, her testimony was damning, to say the least. The jury was out for less than an hour. Michael Holloran was convicted and sentenced to die.

"As night fell, I unwrapped the gun and hiked down to the river bottom and up to his hut. Kirby barked and greeted me, in his way, just like you said. I found Michael on the patio, eating beans out of a can with a fancy spoon. He was sitting down and had his feet propped up on his beer cooler, tipping his chair back and raising the front legs a little off the ground. Real cool he was, until I told him to say his prayers.

226

"He prayed I wouldn't shoot him, but that didn't count.

"I shot once him in the face. He looked a little surprised, and hurt. He didn't try to stop me, though. He just stared at me, like he was trying to figure it all out. He was sometimes a little slow. I didn't have all day, so I shot him again, and again, until finally he fell over backward on his chair. Then I stood over him and emptied the gun. I reloaded it and emptied it again, all over that big ugly face of his. I had plenty of bullets and I wasn't going to stop until I obliterated it. But then my finger got sore and so, after settling one final detail, I called it quits. Kirby was hiding under a bench in Michael's hut. I called him out, calmed him down and he followed me home."

She dabbed her eyes with her skirt, though she didn't seem to be shedding any tears for Rhino Holloran. Killing him, after all, was an act of justice.

But something troubled her.

"I tried to stop them," she said.

Canin nodded. Nickerson and Collick.

"These two dogcatchers, they came by. Before you. All night, people came by. But when they drove by, Kirby barked. They heard him. ... I don't know how else to put it. They kidnapped Kirby. They pulled me out of my shelter and stuck a funny-looking gun to my stomach. The little one, he slapped me and told me he was taking the dog. The big one didn't say much, but he had the gun and looked like he wouldn't lose any sleep if he had to use it. There was nothing I could do. I had no bullets left. I used them all on Michael. They took Kirby and told me not to bother going to the pound, because I wouldn't find him there. And if they caught me snooping around, they'd kill the dog. I didn't care about me – but Kirby ... I told you without telling you, how to find him ... And now, no Michael. No Kirby. I have nothing."

The wrinkles around her eyes collapsed into a contour map of grief and despair. Then, as if struck by a pleasant thought, her face brightened.

Once more, Mesquite Suzy dug into the pile of clothes and rags she was sitting on. She came up with, well, Canin couldn't tell – as she kept it hidden inside her hands. Her eyelids half closed, she spoke in a longing, sentimental tone.

"Of course, that doesn't mean I was lonely all the time," she said.

Her cupped hands spread open like an oyster shell, revealing the horn of Rhino Holloran. Some traces of flesh remained, though most of it had wasted away.

Canin winced. He turned away.

"That doesn't look too sanitary," he said.

"It's … it's, it's all I have left of him."

"Well, could you possibly set that aside for now, under a sock or something?"

"Done."

Canin raised his eyes, and took a big breath of hot, stale air.

Susan Franklin-Mesquite Suzy shook her head. Again, she was sad. No longer sullen and unexpressive, she was now changing moods like a mutating virus.

"Poor Kirby. They killed him. I'm sure of it."

"He's OK. He's with me."

Her face lit up again. "You're a good dog person. I can tell."

"I'm kind of new at it. Um, there's one more thing, Mrs. Franklin."

Canin kneeled forward and took her hands. He held them gently between his own. Her looked into her sun-ripened face.

"Yes?" she said.

He slid his hands away. As sweaty as they were, it wasn't hard. Then, getting to his feet, he plucked the gun from the floor.

"First, I need this."

"Yes?" she asked again.

"It's a little matter of justice."

Stooped over, Canin exited the rug palace and nodded to Sgt.

228

Sterner and Detective Stern, who had been waiting outside. He handed Sterner the gun, as well as the digital recorder he had tucked in his shirt pocket. Without bothering to wipe their feet, the two homicide detectives entered the rug palace and arrested Susan Franklin, AKA Mesquite Suzy, on a charge of first-degree murder.

Epilogue

Ray Canin adopted the pug and got him a county dog tag. Now Kirby was street legal. He didn't wander much from home, though he exercised in the yard by chasing the chicken twice a day. Once after breakfast and once before dinner. It wasn't the same chicken he'd started with. The first chicken, halfway through his second frantic lap around the house, dropped dead of heart failure.

Kirby had his brother to play with, too – Captain Nemo, newly christened as Hoover – the pug nearly given up for dead. Herman had put the dog on a strict traditional diet, cutting fatty foods and all alcohol. And he gave Captain Nemo regular exercise. The dog grew healthier and stronger.

Captain Nemo recovered fully, along with most of his liver.

Herman kept the dog for his own and often brought it over to visit Kirby. The dogs played well together, and enjoyed ganging up on the chicken.

Alison Ford, onetime-TV star, never knew about Captain Nemo's miraculous recovery. Canin told her the dog had been swept away by the swollen Salt River. Canin lied because he knew Captain Nemo was as good as dead if he went back to Alison Ford. She'd have him right back on the bottle. Only this time the damage would be irreversible.

Now with Herman, the pug had a chance.

Alison spent her days outside the pug mausoleum, waiting for Captain Nemo's return. Waiting for her beloved pug to take his place in the empty vault. Waiting and drinking. Waiting and drinking. And hastening her own death. Doctors warned her that her liver was nearly

230

shot. Still, she kept drinking, all the while demanding a spanking new liver, insisting she was too important to start out at the bottom of the liver list, like ordinary people. In truth, she didn't even make the first cut. No doctor in the country was willing to waste a perfectly good liver on a practicing alcoholic.

But Alison Ford just had so many reasons to drink. The loss of her dog. Her failing health. Her growing pile of medical bills. On top of that, she narrowly escaped being charged with stealing her own painting, "Pug on the Moor." Luckily, she worked out an arrangement with the insurance company. They auctioned off the painting and pocketed the proceeds — substantial enough to let bygones by bygones. Alison Ford regretted losing the piece a second time. But what could she do? She couldn't mourn her beloved pugs from prison. She had to be right there for them.

Money was tight and getting tighter. Her shows seemed to have lost their appeal to a whole new generation. They didn't hold up well. The residuals had slowed to a trickle. She lost the well-paying gig as spokeswoman for Denchoo-Sure denture adhesive. And, perhaps the cruelest blow, she was kicked off the ARF board of directors — for getting too cozy with a fraud like Mullard.

Alison Ford was forced to rent out the main house and move into the maid's quarters.

Of course, she had to let go of Dominique, the maid. Dominique, however, was not one to brood about her own bad fortune. She grabbed the bull by the testicles and invested her savings in a 900 sex-talk line just for ex-cons. It was a fast-growing market, and at last report, business was booming.

Susan Pamela Franklin was judged competent to stand trial. She chose instead to plead guilty to second-degree murder, for which she drew a fifteen-year sentence.

Dr. Donald Mullard did not get off so lightly. His body was found in late September, some forty days after he was first reported missing.

A homeless family in search of a better life on the river bottom – dry once again – discovered his remains twisted around the exposed roots of a mesquite tree. The body had no face. Sheriff's deputy said it looked like coyotes, scavengers of the highest order, had eaten it.

The two dogcatchers who had done Mullard's dirty work were charged with multiple counts of cruelty to animals. They were sentenced to 300 hours of community service. The court ordered them to help senior citizens care for their pets. Nickerson and Collick walked dogs and picked up after them in Sun City. They fed cats and cleaned out litter boxes in Leisure World. They were bitten and scratched and had little choice but to take it – or face jail. One 83-year-old woman corrected Collick's grip on her dog's leash by breaking his arm with a cane.

Canin's former and rage-inclined managing editor, Clay Sommerfield, was fired along with seventy percent of the *Scottsdale Monument* staff. It was a routine death-spiral for another newspaper. Forward-thinking media giants ditched print, slashed jobs, went to Web – and failed. Sommerfield landed on his feet, though. He hired on as a public information officer for the state Department of Agriculture. It wasn't hard. All he had to do was avoid calls from the one reporter left covering state government.

Renee Canin, better at breaking hearts, won her divorce from Ray Canin. Renee didn't drop out of Ray's life altogether, though. Quite the contrary, she made repeated demands for half the money Martha Holloran had agreed to pay for the pug's recovery. Renee said her lawyer told her she had a right to it. It didn't matter that Canin never collected on the bulk of the twenty-five hundred dollar fee.

Well, he did get the dog, and he sort of got the girl, Anna Stewart.

Anna had had a falling out with her boyfriend, the legislator from Window Rock. He kept pressing her to move up to Navajoland with him, but she saw herself as too much of a city slicker for a place so isolated.

Not that she went running straight into Ray Canin's arms. On completing her dissertation, she joined the political-science faculty at Colorado State University in Fort Collins. Though Fort Collins wasn't exactly the ideal spot for city slickers, it was good work. And, after five years of enduring mind-numbing critiques in graduate school, she was ready to dish it out for a change.

Anna didn't lose touch, however. She and Ray called each other often and exchanged occasional letters. And, planning ahead, Anna invited him to go camping with her next summer. It seemed a long wait, but Canin gladly accepted, on condition the pug went with them. She agreed.

No other conditions were made. If she just wanted to hike and have a few laughs, he'd be happy. He enjoyed her company. If she wanted more ... well, Canin didn't dwell on that. He only knew he was ready for just about anything, even the occasional beer. He did not, it turned out, have hepatitis.

Anna's cousin, Danny, proved himself a damn-good photographer. His photo essay on Rhino Holloran and Kirby in the river bottom won a Pulitzer. Danny kind of liked the recognition. A month later he quit the *Scottsdale Monument* to take the job he had so long sought – working for Associated Press.

On a recent assignment, he photographed workers resealing the mine shaft that drew in Martha Holloran. She had fallen some three hundred feet to a deep and final resting place. Crews patched the opening with reinforced concrete, then topped it off with soil and cactus. You hardly knew it was there, or what lay below. Like Danny, Ray Canin found a new job, too – just in time to avoid eviction. He became managing editor of the *Maricopa Dog*, a monthly tabloid covering dogs and dog issues in the greater Phoenix metropolitan area. According to the job description, he wrote and edited the stories, took the photographs and did the layout. And sold the ads. He no longer tracked down lost dogs, though a few anxious callers asked for his help. He would tell them to take out a classified.

With a nod from the publisher, Canin hired his own pug to do a food column. Canin bought different brands of dog food off the shelf, and Kirby would try them out. Anything the dog inhaled within a minute got a five-wag rating. The worst stuff got an unceremonious nose-snub.

It was a team effort really. Kirby gave his opinion and Canin put it in words.

Lastly, Bobby Moorehouse got back Mandy, his sheepdog. Under the care of Penelope, Mullard's receptionist, Mandy overcame her nervousness – though she still got sick on car rides.

www.ingramcontent.com/pod-product-compliance
Lightning Source LLC
Chambersburg PA
CBHW071603110726
47908CB00007B/2219